The
A

MW00940543

Toby Oliver

Cover Design: CreateSpace
Republished February 2016
Copyright 2015 Toby Oliver

ISBN-13: 978-1517038380

ISBN-10:1517038383

1

With grateful thanks to David Morris and Jill Langley for their patience and support.

"People, in the long run, are going to do more to promote peace than governments."
Dwight D. Eisenhower

Chapter 1
Mayfair, London

Although the war had been over some fifteen years, London still remained a grey battle-scarred city with only the occasional much-needed flash of post-war colour. Bomb sites still littered the jagged landscape caused by years of relentless German bombing. Rising almost defiantly amongst the surrounding skeletal shells stood the tower of St. George's Church, it had remained largely untouched by the ravages of the Blitz, while a vast swathe of the buildings close by were reduced to little more than rubble.

Mourners began to gather in the porticoed doorway and spilled out onto the street as the hearse carrying an ornate flowered coffin headed off for a private family burial. During the war, many US servicemen, particularly those based at Eisenhower's headquarters near their Embassy, had worshipped at St George's. It, therefore, seemed fitting that Todd Carter, the US Defence Attaché, who had died unexpectedly of a heart attack, should have his funeral service at St. George's. It was icy cold, and the mourners' breath rose as steam in the chill early morning air, and the pale wintry sunshine shone hazily through the mist and cast an almost eerie light on the scene.

Amongst the mourners was Sir Spencer Hall, the Head of MI5, their paths had crossed many times, Todd was not only a colleague but a close friend. They'd first met during the War, when Todd had been in the American Ranger Division, since then he'd become a popular, and somewhat charismatic character in diplomatic circles. Perhaps more importantly, Spencer knew that Todd would cut through the dross, and was a past master at gathering and disseminating intelligence on a need to know basis. There had been no side with Todd; he was someone who Spencer had relied upon to not only speak his mind but to cut through the political froth of diplomacy. They worked well together and had built up a great rapport between their respective intelligence agencies. Spencer was still in turmoil at his loss, and Todd's wife Jackie was understandably grief-stricken.

On the steps of the Georgian Church, Spencer made a point of seeking out Winthrop Alder, the American Ambassador. It wasn't only a social nicety; it was personal. He still couldn't quite believe that Todd, who had always been so full of life, was actually dead. They chatted for a while, made small talk, Spencer expressing how deeply Todd would be missed in London; it was no more than the truth. Alder knew they had been friends since the war, and whilst the war no longer defined their lives, he was acutely aware that Spencer and Todd were inextricably linked by their shared experiences. Alder suggested they should have lunch; Spencer agreed and promised to arrange something in the diary

Alder moved on through the throng occasionally stopping to pass the time of day with those he felt he had to. He was kindly hosting a lunch for Todd's family and a small select gathering of his closest friends and colleagues at his palatial official London residence, Winfield House in Regent's Park. Spencer had politely declined the invite, citing a prior engagement. It wasn't strictly true; if truth be told he simply didn't have the stomach for it, sitting for a couple of hours reminiscing about old times. He would much rather grieve for his friend in private and alone with his thoughts.

Spencer checked his watch; he'd asked his secretary to keep his diary free; he really wasn't in the mood for any heavy duty meetings, at least not just yet. His driver was parked a short distance from St. George's, meetings or not, he still needed to get back to the office. He was on the verge of heading down the wide sweeping steps of the Church when he suddenly became aware that he was being watched. Spencer instinctively glanced across the road and on recognising the

5

slender six foot four inch figure of Jack Stein, leaning casually against the side of a car, he relaxed immediately. It certainly wasn't an official American Embassy car that much he did know. Stein was CIA; they went back a long way. It crossed Spencer's mind that the hangdog expression and soulful eyes hadn't changed much at all during the intervening years. He had a cigarette on the go, but there again he always had a cigarette on the go. He also had the sort of aquiline good looks that women found attractive and was sporting a slight tan, wherever it was from at this time of year, it certainly wasn't from Washington.

Back in 1944 Stein had parachuted into occupied France, by night, as part of a special forces Jedburgh team. The "Jed's" were invariably dropped in advance of the front line, and operated behind Nazi lines to act as a liaison between the Allied military and the local Resistance fighters. The team usually, but not always, consisted of three men: a commander, an executive officer, and a non-commissioned radio operator. One of the officers would either be British or American while another member of the team usually, but not exclusively, originated from the country to which the team deployed.

Jack Stein had been in France for about three months before their paths had finally crossed, by that time he had managed to establish himself with a local Maquis group, helping to arrange airdrops of arms and ammunition, but perhaps more importantly, also fighting alongside them; it was a crucial part of gaining their respect. In real terms, Operation Jedburgh represented the first tangible operational intelligence cooperation in Europe between the British Intelligence arm, the Special Operations Executive, and the American's Special Operations Branch of the Office of Strategic Services.

During the period Stein was operating in France, Spencer had been sent on a separate mission to rescue Virginia Dudley, a leading female agent, from almost certain arrest. Without his help and quick thinking, it was doubtful whether either he or Dudley would have avoided capture and got out of France alive. At the time, the Gestapo had publicly named her as a dangerous spy and hung posters offering a reward for her either dead or alive.

As Spencer and Virginia battled their way through occupied France, they sought temporary refuge with Stein's Maquis group, they came under heavy fire from the SS; the engagement had resulted in an intense firefight that lasted for well over an hour. But their ordeal hadn't ended there; they finished up living cheek by jowl until the group's radio operator could arrange a rescue mission. It wasn't until the last night of the September moon, when the brief lunar window finally allowed the RAF's covert 161 Squadron, who were known as the "Moon Squadron," to fly into occupied terrority and rescue them.

In many ways, Jack, like himself, was a loner, cautious, and invariably suspicious until he felt able to know and trust someone, but in their game, trust certainly didn't come easily. Stein had always functioned well in crisis situations and enjoyed living at full-capacity. Once you had gained his friendship, he was intensely loyal, and in return expected the same unwavering loyalty.

Since the war, of course, their lives had moved on inexorably, just as the world had moved on around them. But whilst they had their own agendas, their own remits and loyalties to their respective organisations, there existed between them a kind of unwavering, undying bond that can only ever be truly borne out fighting for your life in the midst of battle side by side.

Because of Spencer's natural reserve, Stein initially hadn't found him easy to get to know and in some respects, he still remained something of an enigma. Spencer was quite often defensive, but there again he supposed it came with the terrority, he certainly wasn't alone. In Stein's experience, he tended to do everything wholeheartedly, not only with passion

7

but accompanied by a deadly ruthless ability to see the job through to the end. His instincts and perceptions about others were also unfailingly incisive, and if you didn't pass muster, there were no second chances, no half measures.

Spencer crossed over the road to greet him and said with genuine pleasure. 'What the hell are you doing here, Jack?'

Stein broke into a broad grin. 'Much the same as you, I guess, just paying my respects to Carter.'

'I didn't see you inside the church.'

'No, I was running late,' he explained.

Spencer looked at him searchingly. 'It's been a long time.'

'Yeah, too long,' he said with feeling.

'When did you fly in?'

'Yesterday morning.'

'So you're here on business, then?'

'Brennan took it into his head that I should cover Carter's job for a while.'

Chas Brennan was the Director of the CIA. Spencer studied him carefully he had a gut feeling it probably wasn't quite as clear-cut as that. Jack like himself, was by nature a field man, but he kept his thoughts to himself, after all, he wasn't in a position to criticise, he'd been desk bound for the last five years.

Stein noticed the flicker of surprise on Spencer's face and added by way of explanation. 'Only temporarily you understand,' he smirked. 'I can't imagine Brennan wanting me to fill Todd Carter's shoes on a permanent basis, can you?'

'No, I can't,' Spencer said bluntly. 'Did you know Carter well?'

'We met on a training course during the War, but that was about it, he was a good guy, nice family and all.'

'Yes, I'll miss the old bugger. He'd recently taken his foot off the pedal, but he was still doing a great job at the Embassy.' Spencer said, reflectively.

'Yeah, I can see he was probably a pretty good source for you guys.'

Spencer looked at him sharply. 'You know damn well it wasn't like that Todd shot from the hip and didn't take any prisoners. He had a knack for cutting through all the political crap and keeping things moving, to sort the wheat from the chaff and allow us to get on with the day job!'

Jack didn't argue the point. Todd had been good at his job and had the kind of pre-eminence in CIA circles that meant he had the direct ear of the President.

By now Spencer was on a roll. 'Have you ever tried getting a whole bunch of politicians to sing off the same hymn sheet?'

Stein accepted that he hadn't.

'The trouble is it takes time, and you know that in our business time is at a premium.'

Stein drew heavily on his cigarette and eyed Spencer thoughtfully before his face slowly cracked into another broad smile. He decided to change tack he needed to. 'Who'd have thought when we were holed up in that French farmhouse, you of all people would have ended up as the Head of MI5 and with a knighthood to boot!'

Spencer grinned. 'Well, the knighthood came with the job.'

'Yeah, but even so I mean no-one in their right mind would ever allow me to take over from Brennan! Don't get me wrong, you were good, really good, but at heart we're just the same, we're field agents, not desk men.'

'I've lost a few of my rough edges since then,' Spencer protested lamely.

Jack wasn't convinced.

Spencer hesitated, before laughing at his own expense, he had to agree. 'To be honest with you, I have a sneaking suspicion that the men in grey suits probably thought appointing me as DG was nothing more than a damage limitation exercise.'

Jack looked at him questioningly, not quite sure what he meant.

'I've always had a sneaking suspicion that they probably promoted me out of harm's way. In my experience, loose cannons in peacetime tend to have a somewhat limited usefulness.'

Jack pulled a face; Spencer was being self-deprecating, he wasn't only a shrewd spymaster, but also had an innate flare as a counter-espionage expert. He was a hugely formidable figure within British intelligence circles, and also highly regarded on the other side of the Pond.

'Shall we take a walk?' Jack suggested.

Spencer glanced back along the street, spotted his driver standing beside a sleek black Jaguar with his collar pulled up against the biting cold, and gestured to him to stay where he was.

'So what's this really all about Jack?'

'Well, Brennan and I both figured we owed you a favour or two.'

'As I remember it, it's always been a two-way street.'

'I guess so.'

Spencer slipped a pack of cigarettes out of his hip pocket and stopped to flick on his lighter. He drew heavily on his freshly lit cigarette. 'Is there anything I need to know?' he asked warily, instinctively realising that something was wrong.

'Brennan's hauled me off another job State Side he thought it'd be better coming from me.'

Spencer eyed him searchingly.

'Brennan didn't want to go through official channels,' he added by way of explanation.

'Go on.'

'We've come across a piece of intelligence, some high-grade stuff about a KGB assassin.'

'So what's new?' Spencer said bleakly.

Jack swung around to face him, his breath rising as steam in the freezing air. 'This is serious Spence we've stumbled across a plot to assassinate your Prime Minister, Jeremy Haining.'

The colour drained instantly from Spencer's face. Whatever had been running through his mind, a plot to kill Haining had never crossed it. Assassination attempts happened all the time in France; President de Gaulle and his security forces had faced them almost on a monthly basis, but that was France. It was unprecedented in Britain unless of course you included the only Prime Minister to be assassinated whilst in office, but that was way back in 1812.

Jack grinned. 'Yeah, I can see why that would shake you up a little.'

'How reliable is your source?'

'It's Freda.'

Freda was the Codename of a top CIA operative working out of Moscow.

'So why didn't Brennan tip me off?' he said sharply, through a faint haze of cigarette smoke.

'He has, that's why I'm here.'

'That's not what I meant, why didn't he contact me at the office?'

'We have a problem.'

Spencer smirked, waving his hand in the air wafting a stream of smoke in its trail. 'For Christ's sake, Jack, we always have a problem, it comes with the terrority.'

'Freda reckons the hired help might be one of your guys.'

'How sure is she?' he asked frostily.

Stein pulled a face. 'Well, at this stage as sure as she can be.'

'You mean it might be someone current?'

'It's looking more likely to be an ex-agent, but until Freda comes up with the goods, Brennan didn't want to contact you at the office.'

In Brennan's shoes, Spencer would have reacted in exactly the same way. He couldn't fault his logic. Whether the assassin was a member of British Intelligence or the KGB, the prospect of a professional killer loose on the streets of London meant Spencer would have to move fast before his entire world imploded. He was grateful to Brennan and for Stein's timely arrival in London. He could deal with Stein, and right now, he needed someone not only to watch his back but more importantly, he was an American and outside the British Intelligence community.

'You know how it is,' Stein explained, unnecessarily, 'Brennan didn't want to risk sending anything too official through the usual channels.'

'You mean he thought it might be intercepted?'

'Yeah, he did.' Stein took another long drag on his cigarette before flicking the stub into the kerb. 'Fortunately, Todd's death has given us the perfect cover for my being here. As things stand the KGB won't question my posting to London, at least not yet a while.'

'No, I don't suppose they will.'

'So how do you want to play it?'

'Well, that all depends.'

Stein gave him a searching look. 'Depends on what?'

'Why the hell does Moscow want to take Haining out? It doesn't add up. Or at least, it doesn't to me.'

'We're not sure, at least not yet. Freda needs time, but Brennan figured that we needed to touch base. I'll be straight with you Spence, Washington has no more idea about the Soviets' motives than you do.'

It was a small but significant consolation. Spencer shook his head. 'I know Haining has had a few run-ins at the United Nations and with Khrushchev, but even so, you give me a Western leader who hasn't crossed the Soviets at one time or another at the Assembly?'

Stein agreed.

'Besides there's a General Election next year, there's no guarantee Haining will even be re-elected! So what's the rush?'

Stein gave him a long, slow look. 'Whatever's behind the plot there's only one thing we know for certain Freda's source is sound, I mean *really* sound.'

'I'm sure it is,' Spencer said, thoughtfully.

He knew that Freda's access and contacts within the Kremlin were second to none. She had proved to be the CIA's ultimate honey trap and had bagged a high ranking officer in the KGB. So far, she had never let them down.

'So how do you want to handle it?' Stein pressed him.

In the normal run of events, Spencer would have convened a secret Cabinet meeting involving his immediate boss, Stanley Bradshaw, the Home Secretary, the Prime Minister, and the various heads of the security forces, including Scotland Yard's Special Branch. But as things stood, he couldn't run the risk of opening up the meeting too widely. If Stein was correct, and Haining's would be assassin was home grown, and either an ex-British agent hired for the right price or an embedded agent with possible Soviet leanings, then he would have to play it very carefully, and like Brennan, bypass the normal channels of communications. More to the point he would also have to choose a tight-knit team around him, but it certainly wasn't going to be that easy.

13

As things stood Spencer wasn't quite sure what Stein's actual remit was, did it end with passing on the news of the plot? He needed to know exactly where he stood.

'I need you onboard,' he said, frankly, 'will Brennan sanction it?'

Stein looked him in the eye. 'What *do* you think? I'm not a desk man Spence. You know that that's why I'm here. Brennan's given me some slack to help you out.'

Spencer couldn't deny that he was indebted to Brennan for sending his best field agent to London, but he was still between a rock and a hard place. Although he was giving nothing away, Spencer inwardly gave an inaudible sigh of relief. Stein was one down; he just needed to re-group and choose his team carefully.

'Where are you staying?' he asked him.

'The St Philips Hotel.'

Spencer's expression suddenly relaxed into an open smile. 'Old habits die hard.'

Stein returned his smile. 'They sure do.'

Even before the outbreak of the War, the St. Philips Hotel had been used by the UK's secret intelligence agencies as a prime meeting place. It was conveniently located close by 54 Broadway, the MI6 Headquarters, and was also within walking distance of its sister organisations including MI5, and amongst others, the so-called MI8 listening post on the roof of the Passport Office in nearby Petty France. At a later date during the War, St. Philips had also enjoyed the patronage of the OSS and had become almost a semi-official annex for both the British and American intelligence agencies.

'How do you want me to contact you?' Spencer queried.

'I'm in Room 201.' It had been his room of choice during the War. 'We've got to move fast.'

'Give me a break, Jack, will you, you've only just bloody told me.'

He held Stein's gaze. 'I just hope to God you haven't got any other surprises up your sleeve that I should know about, have you?'

'Not just yet,' Stein chuckled.

'Good!' he said, with feeling.

'What do you want me to do?'

'I'll give you a call, but first things first; I'll have to inform the Home Secretary straightaway.'

'From what I've heard you don't get along too well with your Boss.'

'In my experience you deal with Stanley Bradshaw with a long spoon, hold your nose and hope for the best.'

'Well sooner you than me. And then what?'

'I'll have to think about putting a team together. If this goes belly up, it's my ruddy neck on the line.'

'Mine too,' Stein grunted, 'if we end up losing your Prime Minister, Brennan's not gonna be too happy that it happened on my watch either. It's a British-led Operation of course, but the politicians and the hawks on both sides of the Pond will want their pound of flesh and hang someone out to dry, and right now, I guess that's us.'

Spencer flicked his half smoked cigarette onto the pavement and ground it under his foot. As always Jack was spot on, but more importantly, Spencer was grateful he was on side and that he had someone to trust implicitly.

'I'll be in touch,' he said, with a flicker of a smile, and headed off down the street toward his car.

'Remember it's Room 201,' Stein called after him.

Spencer didn't look back but made a throw-away gesture with his right hand confirming that he'd heard.

Chapter 2
The Home Office, Whitehall

The perception in Whitehall, rightly or wrongly, was that Stanley Bradshaw was the real power behind the throne. He always appeared relaxed, personable, supremely confident and perhaps more to the point, deadly. He could, when necessary, be utterly charming and witty, but it was a side of the Home Secretary that Spencer had rarely encountered. Shortly after the end of the war, Bradshaw's career had appeared to be over. He had fallen foul of the Labour Party hierarchy, but like Lazarus, his political career had risen rapidly from the dead over the last decade. He was now older, wiser, and, it was said, slyer than ever. It was also rumoured within political circles that the Prime Minister's increasingly poor health had allowed Bradshaw rather more leeway than otherwise might have been and that behind the scenes he practically ran the country.

His position, or so it appeared, was now such, that nobody could question his political standing. But reading between the lines, and the security reports, Spencer guessed that the situation probably wasn't quite as cut and dried as it appeared on the surface. Although Haining was in poor health, he knew the Prime Minister well enough to suspect that he wouldn't be prepared to give up the reins of power without a fight. He had already made it perfectly clear, that ill-health or not, he intended to run for re-election next year.

The Prime Minister had fought his way out of extreme poverty by sheer hard work and academic ability via his local grammar school. He was someone Spencer could do business with. Haining had let it be known to him that he viewed Bradshaw with healthy disdain, whilst he didn't doubt his Home Secretary's political abilities, their backgrounds were worlds apart. He had once described Bradshaw's family

16

as a powerful political dynasty of intellectuals with a socialist conscience. Due to a series of recent health scares, Haining had admitted, albeit reluctantly, that he had found himself increasingly reliant on his Home Secretary's support. He also appeared acutely aware that there were those within his own Party, who thought he was a man of the past. But he wasn't quite yet dead and buried, even Bradshaw, hungry as he was for power, couldn't deny that Haining was still a force to be reckoned with.

In his own right Bradshaw certainly wasn't a stranger to controversy and amongst his own Labour Party colleagues, he was both feared and admired in equal measure. Even his harshest critics couldn't fault his renowned self-discipline and work ethic. Churchill had once described him as a mix of genius and a master manipulator. Bradshaw wanted total control of those around him; but unfortunately, the Director General of MI5, Spencer Hall, had proved to be the one exception, the one serious fly in the ointment over whom he had no control whatsoever. Although they both shared an almost Machiavellian approach to their work, dominating their every waking minute, it was the only thing they shared in common.

It seriously bothered Bradshaw that he'd never quite managed to get Spencer's measure. Spencer had been around the system far longer than he had. He was also well aware that Spencer's war record was second to none; he'd experienced intense combat, and had been at the forefront of British Intelligence throughout the war. It was a completely alien world to Bradshaw, who had been medically downgraded and excused from being conscripted into the armed forces.

As a consequence, Bradshaw had always found himself somewhat psychologically on the back foot in his dealings with Spencer. He was acutely aware that Spencer knew that his medical downgrading from the armed forces had been signed off by an army doctor, who just happened to be a close family friend of the Bradshaw family. It had been casually but deliberately dropped into one of their terse encounters. He knew full well that prior to his appointment as Home Secretary, Spencer would have routinely not only pulled his security file, but also his medical file. He knew that it wouldn't sit easily with Spencer and that the medical downgrading smacked of family influence.

Outwardly, at least, Bradshaw exuded an air of natural authority, but at times, could appear deceptively quiet, even self-effacing and unassuming. Spencer always thought that it was just an act, a part of an occasional nauseating charm offensive, which he found faintly patronising and had never yet been swayed by.

There was no denying that Bradshaw was an effective political operator, the cool master of a brief, and the sleight of hand. Spencer's predecessor had warned him that behind the greasy smile you had to watch for the knife embedded in your back. No surprise there. Bradshaw came from a political family and was introduced to politics in his childhood. Although they could easily have afforded a private education, he had attended the local grammar school; it was nothing more than a political stance. However, they relaxed their principles when the academically gifted prodigal son won a place at Oxford University.

To Spencer's mind, Bradshaw was all about rhetoric rather than substance. The gold Dunhill lighter and the Saville Row suits didn't quite match his dyed in the wool socialist stance as a man of the people. He smoked a pipe in public, but only the finest Havana cigars in private. Like many politicians, Bradshaw was two-faced, but there was something about him that always set him apart from his peers. He also came with quite a reputation, and although Spencer had never personally witnessed Bradshaw's darker moments, amongst the Civil Service he had earned himself the rather dubious nickname of Krakatoa, after the Indonesian volcano. But there again, he

18

guessed, that his venom was probably spread sparingly, and only aimed against those he could bully into submission or influence. Most of the time, at least to other people, Bradshaw appeared both attentive and engaging, but it was always at a price. It was also extremely difficult working with a Home Secretary who viewed the security services as nothing more than a necessary evil. But there again, Spencer suspected, that Bradshaw viewed him in much the same way.

On returning to the office after Todd Carter's funeral, Spencer asked his secretary, Dawn Abrams, to set up an urgent meeting with Bradshaw's office. Not unexpectedly she had found herself completely stonewalled by his unofficial gatekeeper, Margaret Ellis. The formidable Margaret, or Maggie as she was known, had originally earned her spurs as a junior Labour Party official but had astutely worked her way steadily through the rank and file. Also, by sleeping with Bradshaw, had arguably become one of the most powerful women in politics.

Her official job title was that of private and political secretary. The running joke doing the rounds in Whitehall was that somewhat naively both Bradshaw and Ellis believed they had been entirely discreet about their relationship. Amongst their clerical staff and official drivers, it was an open secret that they were lovers. To Spencer's mind, Maggie was a toxic mixture of ambition, charm and manipulation, underscored by a deep, ingrained sense of insecurity. As a consequence, she retained an incredible sway over Bradshaw. By all accounts the staff at the Home Office had become increasingly frustrated by Maggie's behaviour; she was forever meddling in business that didn't concern her, and putting forward policy ideas that were both way beyond her understanding, but, more importantly, her remit.

Spencer picked up his phone. 'I'm sorry, sir.' Dawn apologised, 'Ellis won't budge she says the Home Secretary's diary is completely full.'

19

'Is the bloody woman still on the line?'

'Yes, sir.'

'Then put her through.'

He waited, the phoned clicked several times before Maggie's dulcet tones came on the line. 'Now what is this all about?'

'I need to see the Home Secretary.'

'Your girl said it was urgent.'

'It is.'

There was a slight pause; he heard a sharp intake of breath. 'I thought that I'd already explained the Home Secretary's diary is completely full, we have back to back meetings this afternoon, and then he's due to travel down to Chequers tomorrow to spend the weekend with the Prime Minister.'

'Perfect.'

'What's perfect?' she said irascibly.

'I couldn't have timed it better.'

He knew that he was winding Ellis up, but that was all part of the game.

'I really do have rather a lot on my plate, can you kindly let me known what this is all about?'

'If I did, I'd have to shoot you.'

She snorted down the phone in exasperation. 'I can't free up his diary; he simply won't agree to it, his meetings have been set in stone for weeks.'

Spencer said, sharply, 'Tell the Home Secretary it's a matter of national security.'

'Not that old nugget,' Maggie said dismissively. In her experience, Spencer had used that card once too often to wangle a meeting with Bradshaw when it hadn't been strictly necessary.

'Tell him,' he repeated coldly, 'that if he doesn't see me this afternoon, it won't only be his neck on the line, but yours as well.' Spencer allowed a silence to fall between them.

She wasn't quite so sure of herself now and instinctively backed down. He heard a noise; it sounded like the ruffling of paper. He presumed that she was checking his diary.

'I might be able to slot you in at 3.45,' she said, stiffly.

'Good,' he said, dismissively, 'I'll put you on hold; you can sort the details out with my secretary *Miss Abrams*.'

*

On arriving at Bradshaw's outer office, Maggie Ellis was waiting to meet him. Spencer could never quite understand Bradshaw's attraction to the woman. For all his faults, and there were many, the man oozed sophistication. He loved the arts and was a renowned collector of paintings and ancient artefacts. Before his marriage Bradshaw's attractive wife, Helen Howe, was a school teacher and was now a successful author in her own right.

Maggie eased herself up from behind her desk; even in her prime, she had never been particularly attractive, which, Spencer assumed was probably why she tried so hard. Even now, in her early fifties, she was heavily made-up and pranced around in ridiculously high stiletto heels and garish tight fitting clothes like some ageing Soho Madam.

'Sir Spencer,' she said, stiffly, 'the Home Secretary is expecting you.'

He inclined his head slightly but barely acknowledged her. On entering Bradshaw's office Maggie hovered close behind him, obviously with the intention of sitting in on the meeting. Bradshaw was seated at a large Victorian desk and was fussing for some inexplicable reason with his cufflinks.

As always he was smartly dressed in a dapper Savile Row suit, accompanied by one of his favourite Turnbull &

Asser shirts, and bespoke black leather shoes from Lobb in St. James's Street. The office was its usual tidy self, the various trays neatly filled with an assortment of files and loose paperwork.

'Spencer, good to see you again,' he said glibly and invited him to sit down, gesturing toward one of two red leather chairs positioned in front of his desk.

Before accepting the offer, Spencer turned sharply to face Maggie. 'I need to speak with the Home Secretary in private,' he announced looking through her, rather than at her.

Maggie Ellis was on the verge of replying, but before she had the chance to respond, Bradshaw decided unexpectedly to cut her short. Generally, he found it often paid not to upset Spencer Hall unduly at least not without good reason.

'Maggie,' he said smoothly, 'would you mind closing the door behind you, please.'

She hesitated. Her eyes as they caught his were stormy, but with difficulty Maggie managed, but only just, to keep her temper in check. For such a Machiavellian character as Bradshaw, it never ceased to amuse those who worked closest to him, just how much hold she could exert. An icy silence fell between them before Maggie eventually turned on her stilettos and flounced out of the office loudly slamming the door behind her.

Bradshaw removed his reading glasses, and thoughtfully placed the tip of the arm in the corner of his mouth, before saying. 'Well Spencer, so what's this all about?' His voice had a slightly bored intonation about it.

Spencer steadily held his gaze; there was simply no easy way of telling him about the plot to kill the Prime Minister, but at that precise moment, the only thing running through Spencer's mind was that no matter how much he tried, there was something about Bradshaw, he couldn't quite bring himself to trust.

'You mentioned to Maggie earlier that it was urgent,' Bradshaw pressed him.

Shaking off his thoughts, he said. 'Yes, yes, I did. Do you mind if I smoke?'

'Feel free.'

Spencer slipped a pack of cigarettes out of his pocket. 'I was at Todd Carter's funeral this morning.'

'How did it go, I take it there was a good turnout?' Bradshaw's manner was clipped, almost perfunctory, as if he was simply going through the motions without any real interest.

'He was very popular,' Spencer said, snapping his lighter shut.

'So I believe.'

'Outside St. George's I met up with an old friend of mine.'

A flicker of irritation crossed Bradshaw's face. 'This better be good, Spencer, I've cancelled a meeting with the French Ambassador about this bloody State visit of General de Gaulle in April!'

'If my CIA contact is spot on and we screw up, then you can forget about de Gaulle's State visit, the French simply won't risk it, they'd call the whole damn thing off.'

At last, he had cornered the Home Secretary's undivided attention. Bradshaw sat bolt upright in his chair. 'Cancel,' he said in horror, 'what on earth are you talking about?'

'I'm talking about a KGB plot to assassinate the Prime Minister.'

A look of complete incredulity crossed Bradshaw's face. 'I'm sorry, Spencer, but is this has got to be some kind of a sick joke?'

'I only wish it were, but do I look like I'm joking?'

Bradshaw shook his head in disbelief. 'No, what are the Americans up to?'

'I'm not sure that I know what you mean?'

'The trouble is, Spencer, you and your CIA friends have lived in a world of deceit and lies for so long you wouldn't recognise the truth if it hit you in the face. You thrive on conspiracy theories; it's your life's blood.'

Spencer drew heavily on his cigarette but didn't respond, there didn't seem to be any point, Bradshaw was on a roll and hadn't quite finished with him yet.

'I'm sorry, I really am, but this whole idea is absolutely absurd, why on earth would the KGB want Jeremy Haining dead. Tell me, why would they?'

Spencer exhaled cigarette smoke slowly through his lips and nostrils. If nothing else, at least, he had managed to extract a reaction, a flicker of emotion from Bradshaw, that in itself was rare enough, he was normally stubbornly inscrutable and wasn't in the habit of giving anything away. He was rattled, so Spencer took his time answering. He looked across the desk at Bradshaw, his expression clouded by contempt, and said coldly.

'Do you honestly think that I'd waste *my* time if I didn't think the threat against the Prime Minister was real?'

Bradshaw shot him a glance, which if looks could kill would have floored him immediately. A senior Civil Servant had once told Spencer, that when the Home Secretary starts being nice to you, it's because he no longer sees you as a threat. Sitting across the desk from him, Spencer felt more than a frisson of satisfaction that hell was more in danger of freezing over before Bradshaw stopped viewing him as a potential threat to his political career.

'So how sure are your CIA friends about this plot to kill Haining?'

'The intelligence comes from their top agent inside the Kremlin.'

Bradshaw's face turned ashen. 'Okay,' he said tentatively, 'so what else do we have?'

24

'I'm afraid it's still early days.'

'Well, surely there must be something.'

'It doesn't get any better.'

Bradshaw gave him a wintry smile. 'It rarely does.'

'The CIA believes the hired assassin is either a current or an ex-British agent.'

He arched his brows questioningly. 'So, is this agent of yours in the pay of the KGB?'

'As I said they might not be current.'

'But they could have been in their pay before they left the Service?'

'I can't answer that.'

'So basically, you don't have a frigging clue!'

Spencer shot him a cold hard look and replied truthfully. 'No, I don't, but given the fact I only learnt about the plot a few hours ago what the hell are you expecting?'

Bradshaw held back; he knew when he'd more than met his match. There was something about the man that radiated a certain inner menace. He let the matter drop; he wanted to move on and hopefully disguise his unease.

'From a security angle, what do you want us to do?'

'I believe the Prime Minister is spending the weekend at Chequers.'

'Yes, he is.'

'I've already instructed the local police to increase their patrols.'

Chequers had served as the private country retreat of the Prime Minister since 1921. During the war, the security surrounding the Buckinghamshire estate had been considered inadequate. Things had changed of course, but even so, the sprawling grounds surrounding Chequers still posed a serious number of security issues, and even with the increased police presence, Spencer was well aware, that it was still woefully undermanned.

'We'll need to take a close look at the PM's diary,' Bradshaw suggested.

Spencer looked at him questioningly.

'We can't expose him to any unnecessary risks.'

'Maybe not, but if we start making too many changes to his diary, the KGB will suspect that we've discovered the plot.'

An expression of horror crossed Bradshaw's face. 'So what are you saying?'

'I'm saying we can't tweak it too much otherwise they'll be onto us.'

'Are you being serious, Spencer?'

'Yes, I am,' he replied coolly, before continuing, 'I've arranged for his official car to be installed with bullet proof glass.'

'You mean it wasn't already?'

'It wasn't thought to be necessary.'

Bradshaw's eyes suddenly flashed with anger. 'So what are you trying to tell me, Spencer, that you're prepared to risk the PM being exposed to some assassin?'

'It's a calculated risk.'

'Yes, it's your calculation, but at the end of the day he'll end up being no more than a sitting duck! '

'I'm well aware of that.'

'Let's not forget, we're talking about the PM's life on the line here!'

'With due respect, sir, there's no other way of dealing with the threat,' Spencer said, bleakly. 'On a day to day basis we'll increase his security, but nothing too over the top to arouse suspicions. The last thing we need is for the Press to pick up on anything and give the game away.'

Bradshaw could see the logic of it, but he was still uncomfortable. He took a sharp intake of breath and said. 'I just hope to God that you know what you're doing.'

Spencer gave him a long, slow look in return. 'So do I, but if I don't, then we both know that it's my neck on the line.'

'Yes, so it is,' Bradshaw said, crisply. 'Without a name, without any serious clues about the identity of the PM's assassin then you're pretty much powerless to act.'

Although he wasn't quite smug, from Spencer's point of view, it was near enough. The trouble was that as much as it pained him, he couldn't disagree.

'So,' Bradshaw said, whipping on his glasses, 'I'll phone the Prime Minister and-.'

Spencer raised his hand and cut him dead.'

'I'd rather you didn't.'

Bradshaw looked at him sharply.

'There's been a security lock down,' Spencer explained.

The Home Secretary's gaze immediately travelled to the bank of phones on his desk and made to reach for the red scrambler.

'With due respect, sir, I'd rather you didn't.'

'Then what the *hell* do you want me to do?' he rasped, irritably.

'I'd rather you told the PM in person.'

'But I'm not due at Chequers until tomorrow lunchtime.'

Spencer held his ground; he wanted the Home Secretary to change his plans.

'Whilst I don't doubt that your CIA sources are impeccable and that there's a serious threat against the Prime Minister's life.'

Spencer interrupted him. 'We can play this one or two ways, sir.'

'Go on,' Bradshaw said, somewhat guardedly.

'As the Head of MI5, I'm duty bound to report to you.'

'Yes, you are.' he answered, stiltedly.

Spencer met his gaze coldly. 'Then, let's put it this way sir, god forbid, but if anything should happen to the Prime Minister over the next twenty-four hours, it'll be down to you.'

Bradshaw breathed deeply, Spencer never, if ever referred to him as sir, and it was beginning to grate on him, it was insincere but had the desired effect of placing him on the defensive. Whatever he was about to say, meant that the ball was finally back in his own court, and as Home Secretary, it was his decision, his responsibility, and his alone. Whilst he had never particularly liked Spencer as a man, in a grudging kind of way, he couldn't help but respect him.

Spencer went on smoothly, something about making a record of their meeting, and that the notes would be made available to any subsequent inquiry. Bradshaw knew only too well that Spencer was good at what he did, and had skillfully, if only temporarily, placed the onus on his decision.

He needed to play it carefully and certainly did not want to allow his venom to boil over. He didn't like taking orders, and least of all from the Head of MI5. Although Spencer hadn't commanded him directly to change his diary plans, and bring forward his visit to Chequers, between the lines, he'd made it quite clear that Bradshaw would be crucified in any subsequent public inquiry into the Prime Minister's death.

Bradshaw's expression closed down. 'Leave it with me,' he said, sharply, and automatically leaned forward and opened his diary. He was due to attend a reception this evening hosted by the Foreign Secretary at Lancaster House, in St. James's. He'd obviously have to make his excuses and also get his staff to contact Chequers to bring forward his visit to stay with the Prime Minister over the weekend.

'I'm sure *Miss Ellis* will be able to make all the necessary arrangements for you, sir.'

28

It ran through Bradshaw's mind there was no doubting that Spencer Hall could be a toxic bastard at times. He chose not to respond to his barbed comment and let it rest. He adjusted his reading glasses and inclined his head indicating that their meeting was at an end.

Spencer pushed back his chair and made to leave, but as he gripped the door handle, he glanced over his shoulder and said. 'Of course, I'll have to inform the Head of Special Branch.'

'Yes, very well,' he said, flatly.

'What about the Police Commissioner?'

'I'll leave it with you to tell both of them the sordid details.'

'May I also remind you, sir, that this situation is for your eyes and ears only, and under no circumstances are you to discuss this with anyone who does not need to know, and that includes your private secretary. Can I have your complete assurance on this?'

Bradshaw looked at Spencer with almost a sneer on his face and said. 'The one thing I do know *Sir Spencer* is when and where to keep my mouth shut.'

'So I have your assurance then?'

'Yes, you do!'

As Spencer closed the door, Bradshaw leaned back in his chair and thoughtfully linked his fingers behind his head. He thrived on controlling those around him, but Spencer was the one serious exception, the maverick in his well-ordered world. At the back of his mind, Bradshaw couldn't help wondering what the secret service had on him. His life had not been entirely scandal-free, although he had largely managed to keep his private life under wraps. His ongoing and sometimes, volatile relationship with Maggie Ellis was an open secret in Whitehall, and that obviously included British Intelligence. He had been forced on occasions to persuade and even occasionally pay journalists to keep his private life out of the Press and the public domain.

Bradshaw suspected that Spencer Hall was simply biding his time and that he not only knew where all the skeletons were buried but was waiting for the right moment to dredge up some past misdeed, and that if push came to shove, he would use it as a bargaining chip against him, and bury his career once and for all.

Bradshaw pressed his intercom. Maggie answered, her tone was sharp, and she obviously still had a strop on.

'I need to cancel the reception this evening.'

'It's a bit late, isn't it, to be pulling out.' She said.

'I'm well aware of that,' he answered irritably, 'and whilst you're at it, get someone to arrange transport for this evening.'

'Transport,' Maggie repeated.

'Yes, contact Chequers and let them know I'm travelling down this evening.'

'But you're not due until tomorrow lunchtime; I'll have to liaise with No10.'

'Just do whatever you have to, tell them it's imperative that I see the Prime Minister today!'

There was a slight hesitation on the line. 'But it's-.'

'Just sort it out will you!'

Bradshaw slammed the receiver down on her. Although he was prepared to indulge her, and give Maggie a certain amount of leeway, even put up with her continual mood swings and volatile temperament, there were times when Maggie knew when to draw a line; the meeting with Spencer had obviously rattled him.

Chapter 3
MI5 HQ

On returning to his office, Spencer asked his secretary to place a call to Assistant Commissioner Luke Garvan at Scotland Yard.

'Can you let his staff know that it's urgent?'

Dawn Abrams had worked for Spencer long enough to detect when there was a certain uncompromising edge to his voice. 'Yes sir,' she said compliantly.

He replaced the receiver, and reached into his desk drawer for a pack of cigarettes and lit one. Whereas he might have usually hesitated to call in Scotland Yard, he knew Luke Garvan well from his days when he was seconded to British Intelligence. Ever since they had continued to remain in touch enjoying the occasional drink not only to discuss business but to put the world to rights. It was an easy relationship borne out of mutual respect.

As Spencer tossed his lighter back into the desk drawer a red light flashed on the intercom; he picked up the black phone from a bank of three. It was Dawn.

'I have Assistant Commissioner Garvan on the line for you, sir.'

'Thank you.'

There was a click as she connected them through.

'Luke,' Spencer said, expectantly.

'This better be important.'

'Why?'

'I'm up to my bloody neck in it.'

'Why what's going on?'

'Don't you ever read the sodding briefs?' Garvan barked down the phone.

Spencer suddenly realised what he meant. 'You mean the State visit?'

The State visit of President Charles de Gaulle in April was causing a number of security issues for both the French police and their counter-intelligence service, the SDECE that needed to be ironed out. Their concerns were legitimate considering the number of attempts on de Gaulle's life, so it wasn't surprising they were anxious to ensure the security arrangements were sound.

'Of course, I've read the bloody briefs, but trust me, this problem's a bit closer to home.'

There was a slight pause at the end of the phone. 'What's wrong?'

'I need your help.'

'What kind of help?' Garvan asked warily.

'It's right up your street.'

Garvan let out a strangled laugh. 'That normally means the shit's about to hit the fan.'

Spencer blew out a cloud of blue-grey smoke from his cigarette. Garvan always had the measure of him; he couldn't deny it. 'Yes, it is.'

He could hear Garvan groan. 'I don't need this; I really don't, at least not right now!'

'Me neither. My courier should be with you in about half an hour or so.' Spencer said, instinctively checking his watch.

'This better be good, Spence!' Garvan snorted down the phone at him.

'You'll need to clear your diary for Monday afternoon.'

'It's cutting things a bit fine, isn't it?

'Yes, I'm sorry, but I've only just found out myself.'

'Do I have a choice?'

There was a slight pause on the end of the line. 'It's a lock down.'

32

Garvan closed his eyes.

'I'll need you to be at St Philips Hotel at 4.30.'

He knew better than to ask why, at least not over the phone, a lockdown meant that whatever Spencer had stumbled across was a matter of National Security. 'Okay,' he said, reluctantly, 'I'll get Pat to clear my diary.' Pat Johnson had worked alongside Garvan for four years now and could be completely relied upon to make all the necessary arrangements. 'But you know that I'll have to run it by the Commissioner first, I just can't drop everything on my desk.'

'Don't worry about the Commissioner it's already been cleared by the Home Secretary.'

Even so Garvan still felt that he needed to cover his own back, and make sure Spencer really did have the clearance of the Met Commissioner to lift him from his duties, especially as he was due to attend another meeting with the French on Monday afternoon, he simply couldn't pull out without some valid justification. The French security guys were difficult enough to deal with at the best of times, and would probably view his absence as a personal affront.

'Don't worry,' Spencer reassured him, 'I've spoken to the Commissioner, he doesn't know the ins and outs of the matter just yet, but I made it clear that he probably doesn't want to get on the wrong side of the Home Secretary.'

'No, I can't imagine he does.'

'So then I'll see you at 4.30 sharp,' Spencer repeated unnecessarily.

'Okay, I'll be there,' Garvan capitulated, before setting the receiver back onto the cradle and summoning Pat to his office.

'Yes, sir?'

Garvan explained that he was expecting a courier from MI5 and that he wanted her to meet him personally at the front gate. Pat guessed that for whatever reason, he didn't want to alert any unnecessary interest at Scotland Yard's main reception desk.

Twenty minutes later Pat returned to the office and handed her boss a plain brown sealed envelope. He thanked her, and waited until she closed the door before picking up a paper knife from the desk drawer, and slicing open the envelope. He wasn't quite sure what he had been expecting, but Spencer's all too familiar spidery scrawl, was typically blunt and to the point and not for the first time completely took the wind out of his sails.

Just when he was beginning to believe that he already had more than enough on his plate with de Gaulle's State visit looming large in three months' time, reading that the CIA had come across a potential plot to assassinate the Prime Minister, suddenly sent his world into free fall. Just when he thought it couldn't get any worse, it just had.

For Christ's sake, if only Spencer had stumbled upon some random nutter who was out to kill the PM, it would almost have been bearable, but knowing this was a major plot and that his hired assassin wasn't some strange weirdo with a grudge, but a highly trained intelligence field agent suddenly brought his world crashing down around his ears. As the senior officer in charge of Special Branch, he was personally responsible for the Prime Minister's security. Haining had always fought against having an overt police presence. He had a trusted armed personal bodyguard, and usually, no more than two police outriders to accompany him on visits around the country. On Garvan's watch, at least up until now, there had never been any major issues, the odd rotten egg or verbal abuse had been hurled at Haining from disgruntled members of the public, but that kind of thing came with the territory. But this was a whole different kettle of fish; it had certainly ratcheted up the stakes.

Garvan still couldn't quite get his head around it, why on earth would the KGB want Haining dead, he might well have publically criticised Soviet policy, but so had every other major western leader. Garvan carefully folded the letter and placed it in his safe, however much he trusted Pat Johnson, he couldn't afford to take any chances, besides it was on a need to know basis, and even the Met Commissioner, at least temporarily, had been left in the dark. He spun the tumbler until he heard it click, and then double checked to make sure it was locked.

From past experience Spencer was adept at playing his cards close to his chest, his rise through the ranks of MI5 certainly wasn't unexpected, but had been aided and abetted with the Prime Minister's approval; it was he, and he alone who had finally approved Spencer's appointment as the Director General of MI5. Haining's decision had not been greeted with universal approval within the intelligence and political community. Spencer's track record was second to none. During the war he had been one of the founding fathers of the Double Cross system, which was in essence, an anti-espionage and deception operation set up by the British Security Service, to infiltrate and capture Nazi agents operating in Britain, and turn them into double agents, to feed disinformation to the Nazi High Command. At heart, Spencer had always been something of a rough diamond, a formidable field agent but not a seasoned desk man. His appointment as the Head of MI5 had forced him to rein in his natural instincts, and at least outwardly, to play along with his political masters, but deep down, Garvan knew that Spencer still wanted to call all the shots.

Chapter 4
Chequers, Buckinghamshire

A dagger of biting cold hit their lungs as they stepped out onto the terrace at Chequers. Fortunately, yesterday's driving snowstorm in Buckinghamshire had ceased, but even so the bitter cold chilled them to the marrow. Gazing out across the parkland Jeremy Haining spotted his police guards on patrol through the grounds. He drew heavily on his cigar and said distractedly.

'There seems to be more and more of the buggers out there every time I look. It really upsets Flossie you know.'

Bradshaw smiled knowingly; Flossie was Haining's much-loved springer spaniel.

'She gets so upset when they're lurking about in the bushes.'

'Yes, I'm sure she does.'

'It's like a red rag to a bull. Only the other day, bless her, she managed to get her own back and bit one of the buggers, not her fault, of course, she's going blind, and they startled the life out of the poor darling.'

Hearing her name, Flossie momentarily looked up and wagged her tail before shuffling off through the snow to continue sniffing her way across the empty flower beds.

Although Bradshaw was an animal lover and had a much loved golden retriever of his own, he couldn't understand how Flossie had become a law unto herself. Haining and his wife were constantly making excuses for her behaviour, on one particularly memorable occasion, when Flossie decided to take exception to a visiting Head of State's leg. All hell had broken loose when she suddenly launched herself down the staircase into the hallway of No10 and sunk her razor-sharp teeth into his flesh before Haining finally managed to grab hold of her.

Bradshaw stood beside the Prime Minister and thoughtfully followed his gaze across the parkland as two armed guards stopped to chat. 'I'm afraid in this day and age it's an increasingly necessary evil,' he said, at length, 'a police presence comes with the job.'

'Yes, I suppose you're right,' Haining snorted.

Bradshaw found himself nervously clearing his throat. 'I had a meeting in London this afternoon with the Head of MI5.'

Haining's brows drew into a frown. 'You mean with Spencer Hall?'

'Yes,' Bradshaw responded, and inclined his head toward the police patrolling the grounds. 'Unfortunately, sir, I'm afraid we've had to increase your security.'

Haining turned to him sharply and demanded. 'Why, what's happened?'

Bradshaw took a sharp intake of breath. 'Apparently MI5 has received intelligence from the CIA about a possible plot.'

'What kind of plot?'

He looked uneasy. 'I'm sorry, Jeremy, but there's really no easy way of telling you this, the Americans have stumbled on a plot to assassinate you.'

The colour drained instantly from Haining's face, that kind of thing, or so he thought, only ever happened across the Channel in France, but was absolutely unheard of in Britain.

'Assassinate me!' He repeated in disbelief. 'Good God, surely there's got to be some kind of mistake.'

'If only there was, apparently the Americans have it on good authority that the KGB is behind the plot.'

'The bloody Soviets!' he rasped gruffly, 'then why hasn't the White House contacted me.'

'Well, with due respect sir, they do appear to have gone through the appropriate channels, or else we wouldn't be having this conversation.'

'But why in God's name do the Soviets want *me* out of the picture?'

Bradshaw took a long deep breath. 'I really couldn't say.'

'I can think of a few political leaders they might want to bump off, but I never thought I'd be on their list.'

Bradshaw carefully adjusted the knot of his blue silk tie. 'Whatever the truth might, or might not be, Jeremy, we simply can't afford to take any chances.'

'So what exactly are MI5 doing about it?'

Bradshaw pulled a face. 'From what I can gather at this stage, they really haven't got that much to go on. Mind you, in my experience, Spencer Hall always plays it pretty close to his chest.'

'Yes, well that's as maybe, but it's my ruddy chest that's likely to have a bullet in it, isn't it!'

Bradshaw was noncommittal.

'So basically, Stan, what you're saying is that until some bloody nutter decides to take a pot shot at me, I'm a ruddy sitting target!'

'I'm sure it won't come to that,' he replied smoothly. 'Spencer said he was going to liaise with Scotland Yard.'

'Well that's very reassuring,' Haining barked sarcastically, and tossed his cigar down onto the terrace and ground it under his foot. 'Considering the gravity of the situation, I would still have expected a call from Washington!'

'I think you'll find that under normal circumstances they would have alerted you personally, but I understand there has been a complete security lockdown. Spencer didn't even want me phoning you on the secure line.'

Haining started to pace; he didn't quite know what to do or say.

'Besides,' Bradshaw continued, 'if the French were ever to get wind of the plot they won't hesitate to pull the plug on the State visit in April.'

38

Haining shook his head. 'No,' he grunted, 'there'd be far too much diplomatic fallout if they call it off this late in the day.'

'Not half as much fallout as there'd be if a bullet ricocheted off you and ended up killing the President of France.'

'You really do have a way with words, Stan, don't you?' Haining grunted.

Bradshaw gave a dismissive shrug. 'I was only trying to point out the facts, Jeremy.'

Haining pulled his collar up against the cold, and said, emphatically. 'Right enough is enough, I want Spencer Hall and Luke Garvan hauled in to see me as soon as possible, but not here at Chequers, I'll see them in London.'

Bradshaw looked at him searchingly.

'Do you understand I don't want my wife to get wind of anything, not a whisper about this plot?'

'Yes, of course, we'll keep everything under wraps. I'll sort something out and check our diaries.'

'No offence, Stan,' Haining said, brusquely. 'But I'd really rather it was a private meeting, you know, just the three of us.'

Bradshaw met his gaze. Haining detected there was a certain amount of reluctance in his Home Secretary's eyes.

'Is there a problem?' he blasted back at him.

'I was just wondering whether it was wise.'

'Wise, what do you mean *wise*?'

'You know how these people are -.'

Haining cut him dead in midstream. 'I think you forget that it's my neck on the line here, Stan. Beside's the three of us go back a long way.'

Bradshaw's face registered surprise.

'I've known Hall and Garvan for years, in fact, our paths first crossed during my time at the Foreign Office in the War,' he said, with a flourish of his hand. 'If I'm being brutally honest, I can't say that it was a particularly pleasant experience, well, at least, it wasn't on my part.'

Bradshaw looked at him expectantly, but it was obvious that Haining had no intention whatsoever of enlightening his Home Secretary about his past history and connection to them.

Haining thrust his hands deep into his overcoat pockets. 'Unlike some people, the one thing you always know is exactly where you stand with them, they're both straight-talking bastards and shoot from the hip, they speak their minds, and there's no side with either of them.'

Although it remained unsaid, he also respected not only their opinions but trusted his two leading security advisers implicitly.

Bradshaw suspected that Haining's comments about them underlined a thinly veiled attack against himself. To the outside world, they were close political allies, but it was simply nothing more than a marriage of convenience. Bradshaw needed Haining's experience and gravitas, and pre-eminence amongst the political elite to claw his way up to power, but now that power was very much in the balance. Haining's ill health was a factor, he was no longer quite the indomitable force that had driven the Labour Party to victory, and he needed Bradshaw, and his growing influence to protect his position. It remained at heart an uneasy alliance, they both used each other to suit their own ends, beyond that, they were diametrically opposed, there was certainly no particular personal friendship between them. Even so, Bradshaw was astute enough to know, that despite Haining's health issues, he was still a force to be reckoned with and that you underestimated him at your peril.

By now Haining was on a roll, and said, sharply. 'Arrange the meeting for Monday evening at No 10.'

Bradshaw narrowed his eyes questioningly.

'My wife is attending some West End Show or other with friends. Nothing formal, you understand,' he said, and almost as an afterthought added. 'Tell them I'll throw in dinner at the flat.'

It was a rare honour indeed to be invited for a meal with Haining; he hardly ever entertained privately. In fact, he positively hated the idea. It was one thing to throw official functions, but that was a duty. Both he and his wife were great hosts, but he loved nothing more than relaxing quietly away from the formality and the pressures in the family's private quarters above No10, or over the shop as he liked to call it.

Bradshaw didn't allow his irritation at being sidelined show. 'I'll have my office contact them right away,' he answered compliantly.

'Make it 7.30, dinner will be for 8 or,' he said, as an afterthought, 'whenever it's ready.'

Haining's gaze once again travelled slowly back across the gardens; there seemed to be some kind of duty change over going on, whatever it was, his bodyguards appeared entirely oblivious to the Prime Minister's interest.

'It's getting cold out here, would you like a drink?' he asked.

Bradshaw readily agreed.

Haining glanced over his shoulder and swore under his breath. 'Flossie!' he shouted, 'don't do that!'

The feisty Flossie had launched herself onto the snow covered lawn and was rolling excitedly on her back in god only knows what, but it was usually fox poo.

'I'll leave you to it, Prime Minister,' Bradshaw said, beating a hasty retreat back to the warmth of the house.

Chapter 5
Coulls Auction House, Bond Street, London

As Virginia Dudley slowly scanned the tightly packed crowd at Coulls Auction House, she was starting to relax, business was brisk, and so far every lot had sold well over its estimated asking price. She'd originally learned her craft at Coulls outlet in New York, but for the last two years had been working in London. The auction room was buzzing; crowded with a mix of private collectors and professional dealers. Virginia was good at what she did and had recently published a critically acclaimed book "The Life and Work of Rembrandt".

Even though the auction was going well, and the sale prices were far exceeding expectation, Virginia still looked pensive; there was some way to go, at least still fifty or so more lots. Even so she still felt a frisson of anxiety; she always did until the gavel came down on the final lot. On auction days, Virginia was usually to be found hovering in the wings, keeping a wary eye on both the auctioneer and the ranks of prospective buyers seated in uniform rows banked around the auctioneer's block.

The latest lot going under the hammer was a recently discovered pre-Raphaelite painting by John Everett Millais. There were two bidders seated on either side of the main aisle who were trying to outbid each other. She knew both of them well, one was from a well-known London art gallery, and the other was representing a wealthy American collector. This was what she loved. There was an almost palpable sense of expectation in the room as they steadily upped the bidding against one another; neither punter was willing to back down, at least not without a fight.

Virginia was watching them with growing interest; that is until her gaze glided slowly across the auction room and her eyes locked onto the figure of Sir Spencer Hall. He was seated beside the central aisle toward the rear of the auction room. On seeing him her heart suddenly missed a beat, and her pulse quickened. His shock of dark hair was now tinged with distinguished flecks of grey, but the tough, good looking face and the penetrating pale blue eyes were still just the same as she remembered them.

He smiled across at her; and even though she managed to look back at him with a cool directness that belied her inner turmoil, her thoughts were spiralling out of control. What the hell was he doing at the auction house, and why now, after all, these years had he decided to slip back into her life? For Virginia, the war had been a dark, desperate time, and without him, and without his selfless bravery she would have faced certain death at the hands of the Gestapo. Whilst she owed her life to Spencer seeing him at Coulls was a complete bolt out of the blue and had shaken her to the core.

The auction had almost started to become a distant blur. Spencer was a ghost from her past, and seeing him sitting in the auction house had dredged up so many poignant memories. Virginia's thoughts tumbled back to France and to a remote farmhouse kitchen, and her battered radio transmitter. At the time, it had been her only lifeline to her controllers in London, and her only means of receiving personal messages and instructions over the BBC French service.

Virginia's French Resistance circuit had been on the verge of total collapse, and the Gestapo were moving in fast to arrest her. A price had been placed on her head, and so Spencer was ordered to mount a rescue operation and parachuted into France. It wasn't just Virginia's resistance circuit at risk, under torture, there was no way of telling how many more lives might have been put at risk.

43

She remembered how they zig-zagged their way across occupied France, dicing with death as they repeatedly narrowly avoided being swept up by the Gestapo. At the time, Spencer had quite literally laid his life on the line for her. Without him and without his skill only one fate had awaited her, torture at the hands of the Gestapo and certain death. If Spencer had not found a way of linking up with Jack Stein's well equipped Maquis group, they would never have made it out alive.

Virginia stared at him gravely; remembering how they'd waited for a rescue flight to England, and how in the turmoil at the lonely remote French farmhouse, they'd spent the night together wrapped in each other's arms. She hadn't slept at all, but believing that she was still asleep Spencer had slipped out of bed to see whether Jack Stein's radio operator had managed to touch base with London and confirm their rescue flight.

Although Spencer had been gentle and loving toward her, Virginia was acutely aware that he'd never quite managed to break free from the tethers that bound him to the memory of Sarah Davis, a beautiful young British agent who had been brutally murdered in the early years of the war by a double agent. It was obvious to anyone who knew, and cared about him that he still loved her, still missed her deeply, and blamed himself for her death. As she held his gaze, she couldn't help wondering, if even now, Spencer was as much a prisoner of the past as she was.

Stein's radio operator successfully managed to contact London and summon up an RAF flight. The following evening with her heart in her mouth, Virginia found herself sheltering in the remote woods a mile or so from the farm house. She remembered peering through the trees and hearing the throbbing engines of the 148 Squadron plane as it banked sharply. This was it, their one and only realistic hope of escape. Snaking low the plane's moonlit shadow cast eerily across the fields. The pilot was aiming for the makeshift runway in the middle of the French countryside, with only the low flickering lights set out by the Maquis to guide him down, when he suddenly forced the nose down and landed on the uneven field.

Once safely down the pilot kept the propellers going, and Spencer bundled her into the aircraft, and within minutes they were off, bumping jerkily over the runway, the fuselage rattling as the pilot opened the engines to full throttle. The plane's engines throbbed noisily, and they were soon soaring up into the clear moonlit sky. Virginia's sense of relief proved to be short-lived, for as they neared the French coast, their flight swiftly turned into a nightmare all of its own as they found themselves coming under attack from the Luftwaffe. The RAF pilot frantically twisted and banked, hoping to God that his crew could return fire. But the deadly Messerschmitt fighter had ripped huge gashes in the fuselage, and they were losing power as fuel leaked from the tanks. The co-pilot was dead at the controls, and now it was touch and go whether they could even make it back to England.

In order to shake off the persistent German fighter they flew frightening low over the Channel and limped back across the glistening moonlit sea on nothing more than a wing and a prayer, with the engines straining to keep them in the air. They never quite managed to reach the RAF Station in Kent and ended up crash landing in some godforsaken meadow, where battered and bruised they clambered out of the aircraft still not quite able to believe that apart from the co-pilot everyone else had miraculously survived in one piece.

Virginia was an American by birth, and as a young woman before the war had enjoyed an affluent lifestyle in Baltimore, attending both Radcliffe and Bernard College, studying French, Spanish and German. She was visiting Paris when the war started and finding herself stranded in France volunteered as a driver with the French Ambulance Service.

45

After France finally capitulated and fell under Nazi control, ever resourceful Virginia bided her time before managing to organise not only her own escape but also that of two girlfriends safely across the Pyrenees into Spain and finally back to England via Gibraltar.

Once back in London, she kicked her heels around for a while but chose to remain rather than return home to her native Baltimore. Through various old friends and new found contacts, her gift for languages soon came to the attention of Britain's newly formed Special Operations Executive, the so-called SOE. She remembered feeling flattered at being approached, but even so, had somewhat warily volunteered her services, and much to her surprise had ended up passing the vigorous training with flying colours.

Before being sent out on a mission, every SOE agent was routinely issued with a small pill-box containing two cyanide pills. They were known as L-pills. The thinking behind their issue, being that it was better to die than be taken prisoner and tortured by the Gestapo. Everyone had a breaking point, and playing mouse to the Gestapo's cat meant agents had a limited life expectancy.

Posing as a representative for a cosmetics company, with the codename 'Bridget,' she was eventually parachuted into occupied territory, landing in a muddy torch lit field. Her mission was to aid the French Resistance and liaise with other SOE agents already on the ground in the area. Virginia's fluency in the language was undoubtedly an advantage, but the Germans were also not expecting a lone woman cycling through the French countryside to be armed to the teeth. Spencer still believed it had given her an edge, and also an element of surprise. But even so working as a courier delivering coded messages to and from radio operators was a nerve-wracking business and more to the point, it was dangerous work and took a particular brand of courage.

By the time Spencer arrived in France, the majority of Virginia's fellow SOE agents had already been rounded up and placed under arrest, and all had gone without exception to their deaths either under torture or within concentration camps. Virginia considered herself lucky to have escaped with her life, but that was in no small measure down to Spencer. Although Virginia had initially served with the SOE, toward the final stages of the war she had transferred and served with the American Office of Strategic Services.

She closed her eyes briefly, since those days the world had never seemed quite the same to her, but more to the point, she could never be the same again.

So why was he here at Coulls? She needed to know. Those penetrating pale blue eyes were still locked mesmerizingly onto hers. He passed her another quick, flicker of acknowledgement. Virginia figured that she had a choice to stay rooted to the spot until the auction was over or get it over and done with and ask him what the hell he was up to. She decided to take the bull by the horns and found herself taking a sharp intake of breath before quietly moving from the wings of the auction house, and heading purposefully down the central aisle toward him. She extended a well-manicured hand, all blood red nail polish, in greeting.

'Well, Spence, what a pleasant surprise.'

He clasped her outstretched hand between his own. 'Ginny,' he whispered, coming to his feet, gently brushing his lips against her cheek.

Virginia's expression was a mixture of fear and defiance. She smiled slightly, and much to her annoyance felt herself blushing, this wasn't the ice cold reaction of old, at least not from the woman who in her young days had remained perennially calm in the face of danger.

'What the hell are you doing here, Spence?'

A slight smile crossed his face. 'I need your help, Ginny,' he said quietly.

Her expression was giving nothing away, and she suggested. 'Maybe we should head to my office.'

Her tone was such that it wasn't so much a question as a command. Virginia had always been considered bossy and self-opinionated, in the early days of her training there had been a number of doubts raised by British Intelligence about her suitability, and whether she would be able to fit into the SOE and accept orders. Even Virginia was the first to admit that she didn't like being directed and always had to be right. But during a training lecture at Arisaig in Scotland, she finally met her match in the shape of Spencer Hall. He'd seen too many people thrive on drama, and Virginia had from the beginning been renowned for the odd histrionic moment. There was something about him, an underlying sense of menace in his eyes and demeanour that had made her finally decide to toe the line. But it was only later on in the war that she discovered he was the most solid, loyal man she had ever met.

During their short, but memorable time serving together in France it also became rapidly apparent to her that the bigger the crises and danger surrounding them, and the more desperate their position, the calmer and more charismatic Spencer appeared to become. Quite simply she owed him everything for his bravery in helping to snatch her from certain arrest by the Nazis.

Spencer followed her out of the auction room and up a narrow staircase to the first floor where she showed him into her office, it wasn't overly large, but he was staggered to find that it was crammed with works of art, either hanging on the walls or stacked up against the furniture. He assumed their owners had brought them in for valuation and that they were destined to be auctioned off at some future sale downstairs.

She gently closed the door and spun round to face him. 'So, what's going on, Spence?' Virginia's tone was formal but polite. 'Why are you here?'

48

'As I said downstairs I need your help.'

'Jesus Christ, Spence, I'm getting a bit long in the tooth now for you to be asking *me* for help. What's passed is past, there's no going back.' Her voice was sharp.

'You look just fine from where I'm standing.'

She brushed over his compliment. 'Whatever it is I'm not interested, I've moved on, I needed to stand back, and make a new life for myself.'

'Have you?'

'You know damn well I resigned from the CIA in 1952, that's what eight years ago now. It's a long time to be out of the game.'

'Eight years or not rumour has it that you've done the odd favour for the CIA since then.'

There didn't seem to be any point in denying it; he obviously knew that she had.

He looked at her, almost indulgently. 'Ginny, you know how it is, no-one ever entirely leaves the Service, it's like being divorced, you might move on and cut the familial ties, but there's always an irrevocable link to the past that can never be broken.'

Virginia's eyes narrowed as she looked at him; it was coupled with an unmistakable hardness. 'What the hell's that supposed to mean?'

'The ties can never be completely severed between us; we're family.'

'Well, maybe in your opinion they can't,' she snorted dismissively.

'Not just mine,' he said smoothly, 'your former colleagues in the CIA want you on board.'

Her face might have looked strained, but she countered defiantly. 'Whatever it is, I really don't want to get involved. I mean it, Spence!'

'Maybe not but I thought you'd like to know that a friend of yours is in town.'

49

She gave him a rather puzzled smile. 'What friend?'

'Jack Stein, I spoke to him on the phone last night; he's really looking forward to meeting up with you again.'

Knowing Jack Stein of old Virginia thought it highly unlikely, they'd never particularly seen eye to eye with one another. 'Go on,' she said wearily, 'I suppose you might as well tell me why you're here.'

Whatever it was, had to be serious, she knew that. As the Director General of MI5, Spencer wouldn't normally have climbed down from his ivory tower to seek her out, at least not if the shit hadn't already hit the fan.

He explained everything to her, the plot, Agent Freda, and how Chas Brennan had dispatched Stein to London. Virginia knew Agent Freda personally; they had worked together briefly in Berlin a few years back, she was one of the CIA's best, if not their very best agent on the current circuit.

Even so Virginia expressed her surprise, wondering if the intelligence was completely sound. Spencer couldn't blame her, but told her they were taking it seriously and had ordered a complete security lockdown, especially as the intelligence indicated that the KGB had taken the unusual step of hiring a contract killer for the job.'

Virginia picked up a pack of Chesterfield cigarettes off her desk and lit one. 'Have we any idea who they've hired?'

'Well that's the rub, Freda couldn't be sure, but it looks like the KGB have managed to bag either a current or an ex-British agent.'

Now she hadn't seen that one coming, far from it, and guessed that as calm as Spencer appeared on the surface, he was between a rock and a hard place.

She blew out a plume of smoke. 'Whatever way you look at it, you really are in the shit, aren't you.'

If there was one thing he could rely on, was that she'd speak her mind, she certainly hadn't disappointed him. 'I guess, Ginny, that's why I'm here.'

'Okay, so what's this gotta do with me?'

'I need to get a team together, a tight-knit one I can trust, and your being an American is precisely why I need you on side.'

He was obviously concerned British Intelligence had been infiltrated by the Soviets, and that the KGB's contract killer might possibly be the tip of the iceberg. It was just a guess; she might have misjudged the situation. After all, she'd been out of the game for a while now and wasn't current. More to the point, she wasn't quite sure what he was expecting of her.

Whilst Virginia wasn't entirely unsympathetic; she said defensively. 'I really just can't drop everything to help out; I've got another auction coming up at the end of the month!'

By now Spencer had moved across the office and casually picked up one of the paintings stacked against the furniture. 'I've heard business is pretty good?' He glanced over his shoulder at her, his smile, whilst not quite smug, was near enough.

'Yes, yes it is,' she said, warily.

He sucked in his lower lip, appraising the turn of the century painting of a Jewish man wearing a kippah selling oranges in a Dutch marketplace. 'So, are Coulls still selling looted art?'

It was a loaded question, and try as she might, Virginia found it an effort to keep the anger off her face. She knew precisely what he meant. Coulls had recently found themselves mired in a high-profile court case, the accusation being, that the auction house was guilty of selling a painting that had been stolen from the National Museum in Warsaw during the Nazi occupation. It had subsequently undergone a

51

number of examinations to determine its authenticity by experts from Warsaw and the National Gallery in London. Virginia had found herself not only heavily criticised by the prosecution lawyers but had been castigated in the Judge's final summation of the case, that as Coulls leading authority, Virginia had failed to make adequate checks into the provenance of the painting. As a consequence, her name had been splashed across both the national and international press. Fortunately, Coulls had stood by her; they'd backed her to the hilt and paid not only their own legal fees but Virginia's as well.

But even before the Warsaw case came to light, there had been rumours circulating that Coulls and other leading international auction houses had unwittingly been selling artefacts looted by the Nazis from Jewish families who had perished in the gas chambers and concentration camps of occupied Europe.

She knew that Spencer was slowly turning up the pressure; there was an underlying inference that, if she failed to play the game, British Intelligence would make it a priority to take a closer interest in the nefarious dealings of London's leading auction house. Whatever way you looked at it, it wasn't only a threat, but blackmail. She couldn't fault him of course, in his shoes she'd have played exactly the same hand, the trouble was, try as she might Virginia knew that Spencer had the moral high ground. The Third Reich had led a systematic campaign to plunder art from not only the Jews but anyone else who had fallen foul of the regime. Although in the immediate aftermath of the war much of the stolen art had been successfully recovered by the Allies, there still remained countless thousands of valuable artefacts that had disappeared without a trace into private collections and galleries that had not been returned to their rightful owners.

Virginia was out on a limb, whilst she'd fought against Nazi Germany during the war, she was also acutely aware that her work at Coulls had unwittingly made her complicit in their war crimes; it was an uneasy mix, and Spencer had justifiably trumped her.

'You've always been a bastard!' she snorted.

He smiled at her; it was half in confidentiality and half in amusement. 'I need your help, Ginny, and I'll get it by whatever means, fair or foul.' He shot her a hard, cold probing stare. 'But it's really not just about me, Ginny; even your CIA friends in Langley have agreed you should be on board.'

So she didn't have a choice, if she decided to kick up a fuss, then it wouldn't only be MI5 leaning on her, but the CIA as well. She looked at him bleakly. 'I just can't walk away from Coulls, not just like that, it's not gonna be that easy, this is my life, I have a great career; it's what I do.'

'I know it is.'

Virginia looked at him almost pleadingly. 'I can't throw everything away, not this time!'

'Trust me, I'll arrange everything.'

She rolled her eyes in despair. 'I've heard that line before! I don't want to lose my job, Spence!'

'Leave it with me, I've got an idea.'

'Yeah, I thought you might have.'

Spencer checked his watch. 'What time are you expecting the auction to be over?'

She pulled a face. 'It shouldn't go much past lunch time.'

'Good, then make your excuses, I want you to be at the St. Phillips Hotel by 4.30.'

'God damn it, Spence, how long have you been planning all this?'

'Not long enough,' he replied truthfully. 'There's just one other thing.'

She met his gaze. 'Go on.'

'I understand that Stanley Bradshaw is a friend of yours.'

Again it was a loaded question. 'Yes, I know Stanley. What about him?'

'How does he strike you?'

Virginia considered her reply carefully. She still wasn't quite sure why it was important to him. 'He's a typical politician,' she answered enigmatically but guessed correctly there was a hidden agenda behind the question.

'A typical politician?' he repeated questioningly.

'Don't get me wrong, I like him, but I know how he operates at close quarters.'

Spencer asked her what she meant.

'Well, we might move in the same social circles, but I'm just an art dealer, not some fancy assed politician. I don't exactly pose a threat to him, do I?'

'I suppose not, 'Spencer agreed.

'Don't get me wrong, he's pleasant enough and great company, but that's as far as it goes.'

'Meaning what?'

'As I said I've seen how he operates.'

'Tell me.'

Her eyes met his, and she said. 'If he thinks you're a threat or if you happen to get on the wrong side of him, well, that's a different matter altogether. Bradshaw won't curse you to your face, that's really not his style, but behind the smile he'll sharpen the knives when your back's turned.'

'I understand Bradshaw and his wife take a keen interest in the art world, from what I've heard he's meant to be something of an expert.'

'Yes, he is,' she answered, guardedly.

'Is it true they've amassed quite a large art collection?'

'I'm sure you already know they have,' she said, flatly.

'As a politician, he doesn't make that much money.'

54

'His wife Helen is a writer, she earns good money, she had one of her books serialised on television recently'.

'Even so, it's still not enough to fund their lifestyle.'

'I really wouldn't know; that's rather more your department than mine.'

'What do you make of Maggie Ellis?'

His relationship with his political secretary was an enduring source of gossip in Whitehall; even their closest friends acknowledged that she held an incredible sway over Bradshaw.

She pulled a face and shrugged. 'What's to know, personally I don't understand the relationship. She struts around like some ageing hooker. I really can't work out the attraction, but whatever it is, she certainly has a cast iron hold over him, but god knows what it is.' She flashed him a smile. 'Maybe it's the sex; I can't think it can be anything else, can you? You've met her!'

He returned her smile. 'What about his wife?'

'What about her?'

'Does she know about them?'

She shrugged. 'I guess she must, it's not exactly something that comes up in conversation.'

'No, I can see that it might not,' he grinned.

'Come on Spence, why all the interest in Bradshaw?'

'As Home Secretary, he's my immediate boss.'

'So?'

'You know me, Ginny, I'm not a natural diplomat; I can't stand all the bloody double talk.'

'So what's new?'

'It's just that with all this going on right now I just need someone with your sixth sense for trouble to watch my back.'

Virginia was only too aware that Bradshaw was viewed as a divisive character, and that no-one was more likely to ignite the ire of his political opponents in the House of Commons. But Spencer knew that he enjoyed a life outside of the Westminster hothouse. He was well-known for having an abiding love of the arts and was considered to be something of a connoisseur in his own right. Whilst Virginia might describe Bradshaw as being thoughtful, charming and insightful; it was a world away from his political persona. But beyond the corridors of Whitehall, he was an entirely different creature altogether from the terse, crafted mannerisms of the seasoned politician.

It was this side of Bradshaw that he needed to cultivate, and to know more about. For a number of years now there had long been unsubstantiated rumours circling Whitehall that his private and political secretary, cum lover, Maggie Ellis had cultivated a number of well-placed contacts in the Soviet Embassy. Whilst they were outwardly above board, Spencer suspected that Maggie's closeness had on one or two occasions possibly compromised her position at the Home Office. Virginia was simply a means to an end, she knew them socially, and could do a little digging around without arousing any suspicion. The beauty of the arrangement was that Bradshaw had no inkling about Virginia's past links to either British Intelligence or the CIA.

Virginia narrowed her eyes as she tried to read his face. 'So what exactly do you want me to do?'

'I'll let you know this afternoon.' Spencer made to leave the office, but as he opened the door, he turned back to face her and said with a smirk. 'Don't be late, Ginny.'

Virginia blew out a plume of grey smoke from her cigarette. 'I won't be.' She held his gaze and said quietly. 'Do you know, Spence, there was a time when I thought you loved me?'

He really hadn't seen that one coming, but Virginia had always been a past master at serving a fastball, and it had completely floored him. Spencer hesitated, he knew all those years ago, he'd been a bloody fool to throw away so much, the chance of happiness. The idea of having an ally, of not being out there entirely on his own had been an attractive idea, quite simply it would have been a godsend. Spencer looked at her carefully as if for the first time. The trouble was he'd thrown it all away; he knew life would have been so different with Virginia at his side. She was still stunningly attractive, clever, resourceful, brave and astute. He'd never doubted that she'd loved him, only that she was still willing to give him a second chance. Spencer knew he didn't deserve her.

He gave her a tired, fleetingly smile. 'I guess it's a little late in the day to say that I did love *you*, I adored you!'

She'd always been known for her fierce independence and spirited personality. But as he stared into those large searching eyes, in his mind he hadn't so much walked away from the relationship, but had mistakenly believed that she was already heavily involved with a well-heeled aristocrat called Henry Palmer-Fortescue, a Guards officer with a large bank balance, but with little in the way of grey matter between his ears. In hindsight, he should have seen that it was never going to last, and it didn't, barely eighteen months and she had probably married him on the rebound.

Virginia's crisp voice and gleaming, ambiguous grin, disguised her feelings. 'Maybe when all this is over you could give me a call?' Try as she might she still couldn't bring herself to hate him, there was simply too much between them. The verbal fencing and the crackling sexuality which had underlain their relationship during the war came flooding back; the trouble was that without Spencer at her side, nothing had ever quite seemed so exciting, so intense.

There was surprising warmth in his smile, coupled with a deep sense of guilt about the wasted years between them. He gently placed his hand in hers and raised it to his lips. Their eyes met.

'Forgive me,' he whispered.

57

In an attempt to conceal the tears burning her eyes, Virginia lowered her head.

Spencer hesitated; he'd been a bloody fool. 'Please,' he begged her, 'if it's not too late, I swear to god I'll try to make it up to you.'

She looked at him through her tears. 'No, maybe it's not too late.'

As he took her in his arms and kissed her, Virginia responded, but Spencer sensed that she was still holding out on him, that he'd have to fight to win her back, to right the wrongs of their past. She'd fallen madly in love with him and had cried like a hurt child when it came to an end. Right now he had no way of knowing what was going through her mind, there was a glimmer of hope, but it was still by no means certain. Whatever Spencer said, and however much he meant it, there'd been too much history between them for Virginia to completely let her guard down. He'd have to work on it, and he'd have to work damned hard.

Spencer closed the door after him. He'd always been a challenge and yet at the same time, there had always been small glimpses of vulnerability. In Virginia's experience, it was a combination that most women found attractive. As much as she might balk at the prospect of returning to the intelligence fold, Virginia had openly confessed to ex-service colleagues, that after the chaos and intense adrenaline rush of war, and as the slow dawning normality of peacetime set in, at times, it had seemed sadly humdrum in comparison. She certainly wasn't alone in her views, most of her friends from the intelligence world tended to share her feelings, that they would probably never feel so alive again as they had during the war. It had been a roller coaster of indescribable intensity and fear that could only truly be understood by those who had lived through those times with the constant threat of death.

When Virginia's SOE circuit was imploding around her, and Spencer was dispatched by London to save her from arrest, he'd commented admiringly that even during training she'd always been tough.

'It's not me who's tough, its life!' she had smiled sadly.

Chapter 6
Victoria Station, London

His alarm went off at the ungodly hour of 5.30 in the morning; Charles Taylor washed, shaved and then packed his bags. He decided to have a full English breakfast before paying his bill at the reception desk of the rather rundown hotel near Fulham Town Hall. He had booked in on Thursday evening for a long weekend. Most of the hotel's clientele appeared to be a mix of travelling salesmen and couples looking for a cheap weekend break in London.

As always Charles was unfailingly polite and thanked the attractive young receptionist for all her help during his stay. He set down his suitcase in the hallway and buttoned up his overcoat before walking the short distance to the bus stop, his feet crunching on the icy pavements. His breath came out as a cloud in the brisk morning air, and the branches of the London plane trees lining the street glistened with a severe hoarfrost in the pale watery sunshine.

By the time he arrived at the bus stop, there was already a queue forming, and the traffic along Fulham Broadway was slowly building as people started to head off for work. The nearby Tube station was also beginning to get busy. Charles set his brown leather suitcase down beside him; it was cold, yes, but he was content watching the hustle and bustle around him, waiting for the No11 bus to arrive and take him to his next port of call, an equally cheap bed and breakfast in Pimlico. By all accounts, it was run by a rather genteel war widow who was reportedly strapped for cash and rented out a couple of rooms in her terraced house on Elizabeth Street.

There were two all-consuming passions in Charles Taylor's life, revenge for past wrongs and accumulating money. He had recently been offered a very large sum of money. He had received an upfront deposit paid into his

Luxembourg account, it was under an alias, of course, he rarely, if ever used his own name. Payment was to be made in francs rather than dollars or sterling, as he believed the transaction was less likely to arouse suspicion. If Charles successfully carried out the operation to assassinate Jeremy Haining, then the contract stipulated the remainder of his fee would be paid into another account in Switzerland, under yet another alias.

Charles had his own agenda and treated everyone and everything with cold, clinical analysis. He was, after all, a professional, and his time spent as a spy had not only taught him to trust no one, but also to be thorough and calculating. Taylor had been suspicious of the KGB's approach, it simply didn't add up; there had to be a hidden agenda, they had more than enough home grown talent at their disposal to assassinate Jeremy Haining, they certainly didn't require the services of a foreign hired killer, especially one who happened to be a former British agent.

He'd thoroughly calculated all the possible risks to the nth degree. He wasn't a fool, it was a top job, and the Soviets obviously needed to distance themselves from any possible diplomatic fallout, and one sure way of doing so was to hire a professional assassin, especially one with a grievance against British Intelligence, if he was caught they'd undoubtedly leave him to hang out to dry.

Taylor's war record had been exemplary, before joining the security service he was awarded a Military Cross for outstanding bravery fighting with the 1st Armoured Division during the Battle of El Alamein. After which he joined the Parachute Regiment. As a gifted linguist, Charles eventually came to the attention of British Intelligence. At the time, he remembered feeling somewhat bemused about being singled out for what seemed like special attention. To be honest, it didn't entirely sit easily with him, but after a little gentle persuasion, he joined their ranks, having decided that the prospect of working behind enemy lines rather appealed to him. Maybe deep down his decision had been fuelled by an insane, if not warped, need for an increasing adrenalin rush and to continue living life on the edge.

At the time, he was young, adventurous and had loved nothing more than the adrenaline rush of battle. Despite the many horrors of his experiences fighting in the Middle East against Rommel's deadly Panzer Divisions, like many other young men of his generation, he naively retained a strange sense of immortality, as only young men can, that he was somehow bullet-proof. By his own admission he was a self-proclaimed risk-taker, but looking back in the cold light of day, Charles realised that he really hadn't thought it through, or appreciated the consequences of his actions. That didn't take away his professionalism, he was good at what he did, but he was also acutely aware during his time with British Intelligence, that the seasoned, Spencer Hall, had sometimes viewed him as something of a wild card, a great soldier, but not necessarily agent material.

Taylor's first posting with the Service had been back in the Middle East, followed by a spell in France helping to co-ordinate a local Resistance Group in the run up to D-Day, and then the bloody bitterly fought aftermath until the Allies managed to finally consolidate and secure a foothold against the occupying German armed forces.

During the War, his path had criss-crossed occasionally with Spencer Hall, but they never worked directly alongside each other, that dubious pleasure came later in August of 1946. Charles remembered it well; it was in Berlin. Spencer had been uncompromising, and still viewed him as a wild card, but Charles had eventually proved himself time and again, and as far as London was concerned he had made himself pretty well indispensable. He had their trust, and ultimately that was all that mattered, that is until things had slowly, but inevitably spiralled out of control. In post-war

Europe there was a great deal of money to be made on the Black Market, and Charles ensured he made a great deal of money.

During his time wheeler dealing in Germany, he built up a number of under the counter high profile contacts before his bubble was finally burst for racketeering. Having been ignominiously dismissed from British Intelligence after his nefarious financial dealings had come to light, and faced with the prospect of starting over again, Taylor had decided that he needed to trade on his skills. He had to do what he knew best, and he needed to make a living, preferably a lucrative one. Quite simply he let it be known that he was up for hire for the right price. He had contacts, of course, some legitimate, but he was more interested in the names and telephone numbers of those, who like himself, had operated outside the law. Initially, business was dry; there was still a certain amount of justifiable mistrust, why employ an ex-British agent, could he be trusted? Was he still in fact covertly working for the Government?

It was a gamble, a high-risk one that could have backfired spectacularly on him. Gradually things moved on; he'd lived on his savings for almost six months, and started to begin to get seriously worried that he was not only running out of money but also options when his first assignment came along as a contract-killer. The money was good; the job was to take out a German antique dealer, a former Nazi, who was selling valuable paintings. On the surface, the contract had seemed almost mundane, but Taylor realised the contract was personal. The paintings were selling on the open market, but dig a little deeper, and he soon discovered that their provenance was mired in the Nazi occupation of France, that they had been stolen from a prominent Jewish family. He had no qualms whatsoever about accepting the Contract, and the fact he was helping a dispossessed family reclaim what was rightly theirs, gave him a sense, that by default, he was providing a service, albeit one that was outside of the law.

After the successful completion of the assignment, Taylor knew that with one assassination under his belt, word would soon spread. Initially, he accepted a few dodgy missions in Spain and Portugal but was acutely aware that he needed to build up a serious profile. In all, it took about two years before he started to gain the upper hand. Now his reputation was such that he didn't always accept the highest bidder. Sometimes if the operation was sufficiently interesting he'd take it, but he was choosy, no more than two assignments a year, anymore would be a risk too far. All in all, he had made a lucrative living since leaving British Intelligence, and he loved his new found life in Monaco, he dabbled at the Casinos but had never been a great gambler; it was more about the lifestyle and the weather that had originally drawn him to the Principality.

*

Even waiting at the bus stop in the biting cold hadn't dented his love of being in England, especially in London. He rarely visited his home city, and then only fleetingly, this was his longest stay for well over eight years. It certainly wasn't by choice, but this job was different. Initially, he had been reluctant to accept the offer, not least because once the deed was done Charles knew that he was unlikely to risk venturing back to England ever again.

He had been away too long, and was slowly reacquainting himself with the streets he'd once known so well, with the huge advertisement hoardings, the wasteland from the war, and the new buildings being erected on bomb sites. The huge development wasn't always entirely to his taste; London's rebirth following its decimation in the war was not entirely without controversy, and it resulted in modernist buildings replacing the familiar and much-loved streets of his youth.

He certainly didn't consider himself to be some vain idealist or a political fanatic; it simply didn't interest him. He always operated ostensibly for the money, but not necessarily just to the highest bidder. To be good at your game, you had to be selective, but he also knew of old that the security surrounding the Prime Minster wasn't particularly tight, and he was sure that he could pull it off.

In the end, he accepted the assignment for one reason, and one reason only, revenge; revenge against his former boss, Spencer Hall. Even so, it hadn't been an easy decision; there was a lot at stake, it was a one off job that would hopefully place him in semi-retirement.

Having taken on the contract, Taylor was under few illusions, that as far as the Soviets were concerned, he wasn't only an ideal choice, but, more importantly, expendable. If he succeeded in killing Haining, then British heads would roll, and Spencer's would be the first to fall on the block. That prospect more than anything had swayed him into eventually accepting the mission, the chance to get even and destroy his former colleague.

Charles had been flown into Heathrow from Ontario, the Soviets having supplied him with a false passport, and various aliases to use throughout the assignment. Living the life of a chameleon, constantly changing his identity and appearance was bread and butter stuff to him, it came with the territory. Since arriving, he had been allotted a single KGB contact, Alexander Bukin, who was the Cultural Attaché at the Soviet Embassy in London. They remained in regular contact, but Bukin was shrewd enough to give Charles some space and not to pressurise him unduly. Communications with Bukin had been deliberately varied; either via a package dropped at the left luggage office of a main line Station in London or by letter. Within the envelope there would always be another deposit slip for the next left luggage office at a different railway station; it was never the same one.

65

Charles would then follow the same procedure and cast an eye around the Station concourse, scanning the crowds to ensure he hadn't been followed. He usually, but not exclusively, decided against going by taxi. In his experience cabbies, by and large, were a talkative bunch, and often too nosey by half, so he invariably opted to travel by tube, it wasn't only anonymous, but more often than not crowded. No-one pays much attention or makes eye contact to their fellow commuters on the London underground.

To mix things up a little, occasionally he would take a train from Waterloo to Vauxhall just to ensure that he wasn't being tailed before coming back on himself. So far, Charles knew that he hadn't been followed. He rarely stayed in one place more than a day or two, and always booked into the next cheap hotel or B&B under a different name. Each of the establishments appeared to share one thing in common; the walls were invariably nicotine yellow, accompanied by an overwhelming stench of stale tobacco.

Direct contact with Bukin tended to be on a weekly basis; he preferred to keep telephone calls to a minimum. They would sometimes meet up on the tube or on the top deck of the No11 bus at a pre-arranged time. One or other of them caught the bus at Sloane Street in Chelsea; a document would be surreptitiously passed between them, and then usually Bukin would get off the bus a couple of stops along the route. They needed to keep it simple, but constantly vary their means of communication.

Whilst Charles needed time to devise a plan, uppermost in his mind was that he needed to cover his own back, and come up with a sound escape route. The Soviets had already accepted that he would need to go to ground for a while, and that escape from Britain wouldn't be easy. The KGB had offered to assist him, as he knew they would, but he needed something tangible. Whatever they said, he treated it all with a pinch of salt, but slowly, as their discussions progressed he'd managed to build up a rapport, or so he hoped, with Alexander Bukin. He was beginning to feel slightly more relaxed about the arrangements. It was also in Moscow's interest, as well as his own, to provide him with a safe means of escape and avoid being arrested in the aftermath of the killing. Whatever way you looked at it, accepting the contract had been a poisoned chalice. For once the initial approach had been made they would never have allowed him to walk away alive, from that moment on he was a dead man walking.

*

The red double decker No11 drew up alongside the bus stop; Charles headed upstairs and sat down in the backseat before instinctively patting his overcoat with its specially tailored poacher's pocket. He breathed more easily; it was becoming something of a habit, but he needed to reassure himself the document was still safely inside. Yesterday afternoon he had been to the left luggage office at King's Cross Station, this was what he had been waiting for, the last piece of information that he needed to help finalise his plans. The document was a copy of the Prime Minister's social and public diary over the next two months.

When Charles finally agreed to accept the assignment Bukin had promised he would be provided with a copy.

"How in hell are you going to do that?" he'd demanded.

Bukin had refused point blank to tell him. "Just be content, my friend, that we'll deliver you a copy."

*

The KGB had been true to their word and over the next week Charles intended checking on the locations detailed in the Prime Minister's diary schedule. Even in the biting cold, it wouldn't exactly be a hardship walking the streets of London. In a way, Charles was actually looking forward to finally drawing up his plans and list of possible venues for the assassination.

He got off the bus in Pimlico and walked the short distance to his new Bed and Breakfast in nearby Elizabeth Street. The landlady seemed pleasant enough and didn't have too many grounds rules. The room itself was adequate, the furniture and decor were somewhat austere and past its best, but he really hadn't been expecting much for the comparatively low cost of the accommodation. With the pleasantries over with, he locked himself in his room and placed the copy of the diary onto the dressing table. He then unlocked his suitcase and carefully unwrapped an elongated leather pouch, inside was a custom made rifle given to him by the KGB, consisting of three separate pieces. He checked all the pieces and once he was content carefully reclosed the pouch.

Charles then moved over toward the window, tweaked the net curtains and stared sombrely down into the street below; and looked both ways just to reassure himself that he hadn't been followed.

Chapter 7
St. Philips Hotel, Westminster

Since the war, the St. Philips Hotel had regularly continued to be used by British Intelligence and on occasions as a venue to interview prospective employees to the Service. The building was shaped like a giant horseshoe around a courtyard with well-maintained tree lined gardens. Jack Stein's last stay at the hotel had been back in 1950. Since then St. Philips had undergone a major refurbishment, the always welcoming lobby now had a certain theatricality about it, dominated by three large sparkling chandeliers, and the newly installed white undulating balustrade balconies and ornate plasterwork. The balconies were accessed via an equally grand double staircase. Even the Hotel's harshest critics were forced to admit that it was impressive.

As Spencer strode toward the courtyard garden Virginia arrived by taxi, he waited for her, and then they headed straight into the hotel. He asked the receptionist to let Mr Stein in Room 201 know that his guests had arrived and would be waiting for him in the lobby.

The hotel's reception staff were fawning over Spencer. His reputation was such that he almost appeared to own the place, simply by doing nothing other than being there. Most of them had no idea that he was the Head of MI5.

It was some nine years since Virginia had last visited the St. Philips; the opulent upgrade had taken her by surprise. It was certainly a far cry from the old days.

'I hardly recognise the place,' she said, her gaze gliding thoughtfully around the hotel.

'No, I don't suppose you do.'

Virginia wasn't entirely sure whether she actually liked the upgrade; there was something missing, was it the atmosphere, or the Edwardian charm of the place. It was probably a combination of both.

'God, I used to love this hotel,' she said fondly. 'It was such a great place to stop off for a meal, to sleep or just get lucky!'

Her sparkling hazel green eyes gave just the merest hint of mischief. Beneath the US East Coast veneer of old money sophistication, there was always an underlying wildness about her. As Spencer held her gaze, he couldn't help thinking that it wasn't an entirely unattractive quality. One thing was for sure, though; she'd always been a handful.

During her time with British Intelligence and in later years with the CIA, many of her colleagues on both sides of the Atlantic had considered her cold, but Spencer had always believed that Stein had hit the nail on the head when he'd once described her as a volcano covered with snow. It had somehow summed her up to a tee; she was a complex mix of emotions, and even before the war had refused to conform to society's expectations of women. She was outspoken, assertive, and also fiercely private. But even so, Spencer was surprised that she had never married again, there had been one or two near misses, or so he'd heard, and looking back, he still felt more than a niggling sense of regret that he hadn't taken their relationship further, but the timing had been all wrong, or at least, that's the way it had seemed. It was all water under the bridge now, but as Spencer glanced at her, try as he might, he couldn't help wondering how things might have turned out between them.

Catching a movement out of the corner of his eye, he turned round, it was Jack Stein on the balcony; he raised his hand in recognition before heading downstairs to meet them.

'My God, Ginny,' Stein exclaimed, with a broad smile, 'you haven't changed a bit!'

She guessed that he was probably just being kind, but maybe not, Jack had always been a smooth talking bastard.

'I've arranged for us to have tea in a private room,' Spencer said.

'Sounds good to me,' Stein smiled, rubbing his hands together in anticipation.

Afternoon Tea at St. Philips was something of an institution, and was a quintessentially British experience. Tea was usually served in the Vaux Court, a large striking room flanked by floor to ceiling gilded mirrors, and an original stone fountain inhabited by large mythical statues. Stein was renowned for having a sweet tooth and the prospect of a large selection of cakes and warm baked scones with strawberry preserve, and Devonshire clotted cream was guaranteed to briefly lighten his mood. So far Spencer was pushing all the right buttons.

'We'll need to hang on here a bit longer,' Spencer said, flatly.

They both looked at him questioningly.

He held their gaze. 'I'm waiting for someone else to join us.'

'Who is it, anyone, I know?' Stein asked.

'Luke Garvan, he's the Assistant Commissioner in charge of Special Branch.'

'Now hold on a minute,' he protested, 'you didn't run that one by me.'

Spencer cut Stein dead; the hard edge to his voice spoke volumes. 'I didn't think I *had* to!'

Stein hesitated a moment, then decided to apologise, he had to accept that it was now primarily a British operation, but more importantly, he had been ordered by Chas Brennan to assist British Intelligence in any way that he could to help track down the would-be assassin. If the President's life had been on the line, there was no way the CIA or any other American agency would have allowed an outside organisation to call the shots. Besides, Spencer wasn't someone you'd cross twice, friend or no friend.

71

'If you must know,' Spencer said, by way of explanation. 'Luke Garvan was seconded to MI5 during the war.'

'But even so, can you trust him? Your police tend to play by the rules.'

'And yours don't?'

'God dammit you know that's not what I meant.'

'Go on.'

'It's just that they don't usually like getting their hands too dirty.' Stein ventured.

'This one's different. I'd trust him with my life.'

It was evident that the conversation wasn't up for further discussion, he'd drawn a line under it, and it was over.

Friendship aside, it was strictly business, there was a lot at stake, and a lot riding on their ability to track down the KGB's hired help. Although the initial intelligence had been sourced by the CIA, ultimately, the operation was a British one, and as the Head of MI5, the final call and responsibility rested solely with Spencer. They exchanged knowing glances, and guessed he didn't particularly care what they thought, but they were both far too seasoned to take offence. He might have cut them dead, but it wasn't personal, they knew that and had worked with him in the field against seemingly unstoppable odds, they both admired his ability to make those around him feel not only comfortable but valued, it was in their experience a rare gift of leadership. Even now, he could summon a deadly thin-lipped menace as easily as expansive bonhomie. It was a deadly combination.

A silence fell between them; Spencer wasn't in any great hurry to break it. Virginia gave him a sidelong glance; the passing years obviously hadn't softened him any.

Spencer eased a pack of cigarettes out of his pocket, and then offered them round, before slipping one between his lips, but as he did so, his attention drifted across the lobby toward the entrance. They both instinctively followed his gaze. The smartly dressed uniformed doorman was welcoming a tall, well-built man, who made a point of thanking him. He was straight-backed, an imposing figure whose movements were deliberate, careful, his hair, once blonde, thick and wavy, was now fading to a light sandy shade flecked with grey.

There was an undeniable commanding presence about him; it had to be Garvan, Stein decided and cast Virginia a meaningful glance. She smiled in response.

Spencer moved across the lobby to meet him; his welcome was warm and familiar, they were obviously easy with one another and were soon laughing at some quip. or other Garvan had made. Spencer patted his back and guided him across the lobby; once the introductions were over, he led them to a private room on the ground floor. As they approached the open doorway there was a great gust of laughter; it was centred on a woman.

She was smartly dressed, a little more sophisticated than Stein remembered, but her hair was still bleached to within an inch of its life. Stein couldn't help but do a double-take, no it couldn't be, what in hells name was Michelle Rookwood doing at the hotel. During the war, she'd been a Double Agent, and if he remembered correctly had been arrested in London by British Intelligence on spying charges. MI5 had turned things around with her, in fact during the war, she'd eventually become a valued agent. MI5's skill in running, what was, in essence, a stable of double agents was still regarded in security circles as a textbook example of how operations should be conducted. By clever handling, and carefully cross-referencing intelligence from their double agents, via intercepted wireless transmissions, MI5 had effectively controlled the entire German Intelligence organisation operating in Britain.

'Say is that really Michelle Rookwood?' he asked, still not quite able to believe his eyes.

'It certainly is,' Spencer answered.

'What's *she* doing here?'

Spencer glanced over his shoulder. 'Michelle manages the hotel for us.'

Stein couldn't disguise his surprise.

'It's a long story.'

'I'm sure it is.'

Michelle excused herself from the three young men she'd been talking to, and headed down the corridor to greet them. 'Everything's ready for you,' she said, addressing Spencer.

He inclined his head but didn't respond. Rookwood's gaze travelled toward Garvan; she knew him well, there was an acknowledgment from him, but it was only slight, and Jack Stein she'd met briefly during the war. He'd aged well, she thought, and was still attractive, but Virginia was a new one on her. Spencer introduced them all. Rookwood was all smiles and showed them into a room resembling a library lined with antique books. A table was set in the centre dressed in a pristine white linen cloth. There was an array of finger sandwiches, freshly baked scones, and a selection of floral themed pastries. Silver teapots, bone china cups and saucers, beside them were crystal flutes filled with Laurent Perrier champagne.

'If you need anything,' she said, 'just press the buzzer beside the fireplace.'

Spencer thanked her.

He waited until Michelle closed the door before taking a seat at the table Virginia sat beside him. Leaving Stein opposite Garvan, he looked at him, but Garvan's blue hooded eyes were giving nothing away.

'Just help yourselves,' Spencer said, gesturing toward the impressive spread.

Stein was the first to fill his plate; he certainly didn't need asking twice. 'So how did the meeting with your Home Secretary go?' he asked.

'It's hard to tell.'

Stein arched his brows questioningly. Even he knew that Bradshaw had a reputation for slipperiness and political thuggery, but guessed that Spencer gave him as good as he got.

'Bradshaw's an arrogant bastard,' Spencer said with feeling, before adding somewhat ruefully. 'But there again, for some reason most people think I am'.

There was an ironical glint in Jack's eye. 'I can't argue with you there.'

Spencer smiled savouring the Laurent Perrier champagne. 'You have to understand dealing with Bradshaw is a little like having a wart on your face, you don't like it, but every day you wake up, and it's still there, and you just have to get on with it.'

Garvan laughed out loud, it was a shared experience and shot him a knowing look.

Spencer swiftly got down to business and began his brief; they all knew they were not only scrabbling around in the dark but that for the time being their lines of communication would have to remain tight. According to the reports received from Freda earlier today, she'd managed to confirm that the KGB's assassin was a former British Intelligence officer who had gone rogue. Although in some ways it was welcome news, Spencer still couldn't rule out altogether that the Service had not been infiltrated. Looking to Stein, he asked him to outline how the CIA had come across the information. In Garvan's presence, Agent Freda wasn't mentioned by name, there was no need, only that a highly placed American spy operating in the Soviet Union was their source.

'Listen, as things stand, the only certainty is that we need absolute secrecy and that for whatever reason the hawks in the Kremlin want to eliminate the Prime Minster.'

'So how far up the chain does this go, all the way to Khrushchev?' Garvan pressed.

'Well now,' Spencer said, 'that's a whole different ball game altogether, and all depends on the power struggles behind the scenes. Right now, the motives behind the plot can wait for another day. My only concern is tracking down their assassin.' Spencer scarcely touched the array of food on offer and lit a cigarette. Blowing out a cloud of smoke, he looked at each of his listeners in turn. They remained silent. So he threw the question out to them, he needed their thoughts.

Virginia said. 'We know the American source is sound, but what doesn't add up is why the KGB would chance hiring a mercenary, let alone an ex-British agent?'

'Exactly, you tell me.'

She took her time in answering. 'We know how they operate, it's how we operate.'

He stared back at her; he wanted her to spell it out.

'We all know there's usually way too many risks hiring an outside trigger man, especially someone with past links to another agency. It's a matter of trust, and this is one hell of an assignment, so why would the Soviets take the chance, as I said it doesn't add up.'

Despite being out of the game for a number of years, it was evident that Virginia still hadn't lost her touch. She was spot on, as Spencer had hoped she would be. 'No it doesn't,' he conceded, 'but in their shoes, what would I do? What would *we* do?'

'Keep it in house,' she shot back in her typical no-nonsense style.

He pulled a face. 'There may well be reasons why we wouldn't.'

'Like what?'

Spencer blew out a plume of cigarette smoke. 'If the shit was to hit the fan, and our agent screwed up a mission, say the assassination of prominent politician, then what.'

She looked at him questioningly.

'You're forgetting something, Ginny, that both the CIA and British Intelligence operate on the 11th Commandment.'

'What's that?'

'Thou shalt not get caught,' he smirked. 'On both sides of the Pond, our political masters demand results. Whilst we might routinely burgle and bug our way across the entire length and breadth of not only our own countries but wherever they decide on the State's behalf, it pays for our worthy, law-abiding politicians to turn a blind eye to the legality of our operations. But only as long as it pays results and they're not personally involved.'

Stein let out his breath with a quiet hiss. Virginia's eyes flickered toward him.

'Spence has a point. If this guy messes up and is arrested, even if he squeals, they'll deny all knowledge of him.'

'Then what's in it for him?'

'Well, I guess that's what we need to find out.'

Garvan intervened and asked not unreasonably. 'So how reliable is this CIA source of yours in Moscow? Is there an outside chance they could have got it wrong?'

'It's good enough,' Stein answered, waspishly.

Spencer leaned back in his chair and stared at each of them in turn. 'Yes, it is,' he agreed, blowing out a stream of smoke from his cigarette. 'Let's not worry about the CIA's source,' he assured Garvan. 'Whatever way we look at it, the rotten apple is apparently a former British field agent.'

'So what exactly do you want us to do?' Garvan queried.

'For a start, we need to keep the investigation low key.'

Stein asked whether he had discussed the threat with the Prime Minister.

'Not yet,' Spencer confessed checking his watch. 'I'm heading off with Garvan to No10 this evening; Bradshaw's already briefed him of course.'

'What about the security arrangements?'

Spencer inclined his head toward Garvan. 'We've increased the patrols around Chequers, his country residence, but posting extra police outside Downing Street is a complete non-starter.'

Security around the Prime Minister was usually fairly routine, he explained, there had never been any major issues about his safety, only the occasional abusive remark hurled from the crowd, the most recent incident being an irate pensioner in Newcastle who had rounded on Haining with her handbag, but it hadn't exactly been a life threatening situation.

'Bradshaw's agreed that we probably shouldn't make any drastic changes to the PM's diary. If we're seen to be increasing his protection, then there's every chance it won't just be picked up by the Press, but the KGB will get wind that we're onto something.'

'So you mean we've got to play cat and mouse with them? Hang around and wait for this guy to strike, is that what you're saying?' Stein's question was met by a wall of empty silence.

It was Garvan who eventually broke it. 'Do you have a better plan?'

'Right now, no, I guess not.'

'We really don't have that much to go on, and unless your CIA colleagues can come up with the identity of the assassin, then whatever way we look at it, we're out on a limb,' Garvan said.

'Yeah,' Stein conceded before countering sharply, 'but, at least, we came up with something!'

'It really wasn't meant as a criticism,' Garvan apologised.

'Nah, I guess it wasn't.'

78

'So where does that leave us? Spencer said, 'at least the latest intelligence report confirms our man isn't current.'

'It's looking that way,' she agreed.

Garvan looked across the table at Spencer. 'So what's your gut instinct, is it someone with a grudge against the Service?'

'Who knows?'

'Or maybe it's more personal than that,' he suggested.

Spencer held his gaze but didn't respond he wasn't quite sure where he was going.

'Let's face it Spence we all know that you've made a few enemies in your time.'

'Who hasn't,' he shrugged indifferently.

'But it's got to be someone who isn't only good,' Virginia cut in, 'but someone who's still at the top of their game.'

He agreed.

'Whatever their motive, be it money or revenge, it really doesn't matter, the bottom line is we'll have to start somewhere. You'll need to go through the files,' she said to Spencer.

'Yes, we will.'

'The one thing we do know is that the Soviets won't have taken the decision lightly, so maybe we should start winding things back a little, and try and work out how the KGB came across this guy in the first place.'

Spencer knew what she was getting at; they needed to focus on a professional assassin, someone who could afford to be selective, who was not only highly paid, but who probably only worked once or twice a year at most. They'd have to start by putting out feelers to Interpol and the FBI, and ask them to check their records for recorded professional contract killings over the last five years or so, and whether there was any particular pattern to them. It was a long shot, but as things stood, they really didn't have anything else to go on. Whoever it was, was unlikely to have slipped up and left the authorities with any tangible evidence to go on, but add into the mix, their suspected hired assassin was an ex-British agent, put a whole different slant on the investigation. As things stood, Spencer and his team had been left trying to play catch up on the KGB.

'Maybe you should check the files for someone with Commie leanings,' Stein suggested.

Spencer agreed, he wasn't ruling anything out, at least not just yet.

'Do you want me to go through the files?' Garvan offered.

Spencer pulled a face. 'So where do you want to start?'

'It's only a suggestion, but I could start by looking at agents who have left under a cloud, or maybe someone with a particular grievance, a score to settle against the Service, or as Jack suggested an ex- agent suspected of having sympathies to Moscow.'

Spencer threw him a weary smile. 'Jesus, how long's a piece a string, how far back do you want to go?'

'That's down to you.'

'I thought it might be.'

'There must be some names that spring to mind.'

'There's more than a few,' Spencer conceded, 'the disaffected, the ones who simply weren't up to the job, I don't mind telling you it's a pretty long list, but even so it's certainly worth a punt.' He surveyed them round the table; all eyes were on him. They were waiting for him. 'There again maybe our man isn't driven by any particular grievance or political ideology.'

'But by what, then?' Garvan pressed him.

'They might simply be motivated by money,' he said. 'Let's face it this job would have commanded a high price tag.'

Virginia thoughtfully twisted the stem of the champagne glass between her fingers, and placing the flute to her lips, she gave him a long, slow look, and said. 'Tell me, and don't go trying to give me any bullshit, Spence, I want to know why the hell you've dragged me out of retirement? You don't need me sitting here,' she said gesturing around the table toward Stein and Garvan. 'There's any number of people you could call upon. I'm not even current, I haven't been active for years, and I haven't a goddamn clue about the Soviet operation in Europe anymore, let alone in London.'

Smiling, he narrowed his eyes and looked at her with wary curiosity. 'That's not a problem Jack's going to bring you up to date on the KGB's main agents and their operations.'

She still seemed dubious. 'So what exactly do you need me to do?'

'To help us track down our assassin.'

She passed him a rather puzzled look. 'I told you earlier Spence I just can't walk away from my job.'

'Don't worry I've managed to sort out everything with Coulls.'

'What do you mean *sort out*?' she asked warily.

He glanced at his watch. 'As we speak a hand delivered letter is winging its way over to John Coulls your Managing Director.'

Virginia suddenly looked alarmed; Jesus wept she knew he was up to something. She sure as hell didn't need this right now.

He explained smoothly. 'It's a letter from the Prime Minister expressing his disappointment that in the past few weeks, a portrait of a former Prime Minister, Benjamin Disraeli, which was purchased in good faith by the Government art collection fund from Coulls in 1957, is now suspected of being looted by the Nazis.' He coldly held her gaze. 'As you can imagine it's not only placed Her Majesty's

Government in a potentially embarrassing situation but after the recent court case at the Old Bailey, it could well prove to be the final nail in the coffin for Coulls reputation.'

She remembered the sale well and had conducted extensive research into its provenance, but now, Spencer had managed to sow a seed of doubt in her mind. The portrait had come from a private collection in Switzerland, but she had paid particular attention to its ownership since the 1930s, everything had seemed totally above board. The Auction House had already faced one embarrassing court case involving allegations of unwittingly selling looted art, but a letter from the Prime Minister had more than ratcheted up the stakes a notch or two. She imagined that on reading the PM's letter, John Coulls' world would suddenly implode; they might have survived one court case with their reputation intact, but taking on Her Majesty's Government was never going to have a happy ending for Coulls. Quite apart from that, Virginia's own reputation in the art world would be totally and irrevocably destroyed.

'That portrait was sound,' she announced, defensively.

Spencer looked pleased with himself. 'But John Coulls doesn't know that, does he?'

'You *bastard*!' she spat at him.

'I'm sorry, Ginny, if there'd been any other way of doing it I'd have done so, But I needed an excuse to get you out of the auction house, and fast, just for a few weeks you understand, it maybe a little longer, there's no way of telling, and what better way than by putting the fear of God into your boss.' He eased himself back into his chair. 'Actually don't you think it was a damned good idea?'

'Not really,' she hissed.

'Disraeli was Jewish by birth, wasn't he?'

'Yes, he was!'

'I just thought it added a rather nice touch.'

82

'What do you mean?'

'The PM would be embarrassed enough to discover a government owned painting hanging in No10 was suspected of being looted, but especially the portrait of a Jewish Victorian Prime Minister.'

'Does he know it's a put up job?'

'What do you think?'

'Okay, so just cut the crap what the hell am I supposed to be doing?'

'The PM has requested that you work alongside the government's own art experts to go over the records and re-check the portraits provenance.'

'But they're sound.'

'As I said John Coulls doesn't know that, and he certainly won't question your absence, for one thing, he'll be too shit scared to cause any fuss.'

'John is a good man, he really doesn't deserve this,' her voice was sharp.

'I'm sure he doesn't, Ginny, but there again there's more at stake here than one man's professional reputation.'

Her eyes blazed with anger at him; she tried reading his face, but it was impossible.

'It's merely a means to an end Ginny, it's not personal,' he responded matter of factly, 'you know that besides Coulls will eventually be exonerated of any wrongdoing, and no-one will be any the wiser about the PM's letter.'

Jack Stein exchanged an amused sidelong glance with Garvan. It was an effort for Virginia to keep the anger off her face; she failed dismally. She rattled off that his actions were tantamount to blackmail, he didn't deny it, why would he? The facts spoke for themselves.

'Right now, Ginny,' he said, coolly, 'I'm in it right up to my neck, and I don't particularly care a fig about Coulls or anything else for that matter. If we fail to track down the

83

KGB's contract killer, then the fall-out if things go wrong will bring the whole pack of cards tumbling down. The blame will be mine, and mine alone, which is why I said to you earlier that I needed someone to watch my back with Bradshaw. At the end of the day he's no different from any other politician, he'll happily sanction my actions, but then scurry off into the background and deny all knowledge of our discussion, leaving me to take all the blame and hang me out to dry. But it just isn't about me, as Head of Special Branch, they'll be sharpening their knives for Garvan as well.' He leaned forward and stubbed out his cigarette into a cut glass ashtray. 'It's just the way the system works, but the trouble is Ginny, I've never yet met a politician I would either trust with a secret or my life. So forgive me if I don't quite share your concerns about your precious bloody auction house!'

Chapter 8
No10 Downing Street

At 7.30pm, sharp Garvan and Spencer were being ushered across the black and white checkered hallway and up the grand staircase lined with portraits of every Prime Minister in strict chronological order, with the most recent incumbents at the top and group photographs of various past Cabinet Conferences at the bottom.

The current Prime Minister was an adept and skillful communicator, and a tough, no-nonsense politician from the old school with an intuitive understanding of political issues. Spencer had always respected and admired him; he'd successfully clawed his way out of extreme poverty by sheer hard work and determination. Putting himself through night school whilst working as a ledger clerk, and then as a representative of the Transport and General Workers Union as a Branch Secretary, he was eventually elected as a Member of Parliament. During the War his eminence as a politician soared when impressed by his skills, Churchill appointed him to a senior role at the Foreign Office in the coalition government. It was the ultimate accolade; Churchill wasn't interested in the colour of his pre-war political allegiances, only that he was the right man for the job. Even now, it still gave him a certain gravitas amongst his parliamentary colleagues.

It was during the war that their paths had first crossed, and ever since, Haining had always surmised, rightly or wrongly, that Spencer's life had been driven by a certain moral ambivalence, in so much, that many of his actions were considered, especially in peacetime somewhat questionable. But that deep down his exploits had always been underwritten by a sense of acting in the national interest. Until being appointed Prime Minister, their paths had crossed subsequently in a desultory fashion, Garvan less so. But throughout Spencer had remained very much a closed book, never once allowing a glimpse into his personal life. The only thing Haining knew with any degree of certainty was that he was still close to Garvan.

Haining had endorsed Spencer's appointment as the Director General of MI5. At the time, Haining had been well aware there was a certain amount of opposition, not only from the likes of Stanley Bradshaw but also within the more conservative ranks of the intelligence community. Spencer might be a little rough around the edges, and the smartly tailored suits couldn't quite conceal the fact that he still looked more than capable of re-arranging someone's face without even drawing breath. He was not only straight talking but more importantly, to Haining's mind was the ultimate spymaster. On the other hand, Garvan's great gift was not only directness, but a detective's analytical mind, and right now, his life depended on both Spencer and Garvan being at the top of their game.

To their surprise Haining was casually dressed when he greeted them, his shirt sleeves were rolled up, and his silk tie had been discarded on the hall table.

'Come in, come in,' he said welcomingly and invited them to take off their suit jackets and relax. He thanked his member of staff for ushering them in and asked not to be disturbed.

'Of course, sir,' the young Civil Servant responded closing the door.

Garvan hadn't seen Haining for a while but knew that his recent bout of ill health had allowed both Bradshaw and Maggie Ellis a great deal of political leeway and influence. Even so, he still possessed a formidable memory. In his prime, he would easily have batted both of them out of court, but judging by his appearance this evening, Haining probably wasn't quite yet ready to throw in the towel and relinquish his control of power. Garvan was pleasantly surprised, whilst he hadn't expected him to be at death's door, he seemed in much better shape than either the newspaper reports or his recent appearances on television indicated. What Garvan didn't know, and Spencer did, was that many of the health scare stories circulating the Press had been leaked by Maggie Ellis. The debate was still out as to whether the leaks were made with or without the Home Secretary's tacit approval, but Spencer had his own suspicions that Bradshaw had been the driving force behind the leaks.

Although Haining wasn't entirely back to his best, he was still a wily old bugger. But it was obvious that whilst the cat was away, the mice will play, headed by his supposed closest political ally, Stanley Bradshaw, and that various colleagues were jostling for position and planning to undermine his authority.

Haining knew all too well what was afoot. However, he figured there was a limit to what any Prime Minister can do to continuously defy those plotting against him, but Haining had an ace up his sleeve and knew how at least temporarily to out manoeuvre his opponents. Whilst he needed Bradshaw on side, he certainly wasn't blind to his towering ambition, so played to his weaknesses, and had recently arranged for his press secretary to leak a story to Fleet Street, that he was considering reshuffling his Ministerial posts. The editorial was an implicit threat and was just enough of one to rein Bradshaw back into place. Even off colour, Haining was still far abler than his Cabinet colleagues, although privately, he admitted that Bradshaw was starting to run him a close second.

Haining liked living over the shop as he called it at No10, but there was a definite demarcation between his private and public life. He enjoyed entertaining in the state dining room and worked on all his official documents held in the so-called "red boxes" in the study, where he also held regular meetings with his officials. The flat was his bolthole, his oasis from the constant pressures of the job, but it was also a place where his grandchildren could run free, scream and shout, and clutter the rooms with their toys, and Flossie, the family's much-loved springer spaniel could stretch out on her favourite bed.

Haining poured them a stiff gin and tonic with a splash of ice, he apologised that his staff hadn't provided them with any fresh slices of lemon, before slumping down on a faded brocade armchair, and asked them to make themselves comfortable. Garvan opted for the adjoining armchair, leaving Spencer the two seater sofa.

Haining placed the tumbler to his lips and savoured his first drink of the day, and since his meeting with Bradshaw at Chequers, he had certainly been sinking down rather more than usual, but he needed it.

'So gentlemen, according to the Home Secretary, it appears that my life is in your hands.'

He threw it out to them, but as an opening gambit, they couldn't fault it.

Garvan explained that as a precautionary measure bulletproof glass had now been installed in his official car, and that security surrounding Chequers had also been increased. He knew all that; Bradshaw had mentioned it to him; he'd seen it all for himself.

He retrieved a guillotine cutter off the side table beside his chair, and snipped off the end of his cigar, then struck a match and placed a large Havana cigar in his mouth, once he was satisfied that it was lit, he slowly inserted the stem between his lips.

'So tell me, have the CIA managed to dig anything else up about this ruddy plot,' he rasped angrily.

'No sir, they have not,' Garvan said, flatly.

He took his time in answering. 'I'll tell you something, Spencer, if you manage to track down this bloody assassin; and I come out of this alive, then I swear to God that

I'll not only hammer those bastards at the Soviet Embassy but in the Kremlin as well!'

Whilst his reaction was laudable, they wondered what he had in mind. It was Garvan who asked.

He immediately inclined his head toward Spencer. 'That's why we politicians have agencies like British Intelligence; they do all the underhand work for us and supply the government with the necessary dirt to turn the screw on our enemies.' The PM's eyes sparkled mischievously. 'And sometimes even against our own allies!'

His words brought the merest flicker of a smile on Spencer's face.

Haining sucked heavily on his cigar. 'Well Spencer, any ideas. Do we have something on the bastards at the Soviet Embassy?'

'We always have something,' he replied, enigmatically.

'Then bloody well tell me *what* it is!'

For some reason, Spencer seemed unusually reticent. 'Listen, Prime Minister, I'm not a diplomat.'

'Good God man, we all know that, but that's not why Her Majesty's Government employs you, is it!'

'No, I suppose not, sir.'

'So spit it out man, what do you have?'

'The Foreign Office won't like it.'

'Damn the Foreign Office let me worry about them.'

'Last year,' Spencer said, lighting a cigarette, 'do you remember Mikhail Panoff, he was the top KGB officer who defected from their Embassy in London?'

'Lord yes, I remember reading about him, quite an interesting character, it can't have been easy for him, weren't his family still stranded in Moscow?'

'Yes, they were, in fact, they still are,' he said, drawing heavily on his cigarette. 'the trouble is, sir, it's all become a little bit messy, but over the last twelve months or so we've carried out an intensive investigation into the KGB's espionage activities in Britain.'

'You mean with Panoff's assistance?'

'Yes, he's been very helpful to us.'

'So where are you going with this, Spencer?'

'We believe there are at least forty Soviet diplomats involved in some form of espionage activities in the UK.'

Haining's face creased up in despair. 'Forty, my God, Spencer, are you really sure about this?'

'It could well be more, in fact,' he continued, 'I'm convinced there are. Most of them are operating out of the embassy, but not exclusively, others are attached to their trade delegations and the Moscow Narodny Bank in Moorgate.' Spencer coolly held his gaze. 'It really is quite a long list Prime Minister.'

'I'm sure it is, but at what point were you thinking of officially informing the government about all this?'

'Only when we could be certain that we'd accounted for everyone engaged in spying, but even with Panoff's help, it still hasn't been easy proving their involvement.'

It was no good, Haining drained his glass, he needed another drink, he offered them re-fills; it would have seemed churlish to refuse the Prime Minster.

'What I'm trying to say, sir, is that once we've managed to neutralise the assassin, if you do decide to go public and expel them, it's going to cause one hell of a diplomatic crises.'

'Then it'll be one of their own making,' he grunted, handing out the drinks.

'It'll end up tit for tat.'

He shrugged indifferently. 'If it does, it does.'

Haining slumped wearily back into his armchair. 'Maybe it might just be easier to kill two birds with one stone,' he suggested.

Spencer viewed him warily. 'Could we, sir?'

The Prime Minister was on a roll. 'We get the Foreign Office to contact their chargé d'affaires, and the Ambassador and read them the riot act.'

'And say what precisely?'

'That we've not only discovered their embassy is riddled with spies, but that we've also come across the assassination plot.'

'With due respect, Prime Minister, the Americans would never forgive you.'

'Would they not?'

'You've got to remember it was the CIA who tipped us off about the plot in the first place. They'll move hell and high water to protect their agent in the Kremlin.'

'So what are you trying to tell me, that Britain's Prime Minister is more expendable than some bloody undercover agent.'

'I wasn't suggesting that at all, only that we need to tread carefully. By all means expel as many diplomats as you like, but my advice is not *just* yet.'

Haining breathed deeply, his cigar resting in the corner of his mouth.

'Give us a little more time to do our job, sir, that's all I ask.'

'I wouldn't mind so much, but the bastard they've hired is one of your people Spencer, one of yours!' he said, stabbing an accusing finger at him.

'We're now convinced that he's not current.'

Haining grunted. 'Whether he's current or not, he can still squeeze a bloody trigger!'

The PM had a point. 'I don't know about you sir, but in my experience, vengeance is a dish best served cold.'

Albeit reluctantly, Haining was inclined to agree, so let the matter rest. 'The Home Secretary told me you're against making any major alterations to my diary, is that right?'

'Yes sir,' Spencer said.

He tensed slightly; it didn't sit easily with him that in reality his security services were prepared for him to be little more than a sitting target. Whilst he perfectly understood the wider picture and that they had their own agenda to track down the assassin, the fact remained there was only one person in the firing line.

'Tell me, Spencer, is that an *order*?'

'No, sir, of course not, it's merely advice.'

He looked at him sombrely.

'We could, of course, cancel all your external engagements,' Garvan intervened, 'but then we'd run the risk of giving the game away to the KGB.'

He gave them a bleak smile. 'So far gentlemen you're not exactly inspiring me with any confidence. I know that you've probably weighed up all the pros and cons.' He slowly eased his cigar out of his mouth. 'But let's not lose sight of the fact, that until you hopefully track down this maniac the fact still remains, does it not, that I'm nothing more than a sitting duck?'

Garvan suggested that it wasn't quite like that; he had been detailed extra security, although admitted under cross-examination from the PM, that it wasn't overtly conspicuous as they couldn't afford to arouse the attention of the Press and give the game away.

'I can assure you we haven't taken the decision lightly, sir,' Garvan continued.

'I'm sure you haven't.'

Spencer intervened. 'If we screw up on this, and God forbid anything was to happen to you, we both know that the next Prime Minister, given the pecking order and his influence, is likely to be the Home Secretary. I don't know about you, but I can't help feeling that he's very unlikely to forgive either of us for losing you.'

A slow, rather bemused smile creased Haining's face. 'Yes, I can see that might be a bit of a career breaker.' He then shot Spencer a cold, hard look. 'I guess, even for *you*!'

'It probably wouldn't be my finest hour, sir, no.'

Even so, Haining couldn't help thinking that hell was more likely to freeze over before Bradshaw managed to get the better of Spencer. He was convinced that he would have something up his sleeve, some angle, some leverage against Bradshaw that would ultimately allow him to call all the shots. He knew from personal experience that the Home Secretary was not entirely squeaky clean.

Bradshaw was clever; he knew that and over the last six to twelve months, when he'd had his heart scare, he knew only too well, the general perception in Whitehall was that Bradshaw had become the real power behind the throne. But Haining still had enough fight in him not to allow either his Home Secretary or his, even more, troublesome private secretary and lover, Maggie Ellis to gain the upper hand. He also guessed, rightly or wrongly, that it was in Spencer's interest to keep the status quo. Haining had always tried to retain the moral high ground, and distance himself from Bradshaw's personal life, which he feared; if it ever became public knowledge, the ensuing scandal might well topple the entire Labour Party government.

He had never quite trusted Bradshaw and had once or twice asked Spencer to covertly keep tags on his Home Secretary. Haining's attitude and dealings with his security services, had on occasions, like Bradshaw's, been somewhat ambivalent. However, on becoming Prime Minister, Haining had informed MI5, that under no circumstances were any members of Parliament to have their telephones bugged, but, having thought the matter through, he then decided that didn't preclude anyone the security service believed might pose a potential threat to his Administration. In many respects, it was double dealing on a grand scale, but British Intelligence had seen it all before, it was what politicians did. Whilst they might openly condemn too much intrusion if it involved national security, and perhaps more importantly, their own political survival, then they were not only willing to turn a blind eye to the legal nuisances, but also to conveniently relax their public stance.

Haining was well aware that MI5 had maintained a permanent file; not only on himself, but his entire Cabinet, and that he had routinely been investigated over the course of his political career. It was no more than their duty to ensure that the main political parties had not been infiltrated by the KGB. Haining was an old hand, even before his appointment as a member of Churchill's wartime coalition government; he knew how things worked, and that although the relationship between Whitehall and the security service was sometimes one of mutual distrust, it was also self-feeding. They each had something to gain from the other; it was a game, a deadly one where each of them needed or wanted to retain the upper hand. The bottom line was that it was a case of you couldn't live with them, but you also couldn't live without them.

'If I play along with your plans,' Haining said at length, 'then I think we have to make one or two provisos.'

'What's that, sir?' Spencer asked.

'We go through my diary and delete any engagements that I'm due to attend with my wife.'

It wasn't up for discussion. They agreed.

'I'm not prepared to expose her to that much risk, it simply wouldn't be fair, and I'd never forgive myself if anything happened to her.'

They were both acutely aware that Marie had been unwillingly thrust into the spotlight by her husband's meteoric rise through the political ranks, whilst she'd loyally supported him, and had never, at least publically complained about her own loss of personal privacy, it had also left their children's lives open to public consumption, and at the mercy of the national press. The prospect of endangering her life was for Haining, a sacrifice way too far. He'd also decided against telling Marie about the threat; there was simply no point in worrying his wife unnecessarily, more than anything he wanted to shield her.

His wife hadn't been scheduled to attend that many appointments with him over the next month, so it didn't appear to pose any particular problem; they suggested that if his staff quietly tweaked the diary, then it shouldn't arouse any great interest from the either the Press or the KGB.

Haining seemed satisfied with their response, but where his wife was concerned, her safety was non-negotiable, he'd never have agreed to any plan that might have compromised or placed her life in danger. As Prime Minister, he accepted that he was fair game, and there was always a risk of some random nutter hoping to make a name, it came with the job, but this was different, and he couldn't allow his family to be placed in jeopardy.

He added between puffs on his cigar. 'There's something else that we need to get straight.'

'What's that, sir,' Garvan queried.

'From now on in I'd like both of you to contact me directly.' He looked at each of them in turn before emphasising. 'Do you understand?'

Haining was well aware there was certainly no love lost between Spencer and his Home Secretary, and knew that his request wouldn't exactly cause him any particular problem, but even so, Spencer wanted the PM to spell it out to him. He didn't trust Bradshaw and more to the point he wanted to cover his own back.

He held Haining's gaze and asked coolly. 'Just so that there's no misunderstanding, I take it then, sir, that you'd like us to keep the Home Secretary out of the loop, is that what you're saying?'

'Not entirely,' Haining answered smoothly, 'there are certain niceties to observe we both know that.'

Spencer returned his smile.

'What I'm saying, gentlemen, is that I don't want to hear anything second hand. Let's not forget that it's my life on the line here and not bloody Bradshaw's!'

He couldn't have made himself clearer.

'I'll instruct my staff that if either of you call, you're to be put straight through to me.'

Spencer exchanged Garvan a knowing look; it didn't go unnoticed by Haining. The civil war between the two architects of the government had been simmering for a number of years now, and whilst Haining had needed his help recently; Bradshaw had lost little time in systematically smearing and destroying the ministerial careers of several colleagues in order to burnish his own position. Bradshaw was biding his time, and Haining was also acutely aware that given an inch, he'd make a concerted attempt to oust him from power.

'By the way,' he said, addressing Spencer, 'I received your message about drafting a letter to Coulls Auction House.'

'Yes, sir.'

'Why are you so desperate to have this woman, Virginia Dudley on your team?'

'She's an American by birth.'

'Is that important?'

'Under the circumstances, yes, I think it is, during the war she was a member of the Special Operations Executive, and more recently she served with the CIA.'

'I'll leave all that stuff in your capable hands, Spencer, after all, I'm only the Prime Minister; far be it for me to question *your* motives,' he only half-joked.

'Have you written the letter, sir?'

'Yes, of course, I have, you obviously thought it was important, and heaven forbid that I should upset my intelligence service!'

Spencer let out a deep-throated chuckle. 'Thank you.'

Haining glanced at the ornate ormolu clock sitting on the marble fireplace; it was almost 8 o'clock, and so stubbed out his cigar. He'd promised them dinner, nothing too fancy mind. Before heading off to the theatre, his wife had placed a stew in the oven for them; in spite of his protests she had also left him written instructions, but even Haining figured he could at least master the art of turning the ruddy thing off. As he invited them through to the kitchen, he explained that Flossie would have to be fed first, before making an aside.

'Funny chap, Bradshaw, why the hell would you want to work alongside your mistress, I've always kept mine in St John's Wood.'

They both laughed in response, but behind his back Garvan mouthed. 'Is that true?'

Spencer was giving nothing away.

Chapter 9
Meeting with Alexander Bukin

Alexander Bukin, Taylor's KGB contact, stared somberly out of the café window; the passing shadowy figures cutting across the road were almost swallowed up by the thick, acrid fog shrouding the capital. As he sat nursing a steaming hot mug of tea, it struck Bukin that Taylor's choice of venue was almost like saying a reluctant, somewhat nostalgic goodbye to all his favourite old haunts. For, after the mission was complete, Taylor would never risk returning to his beloved home city again.

It was strictly business, of course, but he'd never particularly warmed to Charles Taylor. Bukin's entire life had been driven by total loyalty to the mother country and the Soviet State. In comparison, Taylor was a failed British agent, who'd not only fallen foul of the authorities but had subsequently whored his way across Europe and America to the highest bidder. Bukin knew he had made a lucrative living, but there was something about the man that he couldn't quite bring himself to trust. But orders were orders, and he'd been obliged to play the game as the KGB's go-between with their contract killer. To a certain extent, although he was prepared for Taylor to take his time in devising a workable plan, it was what he'd been paid for, but in cutting him some slack, it was only serving to massage his already towering ego.

Bukin sat quietly in the café before checking his watch and taking a sharp intake of breath; Taylor was running late, probably deliberately, he decided. He was an arrogant bastard, clever yes, and good at what he did, but Bukin was worried, not for the first time, that Taylor was beginning to lose his edge. He took another slurp of his tea, maybe he wasn't entirely fair to the man, for deep down there was a part of him that actually wanted Taylor to fail, and in doing so, prove his own worth to his KGB spymasters that he, Alexander Bukin, had been right all along that Taylor might not be able to pull off the mission.

Charles Taylor had taken his time; he'd showered and shaved, then rather vainly checked his reflection in the bathroom mirror, he pulled a face and patted down his still wet hair. Admittedly there were a few more lines around the eyes, maybe he was a little more ragged around the edges these days, but he was still passably handsome, and had never been short of attracting women. After accepting the KGB's contract he'd taken his foot off the pedal, and since arriving in London he hadn't slept with a woman, he'd behaved himself, but God, what he wouldn't give not to be celibate.

Taylor threw on a warm overcoat against the cold and left his lodgings. He was wearing a pair of black framed glasses, and a bespoke suit. His dark woolen overcoat was unbuttoned, and around his neck was a blue silk scarf with white polka dots. As Taylor entered the café, Bukin smiled to himself: he wears his clothes well, this Englishman. The café had been Taylor's choice of venue, it was in the upmarket area of Knightsbridge, and had been a favourite of his since the war. He hadn't visited the establishment for a number of years and had confessed that living abroad had made him rather nostalgic for London. In the old days, when he had been working for MI5, he'd loved nothing more than to have a leisurely breakfast at the café and read the sports pages, for football he confessed to Bukin was something of an obsession with him.

Taylor's voice was mellow, unhurried, he ordered tea and shrugged off his overcoat, folding it carefully over the back of his chair, and explaining seamlessly as he did so, that he preferred not to hang it up in the corner with everyone else's coats. The café wasn't particularly busy, and it didn't usually get so on a Saturday morning until well after eleven. He smiled broadly at the waitress and thanked her for fetching over his tea. Taylor had a way with women; Bukin noted, the girl blushed under the onslaught of his understated charm and fading good looks.

Bukin watched him as he carefully lifted the lid of the white china teapot and slowly stir the hot steaming liquid with a spoon. Since his appointment to the Soviet Embassy in London, Bukin had been amused by how the British appeared to have rather strict procedures for doing most things, and the art of pouring a cup of tea was no exception. Watching Taylor carefully replace the lid and set a long handled silver strainer over the teacup to catch the loose tea leaves from the pot, it was difficult to imagine there was another side to this seemingly fastidious Englishman with impeccable manners, that, of a deadly, ruthless killer. But it was probably part and parcel of why he was at the top of his profession, on face value no-one in their right mind would have suspected Taylor of having a darker side.

Bukin expressed his surprise that Taylor hadn't bothered to turn up in disguise; maybe he hadn't thought it was necessary, but under the circumstances, given the nature of the job in hand, it might be deemed a little careless.

Taylor raised the freshly poured tea to his lips, he appeared unconcerned, and brushed the barbed comment aside, spying, he explained, was like theatre, it required a talent for disguise and acting, but there was a time and place. He asked if Bukin was worried that he might have been followed.

'You can never be too careful, my friend.'

'I'm always careful, Alex,' he said, with more than a touch of arrogance.

Bukin coldly held his gaze but decided to let it rest. On a personal level, he had not been in favour of hiring Taylor for the assignment. Whatever the real reasons behind the Kremlin's decision, it still seemed a risk way too far employing an outsider, not least of all a former enemy agent.

100

But the decision had never been his to make, and so he had obeyed orders, as he always had done, to assist Taylor in any way that he could to successfully carry out the mission to assassinate the British Prime Minister.

The Englishman struck him as being somewhat socially shy; or perhaps he'd just been wary and slightly guarded in his dealings with him, but either way on first impressions, he was not at all what Bukin had expected of a renowned professional contract killer. But over a period of time, as he came to know him slightly better, Bukin began to realise that beneath the smooth, urbane charm, lurked a cold, ruthless individual. Although Taylor's expression rarely gave anything away, there was an undeniable steeliness about him that even Bukin found at times intensely unnerving.

From Taylor's perspective, whatever way you looked at it, the offer had not only taken him by surprise, but he was also acutely aware that his chances of survival were minimal. For once they had confided their plans to him, there was simply no way out. Although he'd seemingly taken his time weighing up the options, refusal would have automatically signed his death warrant, it was a fait accompli. He was damned if he did, and damned if he didn't. As far as British Intelligence were concerned, he'd long since lost his moral compass, and would no doubt view him as nothing more than a mercenary living on his wits and paid by the highest bidder. Even so, until the KGB had approached him, Taylor had always managed to have a degree of autonomy over his life. If he pulled it off and more importantly survived, he'd have to go to ground for several years, whilst the pay reflected the magnitude of the contract there was still a chance, that if he was out of the game too long, the contracts would eventually dry up altogether, and then what would he do? Since leaving the Service he had built up a nice life for himself, when not working he lived in Monte Carlo, played the Casinos and enjoyed a lifestyle way beyond his wildest dreams. He socialised with the rich and famous, was on nodding terms with Prince Rainier and his wife, the beautiful Grace Kelly. Whatever happened, there was simply too much at stake to lose it all.

After accepting a large upfront payment for the contract, Taylor had been assigned the Codename, Agent Pegasus; it was a play on the emblem of the British Airborne Forces, with whom he'd served during the war and had received a Military Cross for gallantry before being recruited by British Intelligence.

Bukin had studied his subject well and had read up about Taylor long before their first meeting. He knew that since the war, Taylor had developed an almost manic obsession for the finer things in life, especially for a fine wardrobe. Rumour also had it, that he had once developed an unhealthy relationship with alcohol, but in Bukin's experience, there was nothing to substantiate the claims, it was probably no more than a rumour. Certainly by Soviet standards, Bukin considered Taylor something of a lightweight. Just prior to Moscow giving the all clear to hire him, Bukin had attended a number of briefings at the Soviet Embassy in London before finally being ordered to fly back to Moscow for a private meeting at the Politburo.

There were many powerful voices within the KGB who were understandably reluctant to outsource the assignment, especially about hiring a mercenary with former connections to British Intelligence. But Taylor's well-documented grievance and falling out with Spencer Hall, was also another sticking point. In Bukin's view, he was concerned that his personal animosity might well end up clouding his professional judgement, and affect his ability to carry out the assignment. But when the order arrived from the Chairman of the KGB, Nicholas Shelepin, that they were to formally hire Taylor, it was left up to Bukin to sort out the finer details and make the initial approach.

It hadn't been easy to set up; he'd eventually managed to track Taylor down, not in Monte Carlo, but Spain where he was living high on the hog for a couple of weeks, having just completed another successful mission to assassinate a wealthy banker who had somehow crossed a powerful Portuguese industrialist. Taylor had numerous successes to his name, and wouldn't normally have crossed the KGB's radar, but some years ago, he had accepted a contract from a prominent Yugoslavian, who wanted to settle an old wartime score against a former member of the SS living in South America. The contract was textbook, his preparation had been meticulous, and fortunately for the KGB, his Yugoslavian contractor had been under their surveillance. As a consequence, they picked up about the mission on their communications, and the fact that Taylor had carried out the mission with clinical precision had impressed them. But perhaps more importantly, the fact that he'd had a well-documented fallout with British Intelligence also made him a name to remember, a mental reference card, and someone they might, given the right circumstances, call upon in the future.

'How goes the planning?' Bukin asked casually.

Taylor's response was non-committal. 'It's going well enough.'

'And the copy of the Prime Minister's diary was it helpful?'

'Yes, of course, it was.'

His voice and delivery were hesitant; he thought about everything, this Englishman, but his approach remained, as always, clinically calculating. 'I'll check out a few more locations later this week, but I've already struck off one or two, they weren't suitable and I'd never been able to pull it off.'

'Do you have everything you need from us?'

Taylor stared at him thoughtfully across the table, and said at length, 'Yes, thank you, I have.'

103

'Are you happy with the rifle?'

'It's a beautiful piece of kit, probably the best I've used so far.' His eyes danced mischievously. 'Are you going to allow me to keep it?'

Bukin lit a cigarette. 'I think not, the rifle will be destroyed, all evidence will be destroyed.'

It crossed Taylor's mind whether that included him as well, but he'd long since learned to hide his feelings, and said smoothly 'I'll say this Alex, Russian sniper rifles have always been second to none,' then added, with the merest hint of a smile, 'but there again I suppose you had a great deal of practice during the War.'

Bukin gave him a wintry smile. Taylor knew full well that Bukin had been at the siege of Stalingrad. The bitter fighting had raged in the City for every bomb damaged ruin, street, factory, house, basement, and staircase. The Russians hadn't given an inch and had made the Nazis fight for every single yard of ground. They'd even fought in the sewers, and every building left standing had to be cleared by the Germans room by room through the bombed-out debris of residential neighbourhoods. Snipers on both sides had skillfully used the ruins to inflict huge casualties on one another.

Taylor figured that one way or another, the experiences had left their mark on the man, that he was, in same way damaged goods. Espionage was after all about psychological tactics, mind games, and retaining the upper hand. The trouble was, Taylor knew that he was on the back foot and that so far, Bukin was calling all the shots, but he wasn't about to make it easy for him. The KGB needed his services, and they needed him to keep his mouth shut.

'Is everything in place?' Taylor asked.

Bukin knew instinctively what he meant. Whilst the detailed planning of the assassination was strictly down to Taylor and Taylor alone, he would never have agreed to the

assignment without a lengthy discussion about an escape route from the UK.

The plan was to fly him out of England using a privately owned plane from a farmer's field near Coolham in Sussex. The farmer in question, Steve Smthye, was well known to the KGB, and was a leading member of the local Communist party; they'd used him before, and he had so far never let them down. He assured Taylor that everything was in hand. Whether Taylor believed it or not was an entirely different matter, his eyes had a faraway look before slowly settling back on Bukin.

But try as he might, Bukin still couldn't help eyeing him with distaste, ultimately, Taylor's only loyalty was to himself, it shouldn't matter to him of course, why should it, but deep down it did. Taylor's enforced early retirement from British Intelligence had been mired in controversy. If the KGB files were correct, and he had no reason to suspect that they were not, he'd been fired not just because of his wartime racketeering, but also because Spencer Hall had begun to suspect that sometimes people, like Taylor, ended up killing because they liked to kill.

There was certainly something about Taylor that even Bukin found unsettling. Sitting opposite him in the café he began to wonder whether Hall had been right all along. Whilst on paper Taylor might be the right man for the job, a professional trigger man, and ultimately the Soviets fall guy, somewhere along the line his KGB Spymasters had missed the point that Taylor had turned into a flawed, cold-blooded killer.

Taylor finished off his tea, shrugged on his overcoat and said he'd be in touch.

Bukin didn't respond. As Taylor headed out of the café, Bukin slumped back in his chair, folded his arms, and followed Taylor's shadowy figure through the cafe window as he disappeared into the thick, clogging acrid London fog.

Chapter 10
The Squire's Holt Café, Surrey

Spencer contacted Garvan at Scotland Yard to say that he wanted him to meet the fifth member of their team. Up until that point, he'd didn't know there was going to be a fifth member, but there again, Spencer had always played things pretty close to his chest, and he really didn't think that much of it.

The Squires Holt was not exactly the type of cheap hostelry that Garvan expected Spencer to frequent. The name was somewhat grander than it seemed; the café was situated just outside of London on the busy main road leading down to Brighton on the south coast. It was a large rundown building with a car park filled with motorbikes, trucks and cars. As Garvan entered the café the smell of cigarettes, stale fat and an array of cooking odours momentarily overwhelmed him.

Spencer was sitting at a table next to another man. He looked up, saw Garvan and beckoned him over. Garvan approached the table, and as Spencer introduced him to his companion, Martin Bell came to his feet to shake his hand. Bell, he noticed, was a small, slim, wiry man with not an ounce of fat on him. He was dressed in what was popularly called bikers clothes, leather jacket, American jeans and leather boots, and he guessed probably rode a Harley Davidson. His clothes were good quality and would not have come cheap.

Bell had a cigarette on the go; he looked Garvan in the eyes and told him that any friend of Mr Hall was a friend of his. Garvan's gaze instinctively glided and set on Spencer, who smiled somewhat lamely in response.

Garvan pulled back a chair and joined them at the table. He'd obviously interrupted their breakfast, they were both well into a plate of bacon, eggs, fried bread, baked beans and sausages, with a pint mug of tea to the right of their plates.

Looking around the place, everything, including the food was on an industrial scale.

Spencer continued tucking into his breakfast. 'I'll need to contact Jack and Ginny later, but I thought you ought to be the first to know that I've a proposal to make.'

Whatever it was, obviously involved Martin Bell in some way.

'We're all agreed that we need to keep a tight lid on contacting one another.'

Garvan inclined his head in agreement.

'Good, so from now on all future communications are going to be made through Martin here.'

Garvan's expression registered surprise, who the hell was this guy; it didn't sit easily with him. Spencer as always, seemed totally unconcerned by his reaction, it wasn't up for discussion, it was his call, he was running the show, if it failed, he'd be the first to fall on his sword, there would be no way back.

He carried on seamlessly. 'No phone calls, everything's to be in writing.'

'So how do we keep in contact?'

He explained that Martin owned a car dealership in South London; just off Lambeth Road under the railway arches and that he'd give him the details. Spencer paused and exchanged a knowing smile with Bell. 'In fact, Martin owns several dealerships, they're owned outright by the Spentar Group.'

Garvan's expression closed down; Spentar was a play on words, Bell's dealership was nothing more than a front, and wholly owned by British Intelligence via a faux holding company. During the war, Garvan and Spencer had both worked for the Double Cross Section whose main aim was to gain control of German agents in Britain, and then to feed disinformation about the Allied invasions of Sicily and Normandy to Berlin. Their section commander at the time was Colonel Thomas Argyll Robertson, who was more commonly referred to by his initials as "TAR". The Spentar dealership didn't leave much to the imagination, being a combination of Spencer's name and Robertson's initials.

Garvan still felt uneasy; Martin Bell was a completely unknown quantity to him, more to the point he didn't quite know where he fitted into the equation. Garvan looked across the table at this small, underweight man and wondered what the hell Spencer was playing at. One puff of wind would have blown this smartly dressed leather-clad biker into next week. Surely to God, Spencer must have someone better, someone else in the organisation, other than this guy to call upon.

Having polished off, his breakfast Bell set his knife and fork down on the plate, drained his mug of tea before wiping his mouth with the back of his hand, and announced that he really ought to get going, and would wait for Spencer to contact him. He pushed his chair back, stood up and reached across the table and shook Garvan's hand again, then touched his forelock in comic salute to Spencer, and swaggered his way out of the café.

As he closed the door, Garvan shot is old friend a penetrating look. 'So, come on, who the hell is he?'

'That,' Spencer said, 'is the best despatch rider the Royal Signals ever had, and probably ever will have.'

Garvan still looked unimpressed. 'That's really not telling me much.'

'We need him.'

'Do we?'

'Don't underestimate Bell, during the war he was well thought of by MI5 and MI6.' Spencer hesitated and pulled a face. 'To be honest with you, for a while, I'm not entirely convinced he quite realised who or what he was working for. Martin's always been a bit of a chancer, but he's sound.' Spencer eased a pack of cigarettes out of his hip pocket. 'The only thing you have to know is that Bell isn't only loyal, but totally professional, and right now that's really all that matters.' As he flicked on his lighter, Spencer suddenly took a sharp intake of breath. 'But what I don't need right now, is the indigestion I'm about to get from this bloody breakfast, god,' he snorted, 'why the hell do I do this!'

Garvan smiled, but he needed to know more about this Martin Bell character, he had a copper's sixth sense that however loyal Bell was to the Service, he had a history, and probably wasn't exactly squeaky clean. He pressed him further.

Spencer leaned back in his chair, looked at Garvan, he had a point, and accepted that he owed him an explanation, and said 'Okay, let me tell you about Bell.'

Back in 1938, Martin Bell joined the army for no other reason that it provided an alternative to being homeless. Before signing up on the dotted line Martin had found himself, it had to be said, not for the first time before the Magistrates Court, having been found with three chickens and a turkey in his possession by a Constable in Wandsworth Bridge Road two weeks before Christmas. There had been a number of petty thefts reported by various local butcher shops in the surrounding area, and the beat Constable suspected that Bell had been responsible for the sudden spate of reported robberies in the run up to Christmas.

At the time Bell had no real excuse, in fact, he'd convinced himself that he was due for a stretch in prison, but as luck would have it, for some reason or other the Magistrate gave him a fine of three pounds, which was quite a large sum back then, but he'd made enough out of his lucrative Christmas trade to pay the fine in full. But just as he'd begun to believe he'd fallen on his feet again, his irate mother threw him out of the family home.

Cold and alone Bell had wandered the streets and eventually found himself outside the Central London Recruiting Office and on a mad impulse went in and joined up. He knew he was joining the army but had no idea he'd just joined the Royal Signals. Within two days he was marching up and down a square in Aldershot and twelve weeks later found that he had been selected for the trade of Despatch Rider. Bell had never been on a motorbike in his life before but took to riding on two wheels like a duck to water.

At last, he had finally found his vocation in life. A life riding on two wheels from one point to another, carrying packages and letters, never asking what they contained and getting them to their final destination on time and to the correct person. For six months Signalman Bell had a free and easy life travelling at speed along the lanes and roads of England delivering his packages and letters to various military Headquarters and Units.

Bell's happy, contented life changed when a certain Herr Hitler decided to invade Belgium, and he found himself a member of the British Expeditionary Force, this wasn't quite what he'd bargained for. At Dover Bell had a motorbike, but by the time he disembarked in France his bike was nowhere to be seen, and he found himself as part of a headquarters signals troop. Bell had no idea what a headquarters signal troop did, but he didn't want to be part of it, and so at the first opportunity decided he would find a motorbike and revert to the job he did best.

His chance came during his second week in France when he found himself with a troop of signallers looking for a location for a forward headquarters. At a crossroads, Bell saw a motorbike combination with two German soldiers looking at a map and obviously discussing where they were. Bell looked longingly at the bike and for the first time since arriving in France, he fired his rifle. More by luck than judgement both his shots found their mark, and the two German soldiers of a reconnaissance regiment fell dead beside the wheels of the motorbike and side car. Bell's comrades showed a combination of shock and horror at what he'd done. Bell unimpressed, decided to claim his prize as his troop officer was still castigating him for firing without permission.

Eleven weeks later and after many scrapes and escapades Bell was at Dunkirk with his German bike, less side car, and waiting for a ship to take him home. He did find a ship, but the sailors would only take him and not his bike. Bell was devastated and apparently had tears in his eyes as he saw his much-loved bike thrown unceremoniously over the side of the ship.

Back in England Bell, now a Lance Corporal, was called to his Commanding Officer's Office and told he had been awarded the Military Medal, for continuing to deliver vital dispatches on his motorbike at the height of the British Army's desperate retreat to the beaches of Dunkirk.

Bell then spent the next four years riding his motorbike over the English and Welsh countryside delivering brown envelopes and packages. He also had a secondary job, that of a black marketeer. If you wanted it, Bell could find it and have it delivered to you. Things were going well, that is, until the now Corporal Bell found himself in a landing craft as part of the first signal regiment to hit the beaches on D-Day. Under fire and pushing a motorbike off the landing craft Bell rushed up the beach. After waiting under cover for an hour and seeing many of his mates killed and wounded Bell sat on his bike, kick started it and rode off the beach and never stopped moving until months later when he found himself as one of the first British soldiers in Berlin.

Late in 1945 Corporal Martin Bell was discharged from the Royal Signals with a bar to his Military Medal and a large amount of money made from the black market in England and Germany.

Ten years after the war Mr Bell was the foremost car dealer in West London with four garages wholly owned by the Spentar Group or more precisely a faux holding company owned by British Intelligence, which was ostensibly run to provide them with a variety of modified vehicles, but at the same time the garages also ran an entirely legitimate business, and under Bell's eye for a good deal, it had become surprisingly profitable.

'So,' said Garvan, 'he was carrying messages around Germany for MI5 and MI6 as well as doing a bit of black market dealing on the side.'

111

'In actual fact he was doing a lot more than that for us, but he was never entirely on the payroll, he was just someone we called upon, and if he could make a few pounds on the side, well did it *matter*?'

'So was he working for you personally?'

'Sort of, I had a few like him doing bits and pieces; you know what it's like.'

'No, I don't. Spence, I just get the impression there were times during the war that both you and Tar had your own private army. I'm still not quite sure how the hell you got away with it?'

'We did what we had to do,' he replied simply. 'Beside's I've used Bell far more since the war.' He drew heavily on his cigarette. 'I've had to rein him in once or twice, he's always lived his life on the edge of the law, but since we appointed him as the manager of the Spentar Group, he's had to keep his nose clean, the dodgy second hand car and motorbike deals are a thing of the past.' Spencer paused, flicking a trail of ash into the overflowing metal ashtray. 'Martin's a typical biker, drinks too much, swears too much and has somewhat questionable morals, but he's the salt of the earth.' Spencer saw the look of doubt etched on Garvan's face. 'I know he might not look it, but Bell's sharp-eyed and just what we need for the job.'

Garvan smirked at him. 'You're right, he certainly looks sharp-eyed I'll give you that!'

Chapter 11
Special Branch, Scotland Yard

Garvan ran a hand over his chin; he'd shut himself away at Scotland Yard to read through a stack of personal files and records from British Intelligence's central registry. Spencer had granted special permission for their removal from MI5 custody, it had caused quite a stir amongst the clerical staff, it was unprecedented. The personnel files were normally sacrosanct, but Spencer's directive had been clear and precise. A special delivery had been made direct to Garvan's office, no-one else at Scotland Yard was granted access, and they were only to be removed by British Intelligence messengers in a secure van.

Having ploughed his way through four sacks crammed with files, he'd placed them into three separate piles in order of importance. The first one contained files of agents who had parted company from the Service under a cloud and who he believed potentially fitted the assassin's profile. The second was a pretty mixed bag and sat on the floor beside his desk; they included a dozen or so former and current intelligence officers with some kind of reprimand against them. The third batch he had dismissed out of hand for not being of sufficient calibre to carry out a first division assignment, or simply didn't have the right background. He'd spent hours meticulously poring over the files, but even so, it was still like looking for a needle in a haystack, and for all he knew, the Soviet's hired assassin might not fit as neatly into the profiling as he'd hoped they might.

Garvan had made his notes in longhand before finally typing up the report himself. It had taken more time than he cared to admit, but it was essential that his secretary and clerical staff were kept out of the loop. For the time being the day job was on hold, the only exception being a couple of long-standing pre-arranged meetings with the French police and President's de Gaulle's security staff about his impending state visit to London; he'd already pulled out of one when Spencer had requested they meet up at the St. Phillips Hotel, but it was the one thing he couldn't duck out of indefinitely without arousing suspicions.

He'd worked long into the night without a break reading the files, and had refused all incoming calls. It had been painstaking stuff and a slow process of elimination, but even so, he still might have missed something, something important and he needed Spencer's help. Whoever they were looking for was obviously well paid, and at the high end of the market, after all, it was a lucrative business. There was more research to be done, but time wasn't on their side, they needed to find someone who was living high on the hog, but that kind of investigation wouldn't only take weeks, but more likely months of thorough investigation and their team was way too small to accomplish anything seriously tangible in that timescale.

Garvan initially suggested double checking with the Passport Office for potential suspects, but Spencer had said he'd be wasting their time, any former intelligence officer worth their salt, especially one who was in the pay of the KGB would have travelled under a number of aliases, and their documentation, even to the trained eye at border control, would have been difficult to spot and all but perfect.

In fairness to Spencer, he had already helped him to weed out a number of potential suspects, but the more Garvan read through the files, he couldn't help wondering why both the CIA and British Intelligence hadn't picked up on a former British spy who was plying his trade and operating as a professional killer on the open market. But whoever it was had somehow managed to escape under their radar, but why, or how had the KGB managed to pick up on him. Had they perhaps used his services before?

114

Garvan contacted Spencer and asked if he'd mind running through the personnel files with him. Visiting Scotland Yard didn't pose a particular problem as only a handful of staff, including the Commissioner, knew that the tough looking man who always signed himself in as Mr Hubbard was, in fact, the Director General of MI5.

Spencer stood at the large window of Garvan's office, gazing out across the river toward Westminster Bridge, thoughtfully watching the handover between sunset and the onset of dusk, it came quickly in winter. The Thames was lapping gunmetal grey against the walls of the embankment; overhead a flock of seagulls were mewing and squawking above the tidal river. They rarely, if ever, ventured this far up the estuary in such large numbers unless there was a severe storm out at sea. The light was fading rapidly, and a necklace of twinkling white lights had begun to flicker into life along the granite stone walls lining the embankment.

On closing one of the files, Garvan said. 'I can't help thinking that I'm wasting my time here.'

Spencer thrust his hands deep into his trouser pockets. 'What makes you think that?' He asked, continuing to gaze across the river.

'Well, how longs a piece of string? I'd need a whole ruddy squad to sort through this bloody lot, but with a lockdown I guess that's not going to happen anytime soon.'

Spencer swung away from the window to face him. 'You have to remember we have certain niceties to observe.'

'Like what?'

'As much as I need Jack and Virginia on board, they wouldn't expect me to grant them access to our files, any more than the CIA would allow me access to their people.'

'I'm not questioning that, but since the war just how many agents have you had fall by the wayside or left the Service under a cloud?'

Spencer shrugged; he hadn't a clue, but to his knowledge there really weren't that many of the right calibre or, at least, anyone who the KGB might be interested in for a sniper job. 'The trouble is it might not be someone with a grudge, just someone who works for the highest bidder.'

Garvan leaned back in his chair and lit a much-needed cigarette and decided to play devil's advocate. 'The trouble is if I didn't know any better I'd place your name at the top of the fucking list.'

A slow somewhat tortured smile crossed Spencer's face. 'That wasn't funny.'

'It wasn't meant to be. I'm just saying things as they are, or at least how I see them!'

Having worked his way through the ranks of British Intelligence, Spencer's bravery and courage had never been in doubt, and in the past, he had often been called in to sort out rogue double agents, or, in fact, anyone British Intelligence needed to eliminate. By the time Garvan worked alongside him, he had already developed a healthy disregard for unnecessary red tape and rules, but in fairness, he certainly wasn't entirely alone. The Double Cross section had been designed around bending and breaking the rule book as a means of outwitting the Nazi intelligence machine; it was quite simply a matter of life or death. No quarter was given or expected on either side.

Garvan was well aware that deep down Spencer was frustrated by the constant restrictions his appointment, as the Head of MI5, had imposed upon him. By nature, he wasn't only a maverick, but a free spirit, who found the nuances and restraints of political diplomacy a complete and utter anathema to him. Spencer played the game, of course; he had to, and he had learnt to keep his mouth shut when dealing with politicians and civil servants who spouted nonsense. They always thought they knew best, without possessing any particular qualification or the necessary experience to make

116

informed judgments on intelligence issues. To an extent he'd learned to mellow with the passing of time, but there was still a certain quietness, an explosive aura about him that he could never quite shake off. His underlying ruthlessness and dead-eyed stare had served to unnerve not only his intelligence colleagues but many of his political masters as well.

Garvan folded his arms. 'Whatever it is I'm looking for, I doubt if I'm going to find it on the files, besides there are not enough hours in the day, and the one thing we don't have is time on our side. I figure we need to start looking elsewhere.'

'I'm open to suggestions.'

'So what do we know about this ex-British operative, not much I grant you, but whoever it is hasn't just suddenly broken through the ranks to become a top-flight operator; he must have been pretty slick in his day, and must have been working successfully on the open market for quite a while.'

Spencer agreed.

'Then maybe we ought to consider that this may not be the first time that he's worked for the Soviets.'

'It's possible,' Spencer conceded.

'So perhaps Jack Stein was right all along.'

Spencer looked at him speculatively. 'What do you mean, right all along?'

'Perhaps our assassin is a communist, some ideological convert, and what better way of proving his loyalty to the cause than by taking on a top assignment, perhaps he volunteered.'

Spencer pulled a face; he seemed unimpressed. 'I really don't see it working like that.'

Garvan asked him why.

'Whether our man is a fully paid up member of the communist party is neither here nor there. The bottom line is that he was once a member of British Intelligence. The KGB must have given it a great deal of soul searching before taking the decision to hire him. They must have asked themselves whether or not he could be trusted, was he nothing more than a plant? As I said before, be it us, the CIA or the KGB, from a security angle it's always safer to keep everything in-house.'

'So *why* have they hired an outsider?'

'It's hard to say, the obvious answer is that, if everything goes tits up, they'll have to distance themselves from the operation. The last thing they can't afford is to be seen to have blood on their hands, it's one thing to take out the occasional well-placed businessman or diplomat, but it's a whole different league plotting the assassination of a top politician, especially someone of Jeremy Haining's stature. If you start assassinating Heads of State, where do you stop? Every kind of decision on that level has a ripple effect, a consequence that ends up being played out on the world stage.'

Garvan exhaled the cigarette smoke slowly through his lips and nostrils. 'Well, it still doesn't make sense or, at least, it doesn't to me. If roles were reversed and you'd been ordered by the government to dispose of some dictator or other, you wouldn't have hired an outsider, no matter how good they were.'

'No,' he said, guardedly, 'but it's not entirely without precedent.'

'What the hell is that supposed to mean?'

'If I was sitting in Moscow I'd have weighed up all the options.'

'What kind of options?' Garvan said, offering Spencer a cigarette.

He accepted and borrowed Garvan's lighter. 'Much the same as you do in Special Branch, you weigh up the risk, choose the right man for the job, especially undercover jobs, you're doing it all the time. But just because I have a particular agent on hand capable of carrying out the operation, doesn't mean to say that they necessarily fit the bill. You have to weigh up all the pros and cons. Occasionally, just occasionally, you might need to look elsewhere, outside the organisation, it's rare, in fact very rare,' he continued smoothly, 'but if I was looking for a fall guy or to screw someone, then I certainly wouldn't discount it out of hand. But as I say each case is different, every circumstance is different.'

Garvan looked at him quizzically.' I'm sorry, but I still can't imagine farming out a top job like this to someone I hadn't used before.'

Spencer wouldn't be drawn further, and he certainly wasn't about to provide him with an example of a previous job. 'Well, I guess that's why we need to figure out why the KGB decided to go with him. They'll want to appear squeaky clean, and distance themselves from any diplomatic fallout. I should imagine their Press lines have already been drawn up in preparation; you know the kind of thing, condemning the assassination of the British Prime Minister.' Spencer exhaled a plume of smoke, before adding with a taut smile. 'Besides, if it goes wrong, and I was them, I really wouldn't fancy some smart arse detective like you pointing an accusing finger in my direction.'

Garvan returned his smile. 'Then why would this guy accept the contract? He must know they'll drop him like a ton of bricks. What's in it for him?'

It was a fair question; even if he succeeded it was unlikely that the Soviets would ever allow him to walk away scot free. There was simply too much at stake; they couldn't guarantee that he'd keep his mouth shut indefinitely. If their man found himself on the wrong side of the law, he might well put up one hell of a plea bargain to save his own neck.'

Like Garvan, he still couldn't quite fathom out why he'd go along with the mission, but could only guess that after the KGB had made their initial approach, there was probably no going back for him. Once the cat was out of the bag, and he'd been made aware of the precise nature of the contract,

119

one way or another his death warrant had already been signed. Perhaps by accepting, he hoped that he might have an outside chance of controlling the situation, but to Spencer's mind, he was nothing more than a dead man walking.

'Come on,' he said, bleakly, 'let's get back to the files, what have you managed to come up with so far?'

'Not much,' Garvan confessed, patting the rather meagre pile of classified personnel files on his desk.

All of them had left the service under a cloud. He knew it wasn't much to go on but was marginally better than nothing at all.

Spencer pulled up a chair, sat opposite Garvan and turned around the in-tray to face him so he could take a look at the files. The first belonged to Frederick Harman; he had worked for a number of years in counter-intelligence before being forced to resign. He was an interesting character, whose loyalties had been brought into question over a number of serious leaks during his time in Berlin. Spencer flicked through a couple of records, before discounting him and tossed the file into the neighboring out-tray.

'What's wrong with that one?' Garvan protested, slightly miffed that all his hard work had been dismissed so lightly.

'Harman couldn't hit a double-decker bus at twenty paces, that's why; he was a good in his day, but not quite sniper material.' Spencer picked up the second file; it elicited a similar reaction. 'Johnson has a warrant out for him,' he said.

Garvan's brows drew into a frown.

'He's got the right profile,' Spencer conceded, 'but the KGB wouldn't entertain anyone wanted by Interpol.'

The top enclosure in the file also indicated that he was on the so-called "watch" list across at least three European frontier posts. Johnson's file swiftly joined Harman's in the out-tray. After another hour of careful sifting and discussion, they came up with three former members who potentially fitted the right profile. Spencer said there was little to choose between them; their names were Baines, Russell and Taylor. They agreed to coordinate their inquiries to see if they could find out their current whereabouts. Without giving the game away, Garvan intended to contact Interpol with a routine inquiry about the three of them, without specifying exactly why Scotland Yard had an interest in them. It certainly wouldn't arouse any undue interest, he also intended asking his deputy, Harry Mackenzie, to check whether they might still be living and working in Britain, it was bread and butter stuff so shouldn't take an inordinate amount of time.

Garvan leaned thoughtfully back in his chair. 'Do you know what I still can't fathom out is why the Soviets are so desperate to see Haining dead?'

'We'd all like to know that one,' Spencer grunted, inspecting a further file that had drawn his attention. 'The only given so far is that the CIA's Moscow agent is 99% certain our killer isn't current, but it's the 1% that's likely to screw us!'

Chapter 12
Elizabeth Street, Pimlico

Taylor was meticulously working his way through the Prime Minister's itinerary over the coming weeks. He had spent the entire day out and about on a recce, dawdling through the streets of West London and reacquainting himself with his bearings. Although he still had a couple of venues to visit his main concern was that he had so far dismissed nearly all of them out of hand as being unsuitable. There was no point in bodging the job; he needed to be sure, to feel comfortable about not only the timing but also the location. He was hoping that the Soviets would allow him a little leeway, even more than they had already, but he guessed that ultimately it probably depended upon their ability to obtain further copies of the Prime Minister's diary. Whoever had passed them the paperwork in the first place, was obviously highly placed, but there were no guarantees there'd be an endless supply, but he'd have to cross that bridge when and if he needed to with Bukin.

After a day traipsing around London and constantly checking that he hadn't been followed, Taylor returned to Elizabeth Street and was looking forward to not only sharing a meal but also his bed with his landlady, the delightful Donna Webster. He let himself in the front door and hurried up the wide sweeping staircase to the first floor and along the corridor to his room. He was about to unlock the door, when he heard a noise, a thud as if someone had dropped something heavy on the floorboards, and then he noticed that his bedroom door was ajar. On leaving earlier Taylor had double-checked, as he always did, that it was securely locked.

Shit, he thought to himself, have I screwed up somewhere. He'd been careful, bloody careful, but there was always a chance that British Intelligence was onto him and had stumbled across the Soviet plot. Instinctively reaching inside his suit jacket, he eased a silenced handgun out of its holster, clicked off the safety catch and carefully nudged the door open.

Donna Webster spun round with a look of undisguised horror etched on her face as she nervously glanced at the floor, beside her lay an open wooden box, its contents had spilled out onto the mat. It was a shame really, Charles Taylor had actually rather liked his landlady. She'd certainly been a cut above the others. She was an attractive war widow, whose late husband had served with the RAF and had been shot down somewhere over northern France, and had perished alongside his fellow crew members. She must have been quite a stunning looking woman in her prime, the sculptured bone structure, the high cheek bones and the fiery hazel eyes made for a striking combination. He assumed that she was probably in her late thirties, or there about, but looked considerably younger. In order to continue living in her large former marital home, Donna had been forced to take in lodgers or paying guests as she preferred to call them.

They'd hit it off straightaway, that first evening she'd not only brought him up a nightcap but had come onto him. At the time, it crossed Taylor's mind that he really ought to rebuff her advances, but a one off shag with an attractive woman wouldn't necessarily compromise the assignment, for a start she'd no idea who the hell he was. Taylor had booked in under the name of Peter Bartholomew, and had told her that he was a travelling salesman, a book dealer, he'd explained. It was always better to lie about subjects you felt at ease discussing, his ex-wife had once worked for a large bookshop in Shaftesbury Avenue, and he had picked up enough to hold a lengthy conversation about the intricacies of the business.

Taylor had meant to stay only a couple of nights, but an attractive landlady with extras had meant he'd thrown caution to the wind and stayed on with every intention of checking out at the end of the week. In hindsight, it had been a mistake, a serious error of judgment, for Donna Webster wasn't only a passionate woman, but was an inquisitive one, whose curiosity had finally got the better of her.

Taylor quietly nudged the door shut and shot her a rather sad smile. 'Oh Donna,' he said, almost wistfully as he set the Luger down on the dressing table. 'I asked *you* not to enter my room.'

'I'm sorry,' she sobbed, 'I-I didn't mean any harm.'

'No, I don't suppose you did,' he answered, stooping to pick up the contents of the box.

'I swear to God I won't say anything!' Donna pleaded, as he carefully inspected the various pieces of his custom made snipers rifle to ensure that nothing had been broken.

How could she have got it so wrong, up until now he'd been the quintessential gentleman, respectful, charming and very caring. He'd made a point of listening, a rare quality in most men, and had sympathised about how she'd been reduced to taking in her guests to keep the roof over her head. Maybe he'd been too good to be true, although her husband had been dead for some sixteen years now, Donna still felt strangely vulnerable, and had almost given up all hope of finding someone who was not only willing to share her bed, but also her life.

By now Donna was physically shaking, god knows who he was, or what he was up to, she didn't want to know. Oh Christ, why did she do it, why did she enter his room, it had been nothing more than sheer impulse, and overwhelming desire to know whether he was married or not. Taylor had said he was a widower, but something deep down had made Donna mistrustful. He was simply too good to be true, he was charming, everything that she'd hoped for; there'd been no one like him since her husband's death. Taylor had been the only man that had given her a semblance of hope that she did have a future, and a chance of sharing her life with someone else.

Taylor calmly held up the scope in his right hand, closed one eye and peered through the lens to see if it was damaged. Fortunately, the high precision telescopic lens had survived intact. That was something, at least, he thought to himself, and closed down the lid of the box, in the background he could hear Donna sobbing quietly to herself.

'I only came into clean your room,' she whispered between sobs.

He snapped down the catch and without looking at her said. 'You told me this morning over breakfast that you wouldn't bother cleaning until after I'd booked out at the end of the week.' He turned to face her. 'Besides, I'd asked you not to.' Whilst his voice gave nothing away his eyes were cold with more than a hint of anger.

'Did you?' she cried, her voice rising in panic.

'Yes, I did,' he said, patting the box with the flat of his hand. Taylor held her gaze; it was deadly, she'd found the box tucked away in the back of the wardrobe.

Donna smiled nervously. She didn't know what else to do, for the first time since her husband's brutal death she'd started to feel alive again, and although she was admittedly rushing things, Taylor had offered so much; suave, sophisticated and impeccably dressed, a dream come true. Maybe she'd still been way too vulnerable to see through the thin veneer. Whoever he was Donna knew that she'd completely misread the situation, and she was scared, scared witless, by the cold stranger now standing in front of her.

A stupid, impulsive desire to know more about him had made her act foolishly and out of character, Donna had always been so careful, there'd been lovers, but they'd never meant anything to her, until now that is, and she'd chosen to hit on the wrong one. He didn't normally return until about

125

5.30 in the afternoon, so she'd taken a chance to sate her curiosity and had grabbed hold of the spare key and searched his room. Initially, there really hadn't been that much of interest until Donna opened up a seemingly empty suitcase; she'd been on the point of closing it when she noticed a zip pocket in the lining of the lid. Donna had hesitated before deciding to take a peek inside only to find a number of passports, there were two British ones, but the others were a mixture of American, Canadian, German and Australian. The identity photograph in each although slightly different was all too familiar, but the names and details were entirely different.

In hindsight, Donna realised that she should have left things alone, but she couldn't, and like a dog with a bone had carried on searching through his belongings until she found the wooden box containing the rifle. By that point, her hands had been trembling in anxiety and having shakily unfastened the clip the contents had spilled out onto the floor. Although the rifle had been in pieces, even Donna could make out the wooden butt of a rifle, and the various metal tubes and the scope all appeared to fit together. She'd been on the point of gathering it all up when Taylor, or Peter Bartholomew as she knew him, had nudged open the door.

Donna held his cold, probing stare with a feeling of utter bleakness. Her charming, gentle lover had been replaced by a complete stranger, the affection and the warmth in which Taylor had held her, had hemorrhaged the moment he'd found the contents of the rifle case spilled out across his bedroom floor.

'I don't care about anything,' she pleaded, 'I'm so-so sorry.'

He didn't respond there was no point.

'I swear to god I won't say -.' Donna never quite managed to finish her sentence, for Taylor picked the Luger off the dressing table and squeezed the trigger. It was all over in an instant. But for one awful moment, for a split second, her

126

expression registered something approaching surprise, before crumpling down to her knees, one hand desperately trying to reach out as she hit the floor. Without thinking Taylor stooped to pick up the spent cartridge off the carpet and slipped it into his jacket pocket.

Taylor stared dispassionately as her body went into a strange convulsive spasm, and a growing pool of blood seeped slowly across the mat and wooden floorboards. He let out a short rasp of air, yes, he conceded, it was a shame, but more importantly, he'd screwed up and had possibly jeopardized the entire operation.

He needed to cover his back, think what to do; there was another lodger staying at the house, James Christian. He was a creature of habit and according to Donna was one of her regular customers. He always left punctually after breakfast at 8.30 sharp; they were on nodding terms with a brief good morning. Luckily, Taylor knew that he had travelled up to Birmingham on a business trip and was staying overnight, and wasn't due to return until tomorrow lunchtime, so, at least, he had a little time to play with to dispose of her body.

*

Later that evening the Royal Academy in Piccadilly flickered with the glow of gas lamps surrounding the impressive courtyard. There was a discreet police presence as a steady stream of official cars swept up to the main entrance. Spencer had secured Virginia Dudley a formal invite from the Foreign Office to the prestigious event. There was to be a private viewing of the many priceless artworks temporarily on loan from the renowned Russian Hermitage Museum; it was to be followed by dinner for a select specially invited guests.

Although the Cold War between East and West meant there was an ever-present threat of all-out nuclear war, the politicians had reached an uneasy stalemate. In the long struggle for global supremacy, that pitted the capitalist West against the communist East, their respective nuclear arsenals were such that if war was declared then, total annihilation was the only sure outcome. In spite of the endless posturing and rhetoric deep down neither the Western democracies nor the Eastern bloc under the all-powerful yoke of the Soviet Union had any real political appetite to press the red button to oblivion.

The once derided cultural diplomacy that had been tentatively conducted by politicians, on either side of the political divide, had recently found a new impetus and credence between the warring factions. It was slow progress, but a small if not significant step in providing a conduit for mutual understanding and co-existence, or, at least, that was the public stance. But behind the scenes there was always an underlying motive about any cultural exchange, there were invariably countless issues to be ironed out, and at various times, both factions correctly accused one another of spying on the other.

Prior to the exhibition at the Royal Academy there had already been a number of other cultural exchanges between the two countries, including a Shakespeare production of Hamlet in Moscow, but the Hermitage was a real coup, and at least publically, was seen as a milestone in helping to break down the barriers between the opposing sides. Jeremy Haining's government believed they had secured, even temporarily, the ascendancy in the cultural cold war game against the USSR, but both sides knew that behind the public handshakes; lay an underlying web of intrigue. In the morning the leading British newspapers would carry the story, it was all part and parcel of a propaganda plan, and the so-called cultural diplomacy.

Along with Virginia's gilt-edged invitation from Roger Simpson, the Foreign Secretary, she had been passed a copy of the guest list and seating plan, something that was

128

normally only available to senior government officials. Later in the week, the Prime Minister was hosting a separate lunch at No10 for the Soviet delegation. Under the circumstances, he'd have to muster every ounce of his renowned diplomacy to carry it off without giving the game away.

As one of London's leading art experts, Virginia's presence wasn't questioned, the marked absence of Bradshaw's wife, to the initiated, raised more than a few eyebrows, but sadly his relationship with Maggie Ellis was such, that the Home Secretary couldn't move a muscle without her prior approval of his official diary. As a result his long-suffering wife was subject to no end of scrutiny and speculation; even so, Virginia was surprised not to see her there. She was an avid collector of fine art in her own right, and her absence was a statement in itself.

The viewing started well enough, even Virginia conceded, that Maggie Ellis was on good form, but there again she always was in certain male company. She'd never warmed to the woman, and could never quite understand how someone who was as politically astute as Bradshaw could have allowed his political secretary to have so much influence over him. In the past he'd always been adroit at keeping his colleagues at arm's length, especially members of staff, but Virginia guessed, that sharing his bed with Ellis had obviously added a certain dynamic mix into the equation, and had made him increasingly vulnerable, whatever way you looked at it, it was viewed as pretty much an own goal.

Rumour had it that her increasing insecurity was inevitably souring both their private and working relationship. Whenever Maggie was absent, there was a palpable sense of relief, not only at the Home Office but also amongst his closest friends. Judging by Maggie's dagger-like expression, it was obvious that Virginia's presence on the top table had somehow displeased her. She liked to hold centre stage, why wouldn't she? But it was nothing more than outright jealousy, she viewed Bradshaw's friendships with other women as a personal slight, it was borne out of nothing but deep rooted insecurity. Perhaps it didn't help that Virginia wasn't only attractive, but that Maggie never quite had her measure, she wasn't only famously blunt and outspoken, but oozed sophistication, and was more than a match for Bradshaw's lover, who often felt out of her depth in Virginia's company. Had Maggie been aware of the role she'd played in the war and her subsequent status within the intelligence community on both sides of Atlantic then, no doubt, Maggie would have been even more uncomfortable in her perceived rivals company than she already was.

There was something about her glacial East Coast beauty, she not only spoke her mind, as Maggie did, but her ingrained haughtiness always managed to place Maggie on the defensive. There was an undeniable chemistry between Virginia and Bradshaw, borne out of their mutual love and appreciation of art, but it was a world that remained a complete anathema to Maggie, and although his relationship with Virginia was entirely platonic, it seemed to fuel his lover's resentment and dislike of the woman; for this was Virginia's world, the great and good of London's art world, the Director of the National Gallery, and the leading art house experts rubbing shoulders with one another. It was a tight-knit community and the Hermitage exhibition wasn't only a coup, but the highlight of their year. It also provided a unique opportunity for the general public to visit the Royal Academy. The exhibition had been sold out two months prior to the official opening. A reciprocal arrangement was destined for the autumn, and a number of artworks from both the Tate and National Galleries were due to be shipped over to Moscow and Leningrad.

It occasionally crossed Virginia's mind whether or not Bradshaw was afraid that if he didn't keep Ellis on side, their increasingly turbulent relationship, could, if handled unwisely, ring the death knell to his political ambitions. There was no way of knowing, but somewhere along the line, he surely must have regretted becoming entangled with Maggie. Even if he did, there was by no way too much water under the bridge, and it was simply too late, he was saddled with her, for good or bad, and most of it seemed for bad.

Virginia had heard rumours recently that Bradshaw had been forced to excuse her excesses, her constant rudeness, and demands on his staff; it was also an open secret within Whitehall's inner sanctum that Maggie's increasing demands and histrionics were steadily eating into their relationship. Maggie's presence this evening, she guessed correctly, was no more than a sop to her insecurity, and a means of placating her.

The private viewing of the Hermitage Exhibition proved an outstanding success, the art correspondents of the national newspapers would no doubt ensure the story was carried in tomorrow's editions, even the BBC news intended mentioning the event.

Whilst the press and other guests were still spilling out onto Piccadilly, Roger Simpson and his wife Beverly, who were co-hosting dinner with the Directors of the Royal Academy and the National Gallery, plus their respective spouses led the select few to the private dining room. Seated opposite Virginia was Maggie, who had a plum position between the Soviet Ambassador, Sergei Topolski and Alexander Bukin. As they chatted together, Virginia couldn't help thinking to herself that Bukin seemed vaguely familiar. The cool light grey eyes shot her a probing stare. She caught his gaze and passed him a smile, not quite of recognition, and assumed he too was wondering where their paths had crossed before.

Virginia had always found that Maggie blew hot and cold, but tonight she was on form, and holding centre stage. Virginia was more than happy to take a backseat; she was there to observe and simply report back to Spencer. Maggie's behaviour and familiarity toward the Soviet guests were beginning to raise a few eyebrows. She was all over both Topolski and Bukin like a rash, maybe she'd had one too many, the private viewing had been liberally interspersed by a steady supply of champagne and vodka shots. Virginia was beginning to sense that she wasn't just overplaying her hand, but was on the point of seriously embarrassing herself.

Throughout the meal, Bradshaw's expression remained self-contained, but there was a hint that beneath the formal politeness; his explosive temper was only just in check. The Foreign Secretary's obvious disapproval of her conduct, whilst unspoken, certainly wasn't lost on Bradshaw. If Maggie had been the wife of a senior British diplomat, Simpson wouldn't have thought twice about having him removed from post it was all becoming slightly embarrassing. The fact that Maggie was Bradshaw's mistress only served to compound Simpson's obvious irritation at her behaviour.

Virginia toyed with her wine glass, half twisting the stem between her fingers; Maggie was still gushing nonsense and flirting outrageously, it's what she did. Across the table Virginia caught Bukin's somewhat bemused smile, they exchanged glances, and then she remembered where she'd seen him before. It was obvious Bukin was a step ahead of her; it was in Berlin, some five or six years after the war. He was a good deal heavier now, the slender, but muscular figure had disappeared under an increasing girth, and judging by the amount of food and alcohol he'd consumed throughout the evening it wasn't particularly surprising. The years hadn't been kind to him, Bukin had become round-shouldered, and not quite the ruggedly attractive man she'd come across sitting in a Berlin café.

Virginia placed the wine glass to her lips; there was more than a hint of mutual recognition in his eyes. A fleeting thought crossed her mind, and she wondered, rather vainly, if she'd changed that much over the years. She shrugged it off, whatever he thought wasn't important, but what was important, was that Spencer was playing some kind of counter bluff. Everything slowly started to fall into place. Although Virginia was a renowned art expert and a close friend of Bradshaw, it was still unlikely it would have been enough to have secured an invitation to the exclusive dinner party without Spencer's intervention. Her presence at the table between the Foreign and Home Secretaries was meant to send out a subliminal message to the Soviet Ambassador and his Cultural Secretary, that the Western intelligence agencies had perhaps discovered the plot to assassinate the British Prime Minister. It was a bluff, of course, their intelligence was still somewhat limited, but the Soviet's weren't to know that. Virginia had been the CIA's deputy in Berlin, and although she'd ostensibly disappeared from the scene, her presence was guaranteed not only to send them into a spin but to send out a warning shot across their bows that they could have got wind of the plot. It might be just enough of a wake-up call for them to pull the plug on the entire operation, admittedly, it was a long shot, but was worth trying.

Virginia couldn't help smiling to herself, there were no two ways about it, Spencer was a clever bastard, he'd not only played her like a fiddle but also the KGB. Questions would be raised, had they been set up, had they fallen into a trap, perhaps their hired assassin wasn't quite what he seemed, a disaffected British agent with a score to settle. Just how sure were they of their man?

Bukin had always been concerned that Taylor might be nothing more than an elaborate plant, perhaps now Moscow might finally sit up and take notice. He caught Virginia's eye, and made some banal comment about the exhibition, yes, she agreed, it was a great success. They were sparring with one another, playing cat and mouse. Whatever way you looked at it, Spencer had played a masterstroke, but even so, there were no guarantees that Moscow would call off the assignment, but without lifting a finger, he'd probably managed to sow a few seeds of doubt in their minds. It was a high-risk strategy, and one the Kremlin now might not want to take to the wire.

Virginia's presence on the top table would undoubtedly set the ball rolling, and Spencer hoped might buy the CIA and MI5 a little more time. He might have miscalculated his opponents, but his gut feeling was that he'd temporarily gained the upper hand, and placed the KGB on the back foot, but how their political masters would respond was anyone's guess.

As the evening drew to a close, Bradshaw offered Virginia a lift home in his official car, he knew that she'd made her own way to the Royal Academy by taxi; it was, in her experience, a characteristically kind gesture. She was really grateful to him as the prospect of trying to hail a cab at this time of night in Piccadilly or teetering to nearby Green Park tube station in black suede high heels wasn't ideal. Especially after a heady mixture of champagne and vodka shots, accompanied by several large glasses of wine.

Leaving Bradshaw happily chatting to the Foreign Secretary in the foyer, Virginia made her excuses and followed Maggie into the ladies toilet, there was a queue; there was always a queue. As they waited patiently in line, they barely passed a word, for some reason Maggie had now taken exception to Bradshaw's offer to give Virginia a lift home. It was all of a piece really; Maggie's mood swings were notorious, and she saw slights where none was intended. Virginia suspected her constant aggressiveness masked a myriad of feelings, not least an overwhelming sense of insecurity.

As Virginia eventually fought her way back out of the ladies toilet, the foyer was still crowded; no-one appeared to be in any particular hurry to end the evening, they were having a great time. She hesitated a moment, her gaze sweeping the scene, Bradshaw was near the main doors in deep conversation with the Director of the Royal Academy. There was no sign of Maggie. She'd been ahead of Virginia in the queue, and she had fully expected to find her in the foyer; it was unusual as Maggie was invariably hovering at Bradshaw's elbow at official events. Virginia had often considered her behaviour cringe-worthy, but as Bradshaw appeared, at least publically, to accept his lover's behaviour, she'd always diplomatically kept her opinions buried and her mouth shut.

Bradshaw's Special Branch detective was hovering attentively near the main doors. He made eye contact with him; it was a signal that they needed to move. Bradshaw instinctively checked his watch. He had an early start in the morning, a Cabinet Meeting at 9.30am; the French President's State Visit was on the agenda. To ensure that he was singing from the same hymn sheet as the security forces, he needed to catch up on the latest security briefs from Scotland Yard and British Intelligence.

A flicker of annoyance crossed his face; it was fleeting, but wasn't lost on Virginia, so she weaved her way across the foyer toward him, and said, breezily. 'So, are we ready?'

'Do you know where Maggie is?' he snapped, sharply.

'I'm not sure.'

Bradshaw's expression had closed down, so she ventured. 'Would you like me to check and see where she is?'

He held her gaze; it was obvious that he was grateful. 'I'm sorry,' he apologised.

'There's really no need,' she said, brusquely, and disappeared back across the crowded foyer.

Virginia second guessed what was going through his mind, the fact that both the Foreign Secretary and the Soviet Ambassador had already made their excuses and left, had therefore placed Bradshaw in a somewhat embarrassing position. His presence meant that the straggle of junior delegates and guests loitering in the lobby, still felt obliged to remain until he finally called it a day. It was a social nicety, but one Bradshaw felt keenly, for all his faults, he was acutely aware that most of the remaining guests were reliant upon public transport to get home. He was holding them up and was becoming ever more agitated by Maggie's absence. Bradshaw moved over toward the exit and decided to have a discreet word with his bodyguard before heading back into the melee of the foyer.

Over the last couple of months Bradshaw had become increasingly concerned that his political standing and pre-eminence was slowly, but inexorably being eroded by Maggie's demands not only on his emotions but, more importantly, his time. In the cold light of day, it was a situation entirely of his own making, but the relationship had steadily spiralled out of control, and had not only distracted him from the job in hand but had also now begun to threaten any future bid to oust Jeremy Haining from power.

Whilst no-one seriously doubted his political abilities, since being appointed Home Secretary, he had more than made a mark as a leading player and had skillfully manoeuvred his way through the endless pitfalls of high office. In the early days not even Maggie's enemies, and there were many due to her abrasiveness, could deny that she hadn't ably assisted him as his all-powerful private and political secretary. But their illicit relationship had resulted in Maggie's behaviour becoming ever more unpredictable and explosive. It hadn't helped any that she was generally disliked by both his political and civil service colleagues alike, and was openly regarded as a disruptive influence.

Before Maggie's arrival on the scene, Bradshaw had always been entirely ruthless in dealing with anyone who stood in the way of his determination to climb the political ladder, and right now, Maggie was perilously close to crossing the line of no return. But even so, Bradshaw found himself facing a dilemma, had they not been lovers, then he wouldn't have hesitated to have batted her out of court. However, their twisted, and sometimes all-consuming relationship, had left him entirely vulnerable. Privately he cursed his own stupidity for allowing anyone, least of all anyone as flawed as Maggie Ellis, to threaten his political standing. Through his own stupidity, he was treading on eggshells without any easy way out of an already difficult situation.

There was no way of knowing for sure, but perhaps deep down Maggie had sensed his change of mood, and his growing despair, that the writing was on the wall, and yet, she not only knew where all his personal skeletons were buried but along the way she had also helped bury them. If her behaviour and unpredictability deteriorated to the point of no return, then he'd have to consider an exit strategy, but the trouble was he knew Maggie well enough to realise that she wouldn't go down without one hell of a fight, that she'd leak stories to the national press and bring their entire world crashing down around them.

Having apologised to his bodyguard, Bradshaw's gaze drifted slowly across the foyer, there was still no sign of either Virginia or Maggie. Bradshaw silently ground his teeth, but suddenly felt the eyes of the Academy's Director inquisitively on him, he needed to play the game, and once again made a point of making polite, albeit somewhat trite conversation about the exhibition.

Virginia retraced her steps across the foyer, although it was beginning to thin out, there was still quite a number of people milling about, reluctant to call it a day. She decided to check out the queue near the reception desk waiting to collect their personal belongings from the cloakroom, but on second thoughts it was a complete waste of time, Maggie certainly wasn't the type to join in an orderly queue, but would have marched up to the desk and pulled rank. The only mystery was why Bradshaw put up with her behaviour.

Virginia was running out of options; the catering staff were still busy clearing the dining room. She decided to head back toward the exhibition; the lights were still on, but it was getting late, and there were only a half dozen or so security staff left in the viewing gallery. There was certainly no sign of Maggie. Where the hell could she be? Normally Maggie clung to her lover's side like a leech and basked in his reflected glory, almost as a kind of affirmation of her own importance.

Having drawn a blank Virginia reluctantly started to head back toward the foyer, she knew Bradshaw would be disappointed if she returned empty handed, but she didn't quite know what to do, that is, until she heard a low, strained voice, it was Maggie's. Virginia spun round in the corridor.

'Thank you,' she heard her say, 'so is everything fixed?'

Where was she? Virginia stood stock still and waited for what seemed like an eternity before she heard a man's voice in answer; it was coming from a small side room off the main corridor.

'Da, lyabov moya,' he said in Russian, before repeating it in English, 'yes, my love.'

Virginia needed to think quickly, although barely audible, she'd immediately recognised Bukin's vodka soaked voice. For him to use such a term of intimacy, they obviously knew each other well, very well. She had a choice, hang around and interrupt them or slink back seemingly empty-handed into the foyer. It was obvious that Bukin had already been rattled by Virginia's presence on the top table. She didn't know whether to chance her luck and interrupt them, but how would it look? Bukin had already recognised her. It started to run through her mind, that maybe she really was getting a little rusty, but Stein had once told her, that espionage was a little like riding a bike, having learnt the basic skills, once learnt, you can never forget.

At the back of her mind, Virginia suspected that for whatever reason Maggie had probably already come under Spencer's radar, and was in some way viewed as a potential security risk. But she was second guessing, there was no figuring how his mind worked, or what his end game plan was. However, the fact she'd been set up tonight wasn't in doubt.

Virginia figured that neither Ellis nor Bukin would chance hanging around much longer. The leading players had already departed the Academy, including the Soviet Ambassador, so she had to make a snap decision, she really didn't want them to see her, so erred on the side of caution and headed back to the foyer.

Seeing that she didn't have Maggie in tow, Bradshaw's face dropped in disappointment. Virginia mouthed an apology to him across the throng; he inclined his head, accompanied by a sad smile of recognition and thanks. To say he was disappointed was an understatement. Bradshaw rarely gave way to displays of emotion, but now was one such occasion.

Virginia had a job to do, but even so, felt a frisson of sympathy for him; she'd always held to the adage that you speak as you find. Bradshaw had never been anything but utterly charming and welcoming to her. But she knew there was a great deal more at stake here than any sense of friendship or misplaced personal loyalty. Spencer was relying on both her skill and training. During the war she'd operated at a time when there were few rules, it was a case of kill or be killed.

Virginia's eyes swept casually around the foyer, before automatically checking her Cartier watch, she couldn't help wondering which of them would break cover first. If she hadn't entirely lost her touch, she reckoned Bukin would be

139

the first to take his leave. She wasn't disappointed, Bukin appeared in the foyer he was all smiles and exuded his usual easy charm. He made a point of congratulating the Director of the Royal Academy again for helping to organise such a successful evening, before making his excuses and heading off to the courtyard where his chauffeur-driven black Zil limousine was awaiting him. It was the ultimate social symbol for any Soviet dignitary; they were a familiar sight ferrying the USSR's top leadership around London.

By now Virginia had slipped on her overcoat and was on the verge of heading back toward Bradshaw when she spotted Maggie re-entering the foyer.

'I've been looking for you everywhere!' she called to her.

Maggie stopped, swung round, before shooting Virginia an angry stare, and hissed. 'What do you mean, looking for me?'

She inclined her head toward Bradshaw. 'We've been wondering where you'd got to.'

'What's it got to do with you?'

'It's just that he's offered me a lift home.'

'Yes, I know he mentioned it to me earlier,' she said, witheringly.

'The car was due to pick us up at 10.30.'

Maggie shrugged indifferently and said sharply. 'That's not my problem, is it?'

Undeterred by Ellis's obvious hostility, she pressed her. 'It's just that we're running late; the Home Secretary asked if I knew where you were.'

Ellis looked through, rather than at her.

'I checked out the ladies and the cloakroom behind the reception -.'

Maggie cut her dead in mid-sentence, acid by now creeping into her voice. 'If you really must know, I went to thank the Chef!'

With that Maggie angrily brushed past her, but as she did so, the merest flicker of a smile crossed Virginia's lips. So the bitch was lying after all, if she'd had nothing to hide, then why not come clean and tell the truth that she'd been chatting to Bukin. It was a small, but maybe not insignificant piece of intelligence against Bradshaw's all powerful political assistant.

Chapter 13
The Investigation

Virginia had been right about one thing; Maggie had already come under investigation by MI5, and long before the plot against the Prime Minister had come to light. Securing Virginia an invite to the Hermitage exhibition had in effect killed two birds with one stone. Not only could she keep a close eye on Maggie, but at the same time her presence as a former CIA agent, seated prominently between the Home and Foreign Secretaries was guaranteed to send out a subliminal message to both the Soviet Ambassador and Alexander Bukin, that the western intelligence agencies may have possibly stumbled across the plot to assassinate the British Prime Minister.

Unbeknown to Virginia for many years a number of unsubstantiated rumours had been circulating Whitehall that Maggie Ellis might have snow on her boots, the expression was a euphemism in security circles for someone who held not only extreme left wing views but was also suspected of crossing the line and had in fact become rather too close to one or two members of the Soviet delegation. In fairness, as Bradshaw's political secretary she frequently attended formal social events in and around London, including both the American and Soviet Embassies. Part of the problem was that Maggie's overly flirtatious behaviour was guaranteed to spark endless speculation. Whenever her behaviour had been brought up in conversation Spencer had always pointed out that it was pretty easy to throw mud, but quite another thing to try and make it stick. On a personal level, he couldn't stand the woman, but that was no reason to take the rumours at face value. His interest in Maggie had always been on the back burner. That is until eighteen months ago when the Prime Minister made it clear that he intended appointing Bradshaw as Home Secretary, and thereby catapult him to the front bench of British politics. In the great scheme of things, up until that point, she hadn't been his highest priority; in fact, she hadn't been a priority at all. There was simply no need, for prior to Bradshaw becoming Home Secretary Maggie's access to classified material had been almost non-existent.

Before any formal announcement of Bradshaw's appointment had been made the routine security checks had started to kick in, and it was at this point Spencer decided that he really ought to take a keener interest in Bradshaw's lover. As the Director General of MI5 he was required to report directly to the Home Secretary, so he immediately set the ball rolling, and his agents started ferreting around. He needed to know whether there was any basis to the persistent rumours surrounding Maggie.

Part of the problem had been that Haining's health was already in decline, and he needed to appoint Bradshaw sooner rather than later. So Spencer took a gamble. He didn't have the authority and the necessary top cover from the Prime Minister to sanction placing Maggie under close surveillance, but he did it all the same. Although it was a technicality, it was an important one, for he was now out on a limb. At the time Haining was in poor health, he'd been in an out of hospital for months, the newspapers were speculating that he would have to stand down. They were a heartbeat away from Bradshaw stepping into his shoes, so he needed to know whether the rumours surrounding Maggie were true or not.

The operation had been kept tight, if they screwed up before they'd completed their investigation, Maggie could well slip through their fingers. He also knew that Bradshaw would come down on him like a ton of bricks and demand to know why MI5 was spying on his trusted political secretary. The trouble was, for the first twelve months or so, they appeared to be wasting their time. MI5 had invested a lot of time and effort into an investigation that appeared unfounded.

He knew that Bradshaw had the ear of the Prime Minister, and was fearful that Haining might find it inconceivable that his closest political ally had unwittingly become a Soviet puppet. He had to get it right and to consolidate the intelligence against her. There was always a chance that his claims and accusations could be dismissed out of hand. Haining knew there was no love lost between them, and that any accusations might be mired in some Machiavellian subplot by British Intelligence to oust Bradshaw from power.

Virginia's report from the Royal Academy of the conversation between Maggie and Bukin was timely. Given the venue and the Hermitage exhibition it wasn't on its own exactly a crime, but the fact she had deliberately sneaked off to speak with him in private, and subsequently lied to Virginia about thanking the chef, had provided him yet another nail in her coffin. The investigation had recently thrown up how Maggie had begun to regularly stay overnight at various expensive London Hotels, and that she was always joined by the same man, who normally booked in under the name of Douglas Parsons. It all seemed to coincide with a dinner at the Soviet Embassy that the first of her hotel stays came to light.

In the morning, Mr Parsons would pick up the bill and then they would go their separate ways, he to the Soviet Embassy, and she to the Home Office. The photographic evidence was staring back at him on his desk, he knew both of them by sight, and his heart began to sink. It was all starting to come together; he now had irrefutable evidence Ellis and Bukin were lovers, but it was far more than that, looking at Ellis's bank records over the last six to nine months she had received regular deposits from a company called Artemis. On paper, they appeared to be a firm of accountants, but on closer inspection it was an entirely fictitious company set up by the Moscow Narodny Bank in Moorgate.

He already had enough on his plate, but the trouble was the investigation had so far thrown up rather more dirt than he expected, and not just on Ellis.

He put pressure on the team; the Soviet Embassy was wired, Bukin's flat was wired as was Maggie's; they must find something. It was a shot in the dark, but the weak link in the chain was always going to be Maggie. She lived in Graham Terrace behind Sloane Square; it was a large house covering several floors, she lived beyond her means, but that had always been her way. Maggie liked to live in style, even with the extra income provided by the Soviets her bank account was rarely out of the red. She had a cleaning lady and a part-time cook. Given Maggie's constant demands staff turnover tended to be on a regular basis. She always posted advertisements for domestic help in The Lady Magazine, an upmarket publication, which given her supposedly left wing views Spencer had always found faintly amusing. But it was a means to an end, and he dispatched two female agents with fake credentials to Graham Terrace. He struck lucky, one was accepted: Alison Matea was slick, charming, ruthless and played Maggie like a fiddle.

Everything was beginning to come together, but when the plot against the Prime Minister came to light he had to prioritise things and had briefly taken his eye off the ball a little, there were so many various strands of intelligence hitting his desk. Maggie might be Bukin's lover, which was damning enough, but he needed something else before he made his move against her, he began to wonder whether there was a direct link to the assassination plot. His gut instinct told him that she was involved, but how the hell was he going to prove it. Although Graham Terrace had been wired, nothing had ever come to light. But Matea came up trumps. Maggie was in the habit of working at home, as Bradshaw's political secretary she viewed removing documents from the Home Office without permission as her right.

But some of the documentation was classified, which was a crime in itself, but she was also increasingly equally tardy in her communications with Bukin. Rummaging around the house, Matea found a number of interesting papers; she photographed each of them in turn and passed the film back to the Office for analysis. One of them proved to be particularly interesting, it was a brief thank you note for a copy of a diary, that appeared to coincide with a larger than normal payment into her account. Was it possibly a copy of the Prime Minister's diary?

The only saving grace so far was that Bradshaw appeared to be an entirely unwitting dupe in Maggie's dealings with the KGB. Although he had always been politically aligned to the far left of the Labour Party, and publicly sympathetic to the communist ideology of the Soviet Union, even Spencer was forced to admit, that at heart he remained an idealist, and his ultimate loyalty had never been brought into question. However, his Achilles heel was, and always would be Maggie Ellis. She wasn't only in the pay of the KGB but had also cleverly executed a honey trap and deliberately targeted and lured Bradshaw into bed. Whilst MI5 had only been able to prove she had been in the pay of the Soviets for the last nine months or so; there was no doubt in Spencer's mind that she had been working for them a number of years and that they had probably groomed her from a young age.

Maggie was now a prime target, not only because of her well publicised political views and closeness to Bradshaw, but she was also a soft touch and given over to flattery at the right price. He guessed that at some point, even before she had hooked up with Bradshaw, that they had approached her. No-one who knew Maggie would deny that on occasions she could be persuasive and superficially charming. But the end result was that Bradshaw really hadn't got a clue that he'd been totally sucked into the KGB's hands, and as a

146

consequence had left himself wide open to blackmail. They now knew every intimate aspect of his life, where the skeletons were buried, and when, and if, the time came they wouldn't hesitate to use their knowledge to gain leverage under a future government headed by Bradshaw. With Haining out of the way, their path was clear.

In many respects the entire investigation had been a double edged sword, if he could build up enough evidence against Ellis, then by association Bradshaw would also find himself fatally compromised. But in the process, other things had come to light that had explained why Maggie Ellis appeared to wield such inordinate control over the normally astute Home Secretary.

What started out as a strictly routine question by his agents to a contact at the Tax Office, concerning Bradshaw's personal accountants, soon opened a Pandora's Box of bank accounts in Switzerland and the Channel Islands. The fact that Bradshaw's accountants had spirited away large sums of money meant that if his financial dealings were to be made public, it would leave him in a very vulnerable position.

Since his appointment, Bradshaw had cultivated a coterie of powerful establishment benefactors, and the subsequent audit trail proved that the deposits to his accounts had come via his contacts. Although on the surface their contributions had ostensibly been unimpeachable, albeit some of their business dealings wouldn't pass too much scrutiny, they were obviously hoping that their generosity would, in the end, be rewarded with either a knighthood or peerage. It was the seedier side of politics that Spencer always found unpalatable.

After being alerted by the Prime Minister's staff of suspected malpractice, Bradshaw's private office had fortunately come under an entirely separate investigation by Special Branch. Garvan and his team had managed to confirm that some of Bradshaw's official finances had been secretly salted away into yet another off-shore account. Although the net was drawing in, he had other fish to fry. Even before his appointment had been formally announced, British Intelligence had received information from their defector, Mikhail Panoff, that there were serious concerns in Moscow that since enjoying a series of postings to Washington, Paris and finally London, and embracing everything the West could offer, Bukin was now considered to be a potential defector. He'd grown to love the finer things in life; it was a world far removed from the austerity behind the iron curtain, his motherland, and his family's austere flat in Moscow. According to Panoff, the prospect of returning to the Soviet bloc permanently had filled Bukin with dread but, more importantly, had raised concerns within the Soviet security service. Although Spencer had always approached Panoff's appraisal of Bukin with a healthy dose of scepticism, he couldn't dismiss it entirely.

Chapter 14

The American Embassy, London

Jack Stein picked up his phone at the American Embassy; the telephonist said one word to him, scrambler. He didn't question it but wondered what the hell was going on. Stein leaned forward and flicked on the switch. He was in London for one reason and one reason only, a security lockdown was just that, and under normal circumstances, even the scrambler was out of bounds.

'Yes,' he said, sharply.

The scrambler clicked into life.

'We have an urgent parcel for you.'

Stein relaxed slightly, for the parcel was a coded message referring to a top secret package delivered by courier. 'When can I expect delivery?'

'16.00hrs, Greenwich Mean Time.'

'Thank you.'

Stein clicked off the scrambler. A direct message from the CIA's HQ at Langley could only mean one thing, or so Stein hoped that their agent in Moscow had come up with something important. Stein glanced at his watch; it was only 11.00hrs. Whatever way you looked at it, the way things stood Spencer was operating on no more than a wing and a prayer. Give Bradshaw an inch and he wouldn't hesitate to destroy him. Maybe Stein should have realised his old friend would have something up his sleeve, for unlike the Prime Minister, Bradshaw had made one fatal mistake; he'd foolishly underestimated his MI5 spymaster. Politicians came and went, the personalities might change, but almost to a man they were driven by self-interest and personal ambition.

For the time being there was nothing Stein could do other than sit it out and wait for the courier to arrive.

At 16.00hrs, dead on the dot, there was a gentle knock on his office door; it was a young junior female clerk.

'There's someone to see you, Mr Stein.'

He looked up expectantly. 'Show them in.'

The smartly dressed CIA courier entered the office carrying an attaché case. 'I'm afraid, sir, you'll need to sign,' he said, producing a piece of paper clutched in his left hand.

Stein took it from him, glanced at the receipt and scrawled his name, at which point the courier handed over the attaché case with a small silver key.

'Where are you staying?' Stein asked.

The courier glanced over his shoulder at the clerk. 'I think it's the St. Philips Hotel.'

The clerk nodded.

Stein smiled to himself. 'How long are you booked in for?'

'That all depends, sir.'

'Depends on what?'

'Whether, you need me to take a package back to Langley or not sir.'

'Thanks, I'll let you know.'

The clerk ushered the courier back out of the office. Stein placed the case on his desk and unlocked it. Inside, pinned to a file was a handwritten note from his boss, Chas Brennan, like the man, it was short and to the point.

"Jack, we're missing you already! Agent Freda's come up trumps, yours ever, Chas Brennan."

Stein flicked open the slender file; it was stamped top secret. His eyes glided swiftly over the first page before fixing on something important; Freda had come up with a codename for their contract killer, Pegasus. But why Pegasus, he wondered. Stein read on, apparently it was Bukin's idea, somehow he'd managed to persuade his cohorts in the Kremlin and the Politburo that it was an inspired choice, given that during the war their man had once served with the

British Parachute Brigade. Their insignia was and still is, Pegasus, the winged horse of Greek mythology. But Freda had also managed to come up with a name, Charles Taylor.

Stein slunk back in his chair and said out loud to himself. 'Holy shit not Taylor!'

It was a lot to take onboard. Although he hadn't been allowed official access or expected sight of the MI5's files, Spencer had run a number of names by him; he knew most of them, either by personal experience or by reputation. Taylor's name had admittedly been thrown in, why wouldn't it, but for some goddamn reason it hadn't particularly stuck out, and Stein had convinced himself it was someone else.

Admittedly, Taylor had been top flight in his day, but so had all the others. Freddy Baines was one of those names, he was a good guy, sound, and had operated behind the Iron Curtain, and had also turned up in South America. Stein always felt it was a shame that he'd left British Intelligence under a cloud, there'd been some kind of difference of opinion, and relationships had soured, so by mutual consent they'd parted company. But Stein had always rated Baines; he was steady, a bit of a wild card, but just the kind of cool-headed professional the Soviet's would have targeted.

Taylor was a bit of a surprise, Stein met him shortly after the war in Germany, everything centred around Berlin, as it still did, it remained a City controlled and divided by both the Allies and the Soviets. He was good, yes, and on the surface, at least, possessed all the right credentials. Taylor wasn't only a decorated war hero but had also proved himself to be an effective spy. Back then he appeared to have everything going for him, or so he remembered, the trouble was, the black market in Europe was thriving, and Taylor had seen a chance of making money, really serious money. He certainly wasn't alone, but he'd become increasingly greedy, and was lining his pockets through a nefarious collection of shady bankers, business and criminal contacts in Berlin. It didn't take long before the intelligence services on either side of the Atlantic Pond realised that Taylor was lining his own pockets. He wasn't only making a fast buck, but at the same time also abusing his position at the British Berlin Station by blackmailing his contacts, both official and un-official to buy their silence about his illegal dealings.

Word had it; Taylor had made a small fortune in Berlin, and gave full vent to his expensive tastes, spending his new found wealth almost as quickly as it came in. Stein seemed to remember that Taylor was living high on the hog, flashing his money around on fast cars and even faster women. He'd grown just a little too blasé, a little too arrogant and self-assured to cover his tracks properly. Comments were made; he was becoming unreliable, and shortly afterwards an official report from the Head of the British Intelligence Station was dispatched to London, a week later Spencer Hall arrived in Berlin to take control.

The intelligence community was like a village, and it soon became common knowledge that Spencer had read Taylor the riot act, he'd not only been on the take but had also exposed himself to being blackmailed by both the KGB and the super-efficient Stasi, the East German Secret Police.

Stein checked his watch again, reached for a notebook inside his desk drawer, opened it and ran his finger down the page before picking up the phone and dialing 9 to get an outside line, and rang the number in the notebook. He waited; it rang several times before being answered.

Martin Bell came on the line. 'Spentar Motors.'

He sounded out of breath; Stein smiled to himself imagining that Bell had probably panicked when the red phone on his desk had suddenly sprung into life.

'Hi Martin, I don't know if you remember me, but I dropped by earlier this week to see your chief salesman.'

Bell instantly recognised Stein's distinctive American drawl. 'Yes sir, of course, I do, when would you like to see him?'

'Well, I guess that I'd really like to seal the deal right away.'

There was a slight pause on the line. 'You mean today, sir?'

'Yeah, is that okay with you?'

'I'll get back to you in ten minutes.'

'Thanks.'

Martin set the receiver down; he needed to contact Spencer and fast.

*

Across London at a café in Kensington close by the Soviet Embassy, Alexander Bukin picked up a newspaper from a nearby table and sat down to enjoy his favourite afternoon treat, a pot of tea accompanied by freshly made cream cakes. Since his appointment to London, it had become something of a ritual, and he was now on first name terms with Hetty, the café's owner. The only downside to the arrangement was that he'd put on more than a few pounds, and had been forced to have his suits tailored to accommodate his growing waistline. He lit a cigarette and settled down to read the newspaper; there wasn't much of interest on the front page, an article about some disgraced Member of Parliament, and a report about the forthcoming State Visit of General de Gaulle. In the meantime, Hetty cheerfully presented him with a freshly brewed pot of tea and an array of cakes on a glass stand. Bukin thanked her, before returning to the newspaper. He turned the page and carefully folded the broadsheet, and was on the point of reaching for a cake when something on the page suddenly caught his attention; it was a black and white image of an attractive middle aged woman under the headline.

"Identity of Richmond Park body discovered."

He recalled reading something or other about a woman's remains being discovered in the boot of a burnt-out stolen car. At the time it had made the front page news, the coroner's inquest had found that the cause of death had not been, as originally suspected asphyxiation, but was the result of a single gunshot wound; the bullet was found embedded in her skull. Due to the condition of the corpse, formal identification could only be formalised by dental records. The victim was identified as being that of Donna Webster, of Elizabeth Street, Pimlico.

Bukin clenched his fingers tightly around the paper until his knuckles turned white. He knew that Taylor had been lodging in Elizabeth Street, the time and date of her death coincided with his stay. In part he blamed himself, he'd suggested the lodging to Taylor, the KGB had used it before, it was a nice place, and there'd never been a problem.

There was no doubt in Bukin's mind that he'd murdered the unfortunate woman, but more importantly, the stupid bastard had ended up compromising the entire operation. Bukin pushed back his chair and headed for the door.

'Are you all right luv?' Hetty called after him.

He half turned and muttered an apology before disappearing onto Kensington High Street and back toward the Soviet Embassy.

Chapter 15
Location: Spentar Motors, South London

By the time Jack Stein arrived at the Motor Showroom, Spencer was already waiting for him in Martin Bell's cramped, claustrophobic office. His desk was spilling over with receipts and sales ledgers. Bell had always had a slick mouth and was a good salesman, but even by his own admission, administration wasn't his strongest point. To keep the taxmen happy there had been occasions when Spencer was forced to call in MI5's accountants. Whatever Bell's faults, he still had his uses; and Spentar Motors was just one of a number of faux businesses set up by British Intelligence.

Jack breezed into the office and accepted a large shot of bourbon from Bell's overflowing filing cabinet. Checking the cabinet over, there didn't seem to be that much in the way of paperwork, but it did contain a large stash of well-used booze. Having poured Stein a drink, and guessing that they'd rather be left alone Bell hurriedly made to excuse himself, but Spencer gestured to him to stay.

'As a member of the team you've got every right to know what's going on.'

Bell hesitated before nervously lighting a cigarette and pulling up a chair, although he'd fronted Spentar Motors for a number of years, Bell knew that in the intelligence world he was a mere minnow to the sharks like Spencer and Stein, and they were way out of his league.

Bell sucked heavily on his cigarette; he'd heard a great deal about Stein, in fact during the war he had found himself delivering messages to Stein's French Resistance circuit in France, but until recently had never met him in the flesh. He wasn't disappointed for there was something about him, like Spencer, which commanded respect. He tried brazening it out, but inside his stomach was beginning to churn. He wouldn't normally be invited to sit in on a meeting with the Head of MI5 and a CIA intelligence officer of Stein's standing.

Stein glanced across at him, whatever he thought about Spencer's decision to include Bell; he didn't miss a beat and continued smoothly, pausing only to take the occasional sip of bourbon. He mentioned the courier from Langley and that their Agent had identified the KGB's assassin. Bell sat tight, he could have been wrong, but suspected that Stein was probably glossing over the finer details. His glass was empty; he didn't know quite what else to do, so he decided to offer them a refill. To his relief they both accepted. He needed to brazen it out, poured their drinks and calmly, or at least outwardly, sat down again keeping a tight grip on his fresh glass.

Spencer thanked him for the refill, before asking Stein. 'So who the hell is it?'

'Charles Taylor.'

Bell almost fell off his chair, Christ, he knew the bugger. Their paths had overlapped during the war. Taylor had come with quite a reputation, a war hero; a battle-hardened soldier, who went on to become one of British Intelligence's leading officers.

Spencer ran his fingers through his hair, his face set firm. 'Taylor was a career man right up to the moment I dismissed him from the Service.'

Stein pulled a face, he knew the score and said sharply. 'Since being fired, it seems that he's been whoring his way around to the highest bidder?'

Spencer was giving nothing away but was annoyed that MI5's sister organisation MI6, whose remit it was to monitor security overseas hadn't managed to pick up on Taylor before now. He took his time in answering. 'I'd feel a whole lot happier if we were dealing with some kind of pre-paid amateur.'

'That was never gonna happen.'

'Back in his day, he was thought to be one of our best agents.'

Stein caught the edge to his voice and asked. 'And you didn't?'

'It doesn't matter what I thought.'

'Well,' Stein said, 'it's your call, my friend, but whatever way we look at it, now that we know Taylor's behind the smoking gun, it's certainly upped the stakes?'

Spencer didn't disagree with him.

'If your Prime Minister ends up being assassinated, then one way or another we'll both find ourselves in the shit.'

'Then we'd better up our game before Taylor gets a chance to take him out!'

'That ain't' gonna be easy.'

'Maybe not, but I'd really like to take the bastard alive.'

Stein smiled tightly. 'It'll be a tall order.'

'Maybe, but we've got to try.'

'At least, we know it wasn't all just about the goddam money.'

'No,' Spencer said, distractedly.

They'd temporarily lost Bell, he wasn't sure what they were on about, seeing the rather perplexed expression on his face, it was left to Spencer to open up and explain how he'd been forced to dismiss him from the Service, and that in all probability Taylor's main motivation for accepting the Soviet deal hadn't solely been for financial gain, but was ultimately driven by a grinding sense of grievance against his former boss.

Turning back to address Stein, he said. 'We've got another problem.'

It provoked an ironic smile. 'Swell, only the *one*?'

Reaching down for his attaché case Spencer retrieved a slender folder, it was a top secret file marked with a distinctive red cross and the caveat "UK EYES ONLY". As he handed it across the table, Stein looked up questioningly.

'Times running out Jack, just read the bloody thing, besides it's my call anyway.'

Stein opened the file and began to read, he took his time; his expression giving nothing away before handing it back without further comment. Bell looked at each of them in turn; he really hadn't a clue what was going on.

'Well,' Stein said, taking a large swig of bourbon, 'that kind of explains why they want your man dead!'

Bell could no longer contain himself, he should have minded his place, but asked what the bloody hell was going on.

Spencer apologised, he knew they must have been talking in riddles to him. 'You've got every right to know.'

He explained everything in detail, the thinking behind the assassination plot to kill the pro-US Prime Minister. That the KGB's masterplan was to replace him with a more sympathetic left-wing politician; his deputy in all but name, Bradshaw, and how his political secretary was a plant. With Bell up to speed, well hopefully up to speed, there was really no way of telling with him, he nodded in the right places, made all the right noises, but Spencer suspected he'd really no idea who exactly Ellis was.'

Taking his time Spencer opened a slender silver cigarette case before slipping a cigarette casually between his lips. 'I'm just waiting on a report from Special Branch.'

'You mean from Garvan?' Stein queried.

'Yes, they've been doing some snooping around of their own.'

'So you'll be ready to go?'

Spencer flicked on his lighter. 'Apart from a few tweaks, all being well we should be able to go live tomorrow morning.'

'You'll hand the report over to the Prime Minister?'

'That's the plan.'

'And then what?'

Spencer shrugged slightly. 'In Haining's position, what would you do?'

'Save my ass.'

Spencer smiled. 'Well, we've given him the ammunition, he'll want to save his own neck first, and then the Governments. But trust me; the one sure thing I know is that Haining won't hesitate to destroy Bradshaw.'

A look of doubt came over Stein's face. 'But you said they were close, will he really buy into all this stuff?'

'Their friendship is no more than a marriage of convenience,' Spencer said, dismissively, 'political allegiances are like shifting sands. When Haining fell ill last year he needed someone on side, someone as powerful as Bradshaw to watch his back, but he can't afford for the government to be tainted, and, whatever happens, he'll need to distance himself from any hint of scandal.'

Stein narrowed his eyes; he wasn't quite sure where Spencer was heading. 'It's your call but why not haul the Ellis woman in now?'

'What would we get from her? Besides, Bukin would never have confided in her. She's no more real idea about Taylor's plans than we do, and wouldn't know him from Adam.'

Stein accepted his point.

If Bradshaw's affair with Maggie Ellis was made public, that alone, would have been more than enough to destroy his career. Her connections to the KGB and his dubious financial dealings were simply the icing on the cake.

In the longer term, Spencer knew that Bradshaw would have eventually used his influence to oust him as the Head of MI5, and replace him with some lame duck, someone perhaps willing to kowtow and play lip service to his decisions, even at the risk of compromising Britain's security interests. Although he'd been the victim of a classic honey trap, Spencer had no doubt whatsoever that Bradshaw's loyalties boiled down to one thing, self-interest.

So far the Soviets had played their cards well, Maggie Ellis had helped them infiltrate the heart of the British government, with Haining dead, Bradshaw was his natural successor, at which point they'd have started to apply the pressure, and upped the stakes by blackmailing him, leaving Bradshaw in no doubt whatsoever who was pulling the political strings.

Spencer had never been stinting in his admiration for Jeremy Haining and hoped to god that once the reports landed on his desk, he'd be grateful his security services had not only fulfilled their duty but had also done the dirty work for him by finally squeezing Bradshaw and Ellis out of the picture. It now left Haining completely unhindered; he'd no longer have to constantly look over his shoulder and wonder when Bradshaw would make his bid for power; it had been inevitable.

Haining was sixty-five now and knew that his political colleagues were starting to circle like hungry hyenas. But in one fell swoop, they'd hopefully saved his Government the catastrophic fallout of the scandal surrounding Bradshaw's private life. It would all, of course, be quietly brushed under the carpet; Haining simply couldn't afford to go public.

Stein leaned forward and flicked his half-smoked cigarette into the overflowing ashtray on Bell's desk.

'The way I see it,' he said, finishing off his bourbon, 'whatever happens this guy Bradshaw is damned.' He paused, before setting down the empty glass. 'You've played a blinder, my friend.'

'Have I?'

'You've taken him down before he had a chance to screw you.'

Spencer said, bleakly. 'If you play with fire you end up getting burned.'

'So that's one down, but Charles Taylor is a whole different ball game.'

Spencer's expression said it all.

'I guess one way or another if we end up losing your Prime Minister,' Stein smiled, 'I have a feeling we've both got a lot of answering to do.'

Whilst Spencer might have managed to cancel Bradshaw out of the equation, if the PM died at the hands of Taylor, then his tenure as Director General would still die along with Haining.'

Stein continued. 'The way I see it we need to draw Taylor away from the Prime Minister.'

'Great, how are we going to do that?'

'Well, I figure we need to use you as the bait.'

Bell instinctively reached for the half empty bottle of bourbon. Jesus wept, up until now he'd only ever been on the periphery of their world, but this was a whole different ball game. They both seemed so self-assured, so matter of fact. Spencer didn't seem at all bothered by Stein's suggestion, but even Bell realised that if Spencer was offered up as the bait to lure Taylor away from Haining, then only one of them would realistically escape with their life.

Chapter 16
Kenton Road, South London

Having ruled out all of the Prime Minister's official engagements in central London, Taylor needed to run through his diary appointments outside of the Capital. It was a temporary fix, but having booked himself into another of the many anonymous cheap lodging houses in Earls Court, Taylor set off in the morning to catch the 10.30 train from Charing Cross station to Herne Bay, a small seaside town on the Kent coast. The former Conservative Member of Parliament had died recently forcing a local by-election. Haining's visit to the constituency was intended to show moral support for the prospective Labour candidate, and to get a few prized editorial leaders in the local press.

Taylor needed to crack on; he might have managed to cover his tracks with regards to Donna Webster, but Bukin was on his case and expecting results. The prospect of a public meeting near the Clock Tower on the seafront was worth checking out, sadly, the location had lacked not only a vantage point but also afforded him little cover.

Having drawn a blank in Herne Bay, Taylor was acutely aware that he was rapidly running out of options. Having methodically worked his way through the PM's diary, he was faced with a rapidly dwindling number of possible locations. There was a Trade Union Conference in Manchester, but he had swiftly discounted it as the hotel's stairs, lifts and exits would all be covered by a mixture of local police and undercover Special Branch officers. Taylor had no desire to get himself embroiled in a potential gun fight, at least not by choice, with the Prime Minister's police protection.

He was becoming more and more uneasy, and was on the point of asking Bukin to give him more time, but he guessed, that all rather depended on them securing another copy of the Prime Minister's diary. But if pushed, he reckoned that it probably wouldn't pose too much of a problem for the KGB, whoever their mole was, they were obviously highly placed. Even so he knew that it probably wouldn't go down too well with them, but he needed to get it right, and he didn't want to rush things. Taylor returned to London with a growing sense of despondency, having systematically worked his way through Haining's diary, and dismissed everything out of hand; there was only one engagement left on the list to tick off.

Taylor opened his copy of Haining's diary, so far, he'd scored everything through in red ink, but before approaching Bukin again, he knew that he needed to validate his excuses, and have visited each of the locations in person. There was one more engagement on the PM's itinerary, it was south of the Thames, an area he didn't know particularly well. He ran his finger down the page, and thoughtfully tapped the entry.

"F*riday - 13.00 - No 38 Kenton Road, lunch, private (Edward Gibson)"*

Taylor vaguely recognised the name; he thought that Gibson had been something to do with the War Office. He checked out the address on his London A–Z Street Atlas, and caught the Bakerloo line to Lambeth North underground station; from there it was no more than a five or ten minute walk to Gibson's house.

Taylor was pleasantly surprised by what he found. Haining's former political colleague lived in a rather ramshackle, albeit large Victorian terraced house on the busy Kenton Road. Facing the terrace stood a dilapidated 1930s red bricked style block of flats that had been severely damaged during the Blitz, and they were now awaiting demolition.

Access appeared to be somewhat limited and from what he could see there wasn't any on-site security, so entering the block would be relatively straight forward. Taylor's attention was drawn to the balconies on the four storied flats, which ran the entire length of the block, each of them offering a clear view of the Victorian terrace, and, in particular, No 38.

Up until now Taylor had run out of options, but this rather unprepossessing location was promising, he could take his time setting up his position on the balcony and slip away from the site into the narrow surrounding backstreets. Although Lambeth North tube station was only about ten minutes' walk away, he'd need a car, yes, he decided, that would be the safest option; it'd take the worry out of being on the ground too long and risk being swept up by the police.

Taylor crossed the road and walked slowly around the perimeter, as far as he could see there were two main access points to the site. The one on Kenton Road was secured by two rather flimsy looking wooden panels secured by a heavy metal link chain. Gaining access wouldn't pose any particular problem, but he'd rather re-check around the back, it was one thing to slip into the site, but quite another to escape unseen. He needed to reassure himself he could safely exit the site after the assassination. Nailed up on one of the panels was an official notice from the Council, confirming that demolition work would commence on Monday, 4th April 1960. Presumably, the severity of the winter had delayed work, even for January it was unseasonably cold and, according to the latest weather forecasts, there was unlikely to be any let up until March.

Although he hadn't passed it by Bukin yet, Taylor had already made up his mind that he needed to bag the Prime Minister's personal bodyguard as well. He couldn't risk leaving him alive, unlike his police outriders, he was definitely armed and was the only serious threat, or so he assumed, to screwing things up.

With Jeremy Haining dead Scotland Yard and British Intelligence would be in turmoil, and in the aftermath questions would be raised in both Parliament and the National Press about the shortcomings surrounding the Prime Minister's security arrangements, and so the blame game would begin, and heads would roll. Taylor was secure in the knowledge that Spencer Hall's would be one of the first to roll, that in itself had been reason enough to accept the KGB's contract.

Spencer's mantra that revenge was a dish best served cold made Taylor smile to himself. Although Spencer's fall from grace wouldn't be made public, the identity of the Head of MI5 being only known to a select few, Taylor was content knowing that he wouldn't survive the inevitable fallout and the ensuing bloodletting. Besides, Taylor still retained several old contacts within the intelligence community to glean all the minutiae of Hall's demise as Britain's pre-eminent spy master.

Taylor suddenly had a spring in his step as he continued to inspect the perimeter. Around the side there was a break in the boarding, it looked as if it had been kicked in, he guessed by a bunch of local kids who wanted to lark around in the empty flats. The blanket bombing by the Luftwaffe had created a postwar playground where children, only limited by their imaginations, played their games and rode their bicycles across the desolate sites. Taylor casually glanced up and down the side street; the coast was clear, so he slipped inside.

The majority of the ground floor windows had been smashed in, it didn't look like random vandalism, but a systematic attempt by the Council's developers to prevent squatters moving in, and delaying the demolition. Some minor work looked as if it had been carried out; a stack of lead piping was lying neatly piled together and was awaiting collection.

Picking his way through the debris Taylor headed for the nearest entrance to the flats. The lobby area was full of rubbish, the usual paraphernalia, broken bottles, empty cigarette packs, discarded stubs and pieces of broken furniture.

He climbed the cold dank stone staircase to the first floor and surprised a number of pigeons who'd made a home on the landing. Taylor didn't know who was more startled, he or the pigeons as they flapped in panic and fluttered off over the nearby balcony. Taylor hated the ruddy things and cursed silently under his breath as he walked through a pile of dried and fresh guano. Thank god it was winter otherwise the place would have stunk to high heaven.

He followed the balcony around until he found himself facing the main road and opposite the neat Victorian terrace where Edward Gibson lived. He looked satisfied; he could really make this work. Yes, he muttered to himself this'll do nicely; he could get in quick, but get out even quicker. But he didn't want to commit himself, he'd need to revisit the site and go over it several times until he knew every nook and cranny, every potential escape route and every pitfall.

He subsequently visited the site several more times, and much to his relief had only ever once encountered a team from the developers. He'd smoothly explained away his presence by saying that he was a Council surveyor. They hadn't questioned him, it seemed reasonable enough; in fact, they'd got along quite well. Taylor had even tagged along with them and produced an official-looking clipboard from his attaché case as they gave him a guided tour of the site.

He'd wanted to weigh up all the options, the block had been severely damaged during the war, and although some half-hearted attempts had been made to clear the surrounding area, it was still littered with debris. The developers led him down into the bowels of the building, via a narrow dark staircase, into what had been the residents' wartime bomb shelter. The dimly lit, dank, subterranean world beneath the flats had been made into a communal shelter for the entire neighbourhood, with thick walls, and an enforced concrete

166

roof. It had provided a relatively safe haven from the bombing. The remains of the original slatted wooden benches ran down the length and middle of the shelter. There were no internal doors which meant that in the event of a near miss, the blast would simply have gone straight through the middle of the shelter without crushing anyone at a closed-in end. More importantly, there were several exits into the surrounding streets. He checked each of them out in turn, and settled on one that opened onto St. Mary's Walk, a narrow side turning at least a street away from the perimeter of the hoarding. Taylor couldn't work out how he'd missed it, for he'd been over the site often enough, but if he hadn't tagged along with the builders he'd probably be still none the wiser. Taylor knew that it probably wasn't going to get much better than this.

He still didn't want to make a knee-jerk reaction and needed to weigh up all his options, so later that day placed a call to Lambeth Council's building department, and pretended he was a neighbour of Gibson's and that he needed to discuss the proposed demolition works in Kenton Road. The clerk confirmed the contract had been awarded to O'Hanlon's a local building firm, and that demolition was due to commence on Monday, 4th April. The same firm had also been commissioned to re-develop the site with a new block of dwellings. The clerk admitted that despite a number of objections to both the scale and design of the re-development, the plans had recently been formally approved by the Council.

Taylor listened politely, he wasn't particularly interested in the whys and wherefores of the proposal, but thought he would play on the fact that he was concerned about the number of local children breaking into the site, and that a large quantity of lead piping had simply been thrown into a heap, and it was clearly visible through the broken hoarding. It was nothing more than an open invitation to some jack the lad looking to make a fast quid or two. The clerk assured him that the piping was due to be removed by O'Hanlon's in two days' time, more importantly, up until the 4th April the only regular contractors on site were surveyors, but they only visited on Mondays and Wednesdays.

It was good enough, but Taylor still wanted to get a better feel of the place. In all, he spent hours reconnoitring the place, going through every conceivable nook and cranny until he was certain this was the one. He'd worked out his escape route, it wasn't foolproof, but nothing ever was.

Chapter 17
Selfridges, Oxford Street, London

The following day one of Bukin's cohorts picked up a message from a safety deposit box in Selfridge's department store on Oxford Street, it was from Taylor. Every so often rather than leaving a message in their tried and tested left luggage lockers at London mainline Stations they used Selfridges.

The message was delivered unopened to Bukin's office at the Soviet Embassy. It was short and to the point.

"I will complete the mission Friday, 22nd January, – lunchtime, see PM's diary."

Bukin duly checked his copy of Haining's diary. His expression registered surprise, the only entry on the 22nd was for a private lunch at the home of a former colleague, Edward Gibson. Bukin briefly placed his hands together as if in prayer, before carefully placing the note back into the envelope. Gibson was a former retired War Minister, but in government circles was still a force to be reckoned with, and had unusually gained mutual respect across the political divide and as a consequence sat on a number of security-related committees.

He'd always assumed that Taylor would need more time to come up with a workable plan, but Taylor's decision was no longer important to him. On Bukin's advice, Moscow had decided to pull the plug on the entire operation, the murder of Donna Webster had forced their hand. They knew Taylor had booked into the boarding house under an assumed name; there was no escaping the fact that he'd broken a cardinal rule to maintain a low profile. The last thing they wanted was to attract police attention, even if Taylor had been using an alias, it was a step too far, and had compromised the assignment, there was no going back, the message sitting on Bukin's desk was clear and to the point, it read.

169

"Vylashchit yego", pull it.

Taylor had recently moved to a cheap hotel in Earls Court. By all accounts, the rooms were overpriced and freezing cold, with only a one bar electric fire for warmth. On leaving Elizabeth Street, Taylor meticulously destroyed all of Donna Webster's ledgers and records. Unless he'd missed something, there was nothing, at least on paper, to link him to the name of Peter Bartholomew, it was an alias, but even so, Taylor hadn't wanted to take any chances.

*

Two hours later Bukin was sitting in a rundown pub in Earls Court. The Crown was the kind of place locals referred to as a "spit and sawdust" pub, where only hardened drinkers of a certain age spent their days, downing pints, playing cards and darts. The walls were a dark shade of nicotine yellow and the stench of tobacco, and stale alcohol was almost overpowering.

Outside the rain lashed unforgivingly against the windows, and as the temperature plummeted in the chill, biting wind it slowly began to fall as sleet. The Crown was run by a large landlady who appeared to permanently have a cigarette on the go. She kept up a constant lively banter, peppered with a steady stream of profanities with her regulars. Bukin sat himself down at a corner table facing the door, minding his own business and nursing a pint of frothy brown ale. He cast the woman a rather bemused look; he could imagine that if some drunk got out of hand, she'd probably handle herself pretty well in a fight and that he certainly wouldn't fancy taking her on, at least not sober.

Bukin lit a cigarette and flicked the spent match into the ashtray. He deliberately avoided eye contact, and retrieved a newspaper from his briefcase, when the saloon door opened again, it was Taylor. Even dressed down in a shabby overcoat,

170

flat cap and scuffed shoes, he still couldn't quite get away with it, and exuded a certain innate style. He was carrying a rather battered umbrella, although he'd shaken it out in the doorway, he trailed a stream of rainwater across the bar.

On seeing him, the redoubtable landlady cut her punters dead on the spot and smiled broadly at Taylor. Although not quite a regular, he'd obviously used the pub before and had turned on his renowned charm with her. She was all over him. Bukin found it all faintly embarrassing. Taylor ordered a pint of bitter, then casually glanced round the bar, and acknowledged Bukin's presence with a slight nod of his head. He paid for his drink and joined him in the corner.

'Good to see you, Alex,' he said, pulling up a chair.

Bukin blew out a plume of smoke, and without any preamble said quietly. 'It's over, my friend, the deals off.'

Taylor narrowed his eyes and looked carefully, with a wary curiosity at Bukin's face. He lifted the glass and took a sip of the bitter, before wiping the froth off his upper lip with the back of his right hand. 'What do you mean, over?'

'You've blown it!'

Taylor's mood turned in a moment, he set the beer glass down on the table, and leaned forward, and hissed through gritted teeth. 'What the hell do you mean, *blown it*?'

'Donna Webster,' Bukin responded, flatly. He had the satisfaction of seeing a frisson of doubt cross Taylor's face. 'We're disappointed, my friend, to be honest, I'm disappointed, we'd expected so much more of you, to be more professional, but Webster was careless, very careless.' Bukin coolly blew out another cloud of smoke, this time deliberately into Taylor's face. 'In fact, it was totally unprofessional!'

Taylor's expression closed down immediately.

'You did *kill* her, didn't you?' Bukin said coolly.

'I had to, she'd been snooping around' he responded bleakly.

'Had to?' Bukin repeated curiously.

171

'She'd been searching through my room.'

'Why?'

'I'm not sure.'

'She must have had a reason.'

'You know how women are'

'So what happened?'

'She found the snipers rifle.'

Bukin regarded him thoughtfully. 'Tell me something, my friend.'

'Tell you what exactly?'

'You come with a certain, how shall I say, reputation, yes, that's the word.'

'Do I?'

'Were you sleeping with her?'

Taylor couldn't very well deny it.

Bukin gave him a long, slow look. On the surface, Taylor's charm appeared effortless, and outwardly, at least, he never took himself too seriously, a trait which had no doubt helped him attract a veritable flotilla of lovers. All in all, it was a deadly combination, but Bukin had always suspected there was a much darker side to Taylor, one that he tried to keep hidden. Maybe the war had left an indelible mark upon the man, for he had confessed that he often awoke in the middle of the night with his stomach heaving, as he found himself back in the midst of the war, where the stench of blood and death never quite left him.

Bukin viewed Taylor as nothing more than soiled goods. Spencer Hall's original decision to dismiss him from British Intelligence had obviously not been taken lightly but had been the right one. He had a gut feeling that Taylor's illicit racketeering was merely the tip of the iceberg, and that somewhere along the line he had developed psychopathic tendencies. Bukin's objections against hiring him had, in the main, fallen on deaf ears. Sadly, the killing of Donna Webster had finally vindicated his objections; he'd been proved right, and rather late in the day, his security chiefs sitting in their ivory tower in Moscow had finally sat up and taken notice. Whatever the rights or wrongs of their decision, it was left solely in Bukin's hands to clear up the unholy mess created by Webster's murder.

Bukin spelled it out in detail to Taylor, how he'd compromised the entire assignment and that Moscow had been forced to pull the plug. There would be another day, and no doubt another opportunity, but one thing was certain, Taylor would not be the man behind the telescopic lens. Even so Bukin assured him that the down payment to his Swiss bank account was still secure, and would be honoured.

Taylor remained tight-lipped; they were playing cat and mouse with one another. He knew full well that as far as the Soviets were concerned he was a busted flush. Personally, he'd always found Bukin quite difficult to read, his broad, granite like Slavic features rarely registered any discernible expression. Taylor briefly held his gaze, before glancing idly out of the window. The sleet was now beginning to stick to the glass; he was fast running out of options and needed to play for time, it crossed his mind that he'd really nothing to lose, so why not take Bukin out. It'd probably give him a day or so head's start and would send both the Soviet and British intelligence services into a spin, and probably allow him just enough of a window to do what he had to do. Taylor had no intention of dropping out; this was his one real opportunity to break even with Spencer Hall. Nothing else really mattered, the financial rewards, the KGB, to hell with them all, either way, he was a dead man walking. Right from the beginning the assignment had always been a one-way street, but it had been one that he couldn't walk away from. Taylor knew that he was damned if he did, and damned if he didn't. Maybe the KGB had played on his weaknesses, his well-known sense of grievance, and his festering hatred for the Head of MI5.

173

Whatever had initially driven the Soviet security services to seek him out, really no longer mattered.

They continued to keep up the pretence of politeness; Taylor declined Bukin's offer of a cigarette, preferring his favourite Gauloises. Taylor opened the pack, and fixed one of the cigarettes in the corner of his mouth; his lighter rasped into life, and he continued to chat through the blue haze of smoke.

'So what happens now?' he asked.

'You're free to walk.'

Taylor couldn't help casting him a rueful look. 'You mean as if nothing happened?'

Bukin shrugged indifferently. 'Why ever not, we've kept to our side of the bargain, you have a large down payment in your Swiss bank account, the fact you screwed up by killing the Webster woman and comprising the mission is down to your -,' Bukin paused for effect, 'down to your inability to keep your trousers buttoned!'

Taylor bristled, he'd have loved nothing more right now than to take Bukin out there and then, but he bided his time, he'd have to wait, to keep a grip on his anger.

Bukin rested his arms on the table, leaned forward; his vodka-soaked breath was in Taylor's face, and in a lowered tone, said. 'Have you any idea, my friend, how long this has taken to set up?'

Taylor looked faintly disinterested. 'No, but I'm sure you're about to tell me!'

'It's taken years of meticulous planning to get to this stage!'

'The PM's diary, I take it you have a mole on the inside?'

Bukin smiled a sad, almost cynical smile. 'What do you think?'

Taylor calmly blew out a swirl of pungent cigarette smoke from the Gauloises. 'Why don't we just cut the crap,

Alex, you and I both know that my assignment was always going to end one way!'

Bukin sat back and looked at him searchingly. 'Was it, my friend?'

It was an effort to keep the contempt off his face, but he did so. What was the point of saying what he already knew, even without Donna Webster's death, and even if he'd managed to nail the job, it would only have been a matter of time before the KGB liquidated him. They simply couldn't have afforded to keep him alive; he was way too much of a security risk, and once the deed was done, he would have outlived his usefulness.

Bukin was an old hand at the game, and sensed something was wrong, seriously wrong, at best Taylor was an unstable maverick, and his pathological traits had no doubt forced Spencer's hand. Since meeting him Bukin's fears had been confirmed, but try as he might, until recently, no-one in the Kremlin had taken his objections seriously.

Looking across the table at him, he could have misread the situation, but sensed deep down that Taylor was on a mission of his own, and had no intention whatsoever of pulling out, but the decision wasn't his to make and wasn't open for discussion. Bukin laid down the rules; they had made arrangements for him to fly out of England. In the morning they'd collect him from his lodging; he would then be driven down to a pre-arranged airstrip on a farmer's field on the south coast, they'd get him across to France, at which point he was very much on his own.

Bukin stretched across the table to stub his cigarette out, and made to push back his chair, but paused. 'Tomorrow, 11.30 sharp, I'll collect you at your lodging house, and have you driven down to the airstrip.'

There was a hint of challenge in Taylor's eyes, but he acquiesced and said he'd be packed and ready to go. Taylor reckoned he would be lucky to leave the lodging house alive, let alone make it to the airstrip. Whether Bukin believed him or not was an entirely different matter, for his Soviet contact was far too professional to allow his personal feelings to show. As he watched Bukin move across the saloon bar and leave the ramshackle pub, Taylor picked up his glass and drained it. He was sure as hell playing with fire but had no intention of falling into Bukin's trap.

*

The light was fading in the late afternoon gloom, but the street lamps lining either side of the road had yet to flicker into life. A dark blue delivery van pulled up opposite a large Edwardian apartment block, the kind that can be found in the smarter, more affluent parts of West London. Keen Street was a quiet residential area, where nothing much ever happened, save for the occasional flashlights shooting off, as newspaper photographers tried to capture the street's most famous resident. Christabel Moore was a beautiful up and coming movie starlet who frequently made the headlines, mainly through her notoriously chequered love life rather than her somewhat dubious acting abilities. But the public loved her, and the press and magazines clamoured for the latest sensational story.

Charles Taylor was behind the wheel of a recently stolen blue van. He kept the engine idling over, glanced at his watch and wound down the window. He'd wrapped up warmly against the biting chill. If he knew anything about his subject, it was that he wouldn't have to hang around too long, because Bukin had foolishly become a creature of habit. In their world it always paid to constantly be on your guard and to trust no-one, but since his appointment as the USSR's Cultural Secretary to London, Bukin had seemingly become complacent, or perhaps too self-assured of his abilities as a seasoned spy, that he had somehow fallen under the radar of

176

British Intelligence, and could outplay them at their own game. Whatever his reasons Taylor knew that it was a potentially fatal mistake; and for someone of Bukin's undoubted experience, it came as a surprise. He second guessed that with his large matronly wife safely behind the iron curtain in Leningrad; Bukin hadn't lost time in enthusiastically embracing everything his western postings could offer.

Having accepted the contract to kill the British Prime Minister, Taylor knew he would be tailed routinely by the KGB; it was no more than he had expected. So had decided to play them at their own game, to test their agents and see just how good they were, and had frequently managed to give them the slip. It was a given that Bukin wouldn't bring the subject up in conversation, it just wasn't done, but it was a two-way street, and in fairness, Bukin would have been severely disappointed if Taylor hadn't realised he was being tailed.

At the same time, Taylor had also needed to cover his own back, his main priority was to know how closely Bukin was under surveillance. As far as he could tell, neither the Secret Service nor Scotland Yard's Special Branch department had detailed a specific "watchers" team to tail Bukin on a twenty-four basis and were relying on covert intelligence. The beauty of the arrangement was that it saved time and effort, and unless there was anything specific the authorities needed to pick up on, they wouldn't have to cover his movements round the clock. The cost would have been prohibitive, and on paper, there were much bigger fish to fry at the Embassy than Bukin.

Bukin's flat would have been bugged, the Soviet Embassy was fair game, and it was a given that it was wired, just as the American and British Embassies were in Moscow, but Taylor needed an additional hook on Bukin. Having already worked out how he was being monitored by the

177

British authorities, he successfully managed to trail Bukin on several occasions without being detected. The first time was after an assignation at a West End café, the second was following a performance of the Bolshoi Ballet in Covent Garden, and, more importantly, he also managed to tail him from the Soviet Embassy to Bukin's Edwardian red-bricked apartment building in Kensington on five separate occasions. He was surprised that Bukin didn't appear to take any overt precautions. On returning from Covent Garden, even his official driver appeared oblivious to the fact they were being followed.

Taylor had always known that he needed a Plan B, an alternative exit plan, knew that his planned escape route had been a one ticket to oblivion, so had taken the precaution of contacting an old friend from the war, Squadron Leader Freddy Seymour-Smith, a former Spitfire pilot, who had always been affectionately known as Smithy. Since leaving the RAF, Smithy had spent his time as a flying instructor at Shoreham airport in Sussex. Taylor had called him to ask a favour.

"Anything dear boy," Smithy had chirped down the phone, "anything at all."

Taylor had asked him whether he could arrange a flight at short notice over to France. It wasn't a particularly unusual request; he did it all the time. Smithy assured him there wouldn't be a problem only that he'd need a couple of hours' notice; he even went so far as refusing payment, it was a favour. Having been shot down over France during the war, Smithy had managed to escape across the English Channel and back to safety, with the help of both the French Resistance and Taylor's intervention.

On setting the receiver down on his old friend, even Taylor had felt a slight frisson of guilt; it was an emotion that he hadn't experienced in years. For poor old Smithy, had no idea whatsoever about his activities after the war, either his life as a secret agent or more recently as a contract killer. Their meetings had tended to be somewhat desultory; Taylor had always told him that he worked in sales. Smithy had never enquired further, nor had Taylor offered up any more information. It simply wasn't necessary they were old friends who enjoyed sinking the occasional few beers in each other's company.

*

Sitting behind the wheel of the blue van, Taylor was self-assured as he waited patiently for Bukin to arrive home on foot from the Embassy. But like Bukin, he had miscalculated the situation, for unbeknown to him, the security authorities not only knew about the plot, but also the identity of the leading players. As a result, Spencer had immediately ordered the "watchers" to mount around the clock surveillance on the Soviet Cultural Secretary. Whilst he was meeting Taylor at The Crown in Earls Court, Bukin's Edwardian apartment block had experienced an unexplained power cut, which was eventually blamed on a team of local workmen carrying out repairs in a nearby building. In fact, the electrical supply had been deliberately sabotaged by Spencer's agents. They were leaving nothing to chance, and the outage had allowed for extra surveillance equipment to be installed. Spencer had also deployed a number of other units, not only in Keen Street itself, but he had also upped the routine surveillance surrounding the Soviet Embassy.

Like Bukin, Taylor hadn't followed his own rules or advice, for once, he'd momentarily not only let his guard down but had also allowed his judgement to lapse. As he pulled up opposite the apartment block, he failed to pick up on the innocuous looking red Austin Post Office van drawn up near the main entrance. A nearby work gang had lifted a manhole cover on the pavement and appeared to be working on a mass of twisted communication cables running beneath the street. They'd pitched up a red and white striped tent to protect them from the biting cold. It was a familiar sight and no-one was likely to question their being there.

But Taylor should have picked up on it, to have questioned it being there, but he didn't, and it was to prove a potentially fatal mistake. He'd taken his eye off the ball and was so intent on watching out for Bukin, that he gave the work gang no more than a cursory glance. It was freezing cold, and the van's windows were steaming up, so he wound down the driver's one; his breath suddenly rising as steam in the blast of cold air. He checked his watch again; it was 5.30pm, and true to form, Bukin was heading on foot along Keen Street to the apartment block from the nearby Soviet Embassy. Taylor smiled to himself, and took his time, reached across the passenger seat and picked up the slender precision rifle supplied by his KGB paymasters. At this distance, it would be child's play hitting his target, and he really didn't need the scope. The silencer was already in place. As Bukin reached the apartment's main entrance, Taylor took aim and lightly squeezed the trigger. It was followed by the expected dull phut. In a split second Bukin recoiled under the impact of the bullet, and in one fell swoop poleaxed onto the pavement. As he crashed to the ground there was an ear piercing hysterical scream from a young woman on her way home from work; Bukin had just that moment smiled at her when the bullet had impacted his head and exploded.

An MI5 agent posing as one of the post office workers ran to his aid, but by the time Bukin had hit the pavement he was already dead and lay in a growing pool of blood. Briefly surveying the commotion across the street Taylor eased off the handbrake and headed off down the street, but failed to notice the driver of the post office van had already been checking him out, and had not only made a note of the vehicle number plate but had also taken a picture of Taylor sitting at the wheel.

The backup agents along the street were frantically signalled by one of their colleagues to follow the blue delivery van. They eased out of the kerb keeping, at least, two cars between them; they were in a black Morris Minor, which were two a penny, the most popular vehicle on the road, so unlikely to stand out from the crowd.

Taylor followed standard procedure, a mile or so down the road he doubled back on himself. The agents were caught at a set of red lights when he passed them going in the opposite direction. They were sandwiched in so there was nothing they could do other than wait until the lights turned green, by that time he was far enough down the road, not to pick up on their Morris doing a sharp U-turn.

'I think we've got the bastard!' the driver hissed.

His Special Branch colleague gave him an anxious sidelong glance. 'He's five cars ahead of us; just as long as we don't get stuck at the fucking lights again we'll be fine!'

The surrounding streets were narrow, and even if they'd fancied their chances on overtaking, they'd probably have found themselves blocked it by on-coming traffic.

'He's taking the second right,' the driver rasped.

They didn't have permission to pick him up; besides they were seriously under-armed to take him on. His colleague picked up the radio from the console, and checked with control; the message was the same; they needed to track the fox to its lair. Orders were orders.

Taylor abandoned the delivery van down a narrow side turning, picked up the box containing the rifle and rammed it into his old leather case. As he did so, the surveillance car sailed past and parked up further along the road. By now Taylor had sussed that he was being tailed.

The driver turned to his colleague. 'Are you okay?'

'I'll be fine, contact control' he said, opening the passenger door, and headed off down the road in pursuit.

It was obvious Taylor more than knew his stuff; he occasionally stopped to glance in a shop window and check out if he was still being trailed. On the other side of the road, Spencer's operative kept a subtle distance, but things kicked off when Taylor headed to the main road and suddenly darted into the tube station. Cursing under his breath, the Special Branch Officer took his life in his hands and weaved his way through the oncoming traffic toward the underground.

By the time he arrived, the ticket concourse was heaving with people and there was no sign of Taylor. The officer reached into his jacket and flashed a police warrant card at the ticket collector and was waved through the barrier. But now what? He knew the Circle and District lines served the station, there were four platforms to choose from, he'd simply have to take pot luck and ran down the creaking wooden escalator. It was crowded, and as he brushed his way down a woman shouted after him.

'Mind where you're bloody going!'

At the bottom, he anxiously checked the tube planner, before systematically searching each of the platforms, but then felt the warm rush of air, and the unmistakable sound of a train. Taylor had vanished on the first available train; it really didn't matter to him where it was going, only that it was heading into the dark, labyrinthine underground network criss-crossing London.

Chapter 18
MI5 HQ, London

The morning after Bukin's death the photographic evidence landed on Spencer Hall's desk. The fact that one of his two-man surveillance teams had lost contact with Taylor at High Street Kensington tube station wasn't helping his mood any. He'd already balled out the team leader, but having read the report, he wasn't entirely surprised Taylor had given them the slip. Even so, Spencer couldn't help wondering if Taylor might just be losing his edge, for, at his height, he'd have eyeballed the reconnaissance team long before they'd had a chance to photograph him. Back in the day, he'd been the ultimate professional, even his racketeering had been slickly managed and earned the devious bastard a small fortune.

Further copies of the photographs were dispatched, via Martian Bell, to Jack Stein at the American Embassy, and to Garvan at Scotland Yard. Although they'd temporarily lost contact with Taylor, things were still moving forward and gathering pace. Agent Freda's CIA controllers reported that Donna Webster's death had compromised the entire operation and that even before Bukin's death the KGB had already decided to pull the plug on Taylor's assignment.

It was all slowly beginning to add up, Taylor had obviously not only fallen foul of the Soviets but had taken it into his head to buy himself some much needed time. News of Bukin's death had ricocheted around the intelligence communities on both sides of the Iron Curtain. Taylor was now a dangerous lone wolf with nothing to lose and had made the situation even more combustible than it had been before Bukin's murder. He'd certainly set the cat amongst the pigeons, the diplomats and politicians were momentarily in complete freefall, and behind the scenes accusations in London were flying left, right and centre.

183

Spencer knew his man, knew Taylor well enough to realise that although the Soviets might have pulled the plug on the operation, Taylor certainly wouldn't let it drop; he had his own agenda and could only be sated by one final confrontation. Bukin's assassination had been a calculated gamble; at best he was probably hoping the ensuing turmoil would temporarily force MI5 to take their eye off the ball.

Taylor's photograph was now being openly circulated around Scotland Yard in connection with the murder of Donna Webster. The grim discovery of her body, which had been burnt beyond all recognition in the boot of an abandoned car, had initially left the authorities at the post-mortem examination trying to determine the exact cause of death and also to identify the gender, such was the extensive fire damage to the vehicle; in the end, identification could only be confirmed by dental records. At the time it had made the front page news, the coroner's inquest had eventually ascertained that the cause of death had not been as originally suspected asphyxiation, but the result of a single gunshot wound; as a bullet was found embedded in her skull.

Only a select few, including Garvan's deputy, Chief Superintendent Harry Mackenzie, were made aware of Taylor's involvement with the slaying of Alexander Bukin and also his real identity.

To hell with the security lockdown, all bets were off. Spencer reached across his desk and pressed the intercom button, his secretary answered.

'Yes, sir?'

'Get the Prime Minister on the line right away, use the scrambler.' Spencer hesitated before setting the receiver down and said. 'You'd then better call Jack Stein!'

*

Four hours later Spencer arrived unannounced in Maggie Ellis's office; it was completely unprecedented for the Head of MI5 to arrive at the Home Office without a prior appointment. Maggie looked up in surprise. Spencer treated her with glacial coldness, but that wasn't particularly unusual. He nodded briefly, then turned away from her and without bothering to speak walked straight through into Bradshaw's office unannounced.

Maggie couldn't keep the anger off her face and flew after him. 'What the hell's going on, you just can't walk into the Home Secretary's office without permission,' her voice rising in rage.

Once inside Bradshaw's office, Spencer swung round to face her, his expression set like granite. 'Leave us!' he spat at her venomously.

Taking a sharp intake of breath, Maggie wasn't budging anytime soon and held her ground, it was Bradshaw who intervened. 'Maggie,' he said, evenly. 'Just close the door behind you, will you.'

Maggie still hesitated, but the look on Bradshaw's face said it all, and she reluctantly made a tactical retreat into the outer office, to find herself confronted not only by Assistant Commissioner Garvan standing beside her desk but by another imposing figure standing with his back against the large Georgian window overlooking Whitehall. She'd never seen him before, and could only presume he was a Special Branch colleague of Garvan's. Maggie's breath came fast through her mouth, she was scared, her first instinct was to flee, but she stayed rooted to the spot, fear flooding her mind. Garvan formally introduced the stranger as Chief Superintendent Mackenzie, by now things were starting to become a blur to her.

She began to eye both of them warily, and when she spoke her voice was taut but conveyed her fear. 'Will someone please tell me what in god's name is going on here?'

185

'Miss Ellis,' Garvan said, harshly, 'we have reason to believe you have committed offences under the Official Secrets Act. I am therefore arresting you on suspicion of spying.'

Maggie began to shake her head in disbelief and instinctively reached toward the desk to steady herself and started to sob that there must have been some terrible mistake; that they'd got it all wrong; someone had set her up, that explained everything, yes, that was it, she cried.

Garvan raised his hand to silence her. 'Chief Superintendent Mackenzie will be taking you to Bow Street police station.'

'Bow Street?' she repeated.

'Yes, Miss Ellis, you may, of course, contact your lawyer, but you'll need to do that at the station.'

Maggie made to speak, but realised it was pointless pleading with them, and silently scooped up her handbag before leaving the office with Mackenzie.

*

'What's going on?' Bradshaw demanded of Spencer.

Without answering, he placed an attaché case on the corner of Bradshaw's desk, opened it and handed him a letter.

The Home Secretary looked up questioningly. 'What's this?'

'I think you'll find, sir, it's your letter of resignation.'

Bradshaw's eyes narrowed as he tried to read Spencer's face, but it was impossible. The letter had been typed on headed paper, his own official Home Office paper. He sat back and removed his glasses and tossed them down on the desk

'Why the hell should I resign?'

'Personally, sir, I can think of any number of reasons.'

'I'm sure you can!' he responded coolly, before placing the letter on a large green inkpad. 'What makes you think I'll sign?'

'You really don't have a choice.'

Bradshaw snorted derisively 'I think you'll find that decision lies solely within the command of the Prime Minister, and *not* the Director General of Her Majesty's secret service.' His voice was witheringly condescending.

With brutal efficiency, Spencer handed him another letter from his attaché case. 'Open it,' he commanded, sharply.

Bradshaw opened it and hesitated, his gaze briefly resting on the embossed headed paper of the Prime Minister's office before settling on Jeremy Haining's spidery signature.

Spencer explained, rather unnecessarily. 'I think that you'll find the Prime Minister has already accepted your resignation.'

Bradshaw's world suddenly imploded, for the life of him he didn't quite know how to react, he was totally bewildered. He tried to conceal his uneasiness, but ended up swaying to and fro in his stylish swivel chair, and nervously adjusting his tie and fiddling with his heavy gold cufflinks. The government's gifted master tactician and arch political manipulator had been slickly outmanoeuvred by his old adversary. He simply hadn't seen it coming, and his customary coolness started to slip, and he began to falter. He leaned forward and slowly, deliberately, placed his palms over the two resignation letters, before taking a long deep breath. 'Will you do me a favour, Sir Spencer?'

The sudden formality wasn't lost on Spencer. 'That depends,' he replied, non-committedly.

'Let's just cut the bullshit, shall we, as Home Secretary I think you owe me that much, don't you? Just tell me straight what's going on.'

He came back at him matter of factly. 'Miss Ellis has been placed under arrest.'

Bradshaw's face contorted in disbelief. 'Good god man, what are you talking about?'

Spencer explained everything to him, Maggie's connections to Alexander Bukin, and the KGB, that she'd been in their pay, and was complicit in the assassination plot.

'Let's just say,' Spencer said, smoothly, 'that your relationship with Ellis wasn't entirely exclusive.'

Bradshaw's eyes had a faraway look. 'What in hell's name is that supposed to mean?'

'We know that she's also been sleeping with Alexander Bukin.'

Bradshaw lowered his gaze, he frowned, and slowly swivelled the chair toward the window. 'Are you seriously telling me that Maggie was involved in the plot to assassinate the Prime Minister?' he said, mechanically.

'Yes, she was.'

Whilst Bradshaw took a sharp intake of breath his expression didn't falter. 'Then I would appear not to have any choice, other than to fall on my sword,' he announced brusquely, and swung the back chair to his desk, put on his glasses and without demur he picked up his pen and signed the resignation letter, then handed it over to Spencer. 'So what happens now?'

'You'll make a formal statement in the House of Commons.'

Bradshaw narrowed his eyes and placed his hands together as if in prayer, and appeared to mull the matter over before seeming to be on the point of responding, but Spencer cut in, and added, bleakly. 'The Prime Minister has already made the decision.'

Bradshaw whipped his glasses off his face and held them lightly between his fingers. 'I think you'll need to spell that one out to me.'

Spencer said dispassionately. 'The arrest of Miss Ellis will make front page headlines. The British Press will be clamouring for answers, and will have conspiracy theories printed left, right and centre. I daresay some of the newspapers will call for you and the Prime Minister to resign. One of you will have to fall on their sword, and it's not going to be the Prime Minister!'

Bradshaw took a sharp intake of breath, a look of resignation on his face. 'How much of this will be made public?'

Spencer continued seamlessly. 'Well, we all know how things stand, sir, neither Moscow nor the Prime Minister will want to wash all their dirty linen in public. But I think you'll agree that a sex scandal involving a Russian spy and the Home Secretary is one thing, but the assassination plot is probably best left out of the public domain.'

Bradshaw looked through him, rather than at him. 'So, I'm to be the sacrificial lamb.'

'If you don't resign you'll bring down the entire government, is that what you want?'

'No,' he said wistfully, 'you're right.' He could see the headlines already, disgraced Minister, Stanley Bradshaw, has been forced to resign, and his relationship would probably go down in the annals of history as an infamous political scandal. He needed to walk away from the life that he loved, for no other reason than to salvage what was left of his relationship with his wife.

'The Prime Minister's office has already drawn up the press lines.'

Although a slight cynical smile crossed Bradshaw's mouth, he remained stony faced. They'd thought of everything, but there again why wouldn't they. He had not only been completely outmanoeuvred by Spencer but more crucially by Maggie Ellis. He'd fallen for her hook line and sinker, but how long had she been working for the Soviets? However long it was, Spencer wasn't about to tell him. But he'd been a fool, a bloody fool, not to have seen that he'd been set up by her, and in the process had thrown everything away, his career, and, more importantly, his marriage. All in all, it had been a classic honey trap, but he'd only himself to blame.

'For what it's worth I swear to god I'd no idea,' he whispered huskily, 'I'd no idea about Maggie.'

Spencer almost felt a fleeting sense of sympathy for him, albeit that it was short lived. He made to leave the office, but as an afterthought turned back, and said. 'I'm sorry; I forgot to give you this.' He reopened his attaché case and handed over a file.

The file was marked in red ink "Prime Minister's eyes only". Bradshaw glanced up at him questioningly. 'What's this?'

'It's a security report.'

'They're normally two a penny,' Bradshaw countered derisively.

'Not *this one*, sir!' he snapped with his usual innate assurance. 'The Prime Minister asked me to pass you a copy.'

As Spencer closed the door on him, Bradshaw reluctantly opened the file, and instinctively reached for a cigar and lit it. It didn't take long for him to realise, that even without Maggie's connections to the KGB, his position had already become completely untenable, for MI5 had discovered how and why Maggie had managed to wield such an inordinate amount of control over the normally astute Home Secretary. It wasn't just pillow talk; it went far deeper than that.

Everything was there in black and white, his business dealings, how his accountants Abacus Limited, had opened bank accounts in Switzerland and the Channel Islands. It had been a standard tax avoidance measure, and although not strictly illegal, it probably hadn't been the wisest of moves for a committed left wing politician, who had always railed against the inherent evils of capitalism, and had consistently presented himself as "a man of the people." Perhaps even more, damning was that the funds from his coterie of powerful establishment business contacts, whose contributions and funding of his parliamentary office had ostensibly been unimpeachable, had been steadily syphoned off into his Swiss accounts. The fact his benefactors business dealings probably wouldn't pass too much in-depth scrutiny by either the tax office or Scotland Yard's fraud squad only compounded the situation.

Bradshaw closed the file; he'd read enough, and leaned back in his chair and softly exhaled a cloud of cigar smoke. Spencer had fulfilled his brief; it was no mean feat to take down the Home Secretary. He'd managed to outplay him, but so had the Prime Minister, the one thing Bradshaw knew for certain, was that politics was ruthless, and the moment you ceased to be of use, you could expect no mercy.

Chapter 19
Kenton Road, South

Late on 21st January, a message came through from Agent Freda to the CIA's Headquarters in Langley, Virginia, it read:

FRIDAY, 22ND JANUARY, KENTON ROAD – PM APPOINTMENT – PEGASUS - IT IS A GO – REPEAT - IT IS A GO.

When the information dropped on Spencer's desk all hell broke loose; Pegasus was Taylor's KGB codename. He needed to think on his feet and fast. It was still the Prime Minister's call, he could have backed out, called off his appointment, but bravely decided to go through with it; he wanted to nail the bugger once and for all.

It was after dark by the time Spencer travelled to the site and after consulting Garvan, they immediately moved in a number of covert Special Branch units and MI5 agents in and around Kenton Road. In addition, there were a number of undercover officers from Scotland Yard's Central Investigation Department in reserve. In order to limit the amount of through traffic, Garvan arranged for road restrictions and diversion signs to be set up immediately. Traffic cones were placed at the main crossroads, and a number of notices had been strategically set up announcing road closures were due to emergency repairs to a water main. At short notice Martin Bell had managed to secure them four heavy duty trucks, including one from Thames Water. Spencer didn't ask questions, where Martin was concerned it sometimes paid to turn a blind eye to his methods. They soon got to work and even dug a large gaping hole in the road.

Quite what the local council would make of their handiwork was another matter.

*

On the morning of 22nd January, Taylor washed and shaved in a shabby hotel room in Barons Court, on the Pallister Road. It was still early, but he couldn't sleep, and he needed to clear his head, to meticulously go over the plans once more in his mind. He tweaked the dusty net curtains and stared somberly out of the window, and once again checked whether he was under surveillance. Although removing Bukin out of the equation had been necessary, it had still left him rattled. He'd taken him out cleanly enough but had made a basic rooky error. For up until then Taylor had always believed that he possessed a sixth sense for trouble; but as he'd pulled up opposite Bukin's apartment block, it wasn't that he hadn't noticed the post office van, or the gang working on the communications lines, it had even fleetingly crossed his mind that they might be undercover Special Branch or Secret Service agents. He'd calmly given them the once over, but had dismissed them out of hand. It was a fatal mistake and had seriously dented his confidence.

After shooting Bukin, he'd laid wide awake most of the night not only churning over his plan to kill the Prime Minister but his mistakes outside the apartment block. He'd been lucky and couldn't afford to mess up again, at least not without being punished.

His mood hadn't lightened any when the receptionist delivered the morning paper to his room. The Daily Mirror's headlines were still dominated by Bukin's killing; the story ran how the authorities were following up a number of leads. Jeremy Haining had apparently passed on his personal condolences to the Soviet Ambassador and assured him that Bukin's killer would be brought to justice. It was the usual

193

gobbledygook, but a veritable master class in double-dealing diplomacy.

The editorial was one thing, but as Taylor turned the page his eyes locked onto a black and white picture, it was a damn good one and had obviously been taken whilst he was sitting in the van outside Bukin's flat. He slunk back in the armchair, and thoughtfully linked his fingers behind his head. It had obviously been released by MI5 that much wasn't in doubt.

Beneath the picture ran the line: "*Scotland Yard have released the photograph of a man they want to question in relation to the murder of a London landlady, Donna Webster. A reward of £100 is being offered by the Webster family for information leading to the arrest and prosecution of a man sought in connection with her murder. Police are seeking to trace Charles Taylor, who maybe travelling under several aliases, including Peter Bartholomew. Taylor is aged forty-five, around six foot one and of slim build. Anyone who sees Taylor should not approach him, but call the police on Whitehall 1212.*"

Clever, very clever Taylor mused; there was no doubt in his mind that Spencer was the driving force behind the article. The newspaper editors obviously would not have a clue about his former life as a British agent, or that he was behind their front page headline, for the murder of Alexander Bukin. That nugget of information would surely have let too many cats out of the bag as there was only so much information the authorities were willing to share with the general public. It was a skillful subliminal message that was not only aimed personally at Taylor but also directly at the KGB that the net was closing in around their hired assassin. It had meant to unnerve him, and it hadn't missed its mark.

What Taylor didn't know, was that news of Bradshaw's resignation and Maggie Ellis's arrest on espionage charges had been temporarily suppressed by the authorities under a D-Notice, which was a means of warning the media not to publish intelligence or a story that might damage national security,

Taylor hurriedly shook his thoughts away and slipped a pack of cigarettes out of his hip pocket and began to wonder how his old friend Squadron Leader Freddy Seymour-Smith would react when he read the newspapers. There was no point in phoning him. Taylor would find out soon enough if he managed to make it in one piece to Shoreham airport.

He couldn't afford to hang around at the hotel any longer, so hurriedly fastened his Rolex onto his left wrist; he didn't bother packing, he wanted to travel light with just the rifle box and two handguns, one in a holster and the second in his overcoat pocket, along with a stash of ammunition. If all went well he'd escape with his life, but if it didn't, then dead or alive he would create enough collateral damage to bring down Spencer Hall, and that was motivation enough to see things through.

With infinite care he checked the sleek wooden box containing his custom made snipers rifle, and placed a passport into his jacket pocket. If he was successful in taking out the Prime Minister, he intended travelling under the alias of Gunter Brandt, he spoke fluent German, so it was an easy fix. He then slipped on a pair of horn-rimmed glasses with clear lenses, opened a red tub of Brylcreem and slicked back his hair before checking out his reflection in the wardrobe mirror. It was more than enough he decided to fool the average beat copper from picking up on him.

He buttoned up his overcoat, wrapped a woollen scarf around his neck, picked up the wooden box, and placed it inside his leather briefcase, it fitted comfortably, then disappeared out of the hotel via the rickety old metal fire exit at the rear of the building; he knew it was only a matter of time before the staff picked up on the newspaper reports.

Three hours later the Prime Minister's chauffeur driven car swung out of Downing Street accompanied by one further vehicle and three, rather than his customary two police motorbike outriders. The third was in the unlikely shape of Martin Bell, he'd initially resisted the idea, true he had been a dispatch rider during the war, but close armed protection wasn't exactly what he'd been trained for, supplying cars for the security service was one thing, but risking his life for the sake of some bloody politician he figured was best left for the gung-ho types like Stein and Spencer.

The security detail was still seemingly low-key, the only difference being that Garvan's Deputy Harry Mackenzie was in the front passenger seat of the PM's car, and at the wheel was Haining's personal bodyguard, Simon Buckmaster, an old hand who'd been with the Prime Minister for a number of years. In the rear of the vehicle sat a smartly dressed blonde, to the casual observer she was probably either a secretary or a senior Party official. At first, Haining had baulked at the idea of Virginia Dudley accompanying him in the car, but after a little gentle reminder from Spencer that during the war Dudley had not only controlled an entire SOE circuit in France but had been one of British Intelligence's finest agents did he eventually relent. Even so, he still felt faintly embarrassed that he was being protected not only by an attractive blonde but an American to boot.

Behind the PM's car was a large black Rover 105 with a supercharged engine, it was a very different beast from the normal popular production line vehicles. Driving was Garvan, with him were Jack Stein and sitting in the rear was Spencer Hall.

The Prime Minister's small cavalcade headed down Whitehall before taking a left over Westminster Bridge and travelling the short distance to Kenton Road and the home of Edward Gibson.

By the time they set off from Whitehall, Charles Taylor had already slipped unseen via the subterranean tunnels beneath the flats in Kenton Road and had taken up position on the balcony overlooking Gibson's house. He pulled up the collar of his overcoat and adjusted his thick woollen scarf against the biting wind. He glanced down the road; the Prime Minister's cavalcade hadn't yet come into sight. He slunk back out of sight behind a pillar and calmly clicked on the silencer. It had also become second nature as he skilfully wound it onto the barrel of the rifle and then slipped the telescopic sight into it. He calmly raised the rifle and squinted down the sight, once he was happy, Taylor then loaded the ammunition into the breech.

When Bukin had first handed over the custom made rifle, Taylor had immediately taken himself off to Epping Forest, in Essex, to get a feel for it. The silencer had made a quiet, pleasing phut; it was well balanced, in fact, he considered it to be nothing short of a work of art, and was by far and away one of the best rifles he'd ever used. The three parts fitted comfortably into the wooden box; it was light to carry, and more importantly easily slipped into his battered old leather case.

Taylor glanced at his watch and again surreptitiously checked over the balcony, there was still little through traffic, a set of roadworks near the cross junction adjacent to the park meant that access to Kenton Road had been restricted. He hadn't bargained on that happening; there'd been no sign of it yesterday. Maybe he'd missed something. It also ran through his mind that Spencer might be onto him. He'd screwed up once already with Bukin, and he couldn't afford to do it again. Either way, there was no turning back.

As Taylor glanced to his left, he caught a movement; it was what he'd been waiting for, the Prime Minister's small cavalcade drew up and came to a halt outside Gibson's terraced house. There were three police outriders and a backup car, but nothing out of the ordinary, at least not enough for Taylor to think anything was amiss. As Chief Superintendent Mackenzie jumped out of the passenger seat and opened the rear door of the Prime Minister's car a sudden blast of cold air filled the interior. Buckmaster, Haining's bodyguard, who was at the wheel, glanced nervously over his shoulder as Haining accepted a helping hand out of the car from Mackenzie.

Taylor felt his pulse begin to quicken, but took his time; he assumed the Prime Minister's car had bulletproof windows. He had to shoot his personal bodyguard; it was a given that he was armed and needed to be taken out of the equation.

Nervously scanning the surrounding area, Martin Bell pulled alongside the backup vehicle. Taking everything in inch by inch, there were few people walking along the street, and the nearby roadworks had luckily reduced the usual flow of heavy traffic. He almost started to relax, but as his eyes fixed on the block of flats opposite Gibson's house, his thin, pale face suddenly tightened. He noticed a figure on the balcony, the hair might be styled differently than he remembered, and the horned rimmed glasses were new, but he'd recognise Taylor anywhere as he coolly raised the deadly high-velocity rifle and squinted down the telescopic sight. He needed to move fast and gestured urgently toward Spencer and Stein.

'Nine o'clock, the bastards at nine o'clock!' he shouted, frantically.

Stein was already out of the backup car and had opened the rear door for Spencer; he half turned to where Bell was pointing. Without thinking, Stein instinctively lunged toward the Prime Minister and tackled him. As they crashed to the ground, the gentle phut of the rifle was almost inaudible. The elderly Haining groaned under the impact of Stein landing on top of him. It all happened in a split second; Spencer drew his PKK as Stein rolled off the Prime Minister onto the pavement.

'Holy Christ!' he gasped, holding his side as blood poured from a gunshot wound where the bullet had torn into him.

Taylor cursed under his breath but didn't miss a beat; he'd never messed up an assignation before, if only that bloody fool hadn't got in the way both Haining and his bodyguard would be dead by now. He scooped up the rifle case and headed along the balcony toward the nearest staircase. By now Virginia was already half way across the road; she'd drawn a pistol and ordered Bell to follow her. He momentarily hesitated, he hadn't bargained on being dragged into some kind of hand to handgun fight with someone of Taylor's calibre, but followed her all the same.

Spencer helped Mackenzie bundle the shaken Prime Minister back into the car. 'Are you all right, sir?' he asked.

Haining collapsed in a heap onto the rear seat. 'Never mind me, what about -.'

He never had a chance to finish his sentence; Spencer slammed the door shut on him, and yelled at his bodyguard. 'Just put your bloody foot down and don't stop!'

Buckmaster had already been ordered to keep the engine idling over, so thrust the gear lever into first and crashed the accelerator to the floor. The two remaining motorbike outriders joined them.

Garvan had still been seated in the backup car when he realised what was happening, so reached for the receiver on the middle consul; the phone had a direct link to Scotland Yard's operation room. They'd already positioned a number of units in the surrounding area. Although the roadworks had successfully reduced the flow of traffic through Kenton Road, Garvan now ordered it be closed off completely. He also told them to set up a cordon to prevent any pedestrians wandering into the line of fire. It was only then that he asked for urgent medical assistance.

Mackenzie desperately tried to help stem the flow of blood from the wound. Stein was by now drifting in an out of consciousness. Spencer glanced down at his friend; he wanted to stay, but Mackenzie was doing all he could to save his life.

Mackenzie looked up at him, 'Go on; he'll be fine,' he lied.

Spencer knew that he wasn't, but moved on, there was no point hanging around. As he ran across the road leaving Garvan to coordinate both his own agents and Special Branch Units, there was now only one thing on his mind, to take Taylor down.

*

Virginia found a break in the hoarding and shoulder barged her way through; Martin was only just managing to keep up with her. He was gasping and trying to catch his breath, he'd always promised to give up the cigarettes, but had never quite enough willpower to kick the habit.

'Are you tooled up?' she snapped at him.

He fumbled inside his police uniform and produced a pistol.

'Jesus wept,' she snarled at him, 'do you know how to use the fucking thing!'

She might have been out of his league, but he bristled. 'What the *fuck* do you think?'

A bemused ripple of a smile crossed her face. 'Just do as I do!'

Taylor had a head start on them, and Virginia knew that he must have weighed up all the options, and would have factored the unexpected into his planning. By now he obviously knew British Intelligence was on to him and had surrounded the site, but he was an old pro at the game, and whatever else he was, Taylor wasn't a fool. In his position, she'd probably have gone to ground inside the building for a while and wait until the dust settled a little and take stock rather than make a sudden desperate bid to escape, but maybe he had other plans.

Panting in hot pursuit Bell followed Virginia as she headed the way up the stone staircase to the first floor, and crept along the balcony, they gestured to one another, to wait and listen. They edged their way along the balcony, but there was no sign of him. He'd gone to ground. Having reached the end of the corridor facing onto Kenton Road, they followed the balcony around the side of the building. It seemed likely that Taylor might have taken refuge in one of the disused flats. Her instinct wasn't wrong. Taylor was wondering how much lead time he had. He'd been through the building enough times to know that he more than had the edge over them. But as he tentatively checked out one of the doorways a bullet suddenly whanged into the wall beside him.

Taylor flinched, he recognised Virginia, and fired off a defensive volley, and hurried off through the maze of walkways and interconnecting stairs toward the rear of the building. The bastards were too close for comfort, and he was up against it. He certainly wasn't as fit as he once was, but he guessed. Hopefully, neither were they. Occasionally, he'd half turn and fire off another couple of rounds; they'd dive for cover wherever they could find it, bullets were ricocheting off the walls and the stone floor. Virginia steadied her gun with two hands, fired off two rounds, but Taylor had disappeared round the corner down another flight of stairs.

He continued heading toward the rear of the building, his mind whirred frantically, Spencer had managed to set up a trap, but how long had he known about the location? Probably not long enough, otherwise, the security would have been a great deal tighter. But the fact that Jack Stein had been in the Prime Minister's cavalcade was telling, it meant only one

201

thing; it wasn't only British Intelligence that was onto to him, but the CIA as well.

Taylor crashed down the rusty old fire escape, by now his lungs were starting to burn up, and he was having difficulty catching his breath. Jesus wept Taylor thought to himself, he was more in danger of having a heart attack than being taken out by a bullet, but just then another shot rang out, his last hope was to make it down into the basement, and to the old air raid shelter, where there was an exit onto St. Mary's Walk, the narrow side turning where he'd parked up his car earlier.

Sweat began to bead on Taylor's forehead; he swiped the sweat out of his eyes. They were close on his tail, so Taylor crouched down on the metal staircase and fired off another defensive volley. He heard a groan, maybe he'd struck lucky, but he wasn't about to hang around to find out, and so jumped the final flight and landed awkwardly badly jarring his left ankle, stumbling, he winced in pain, his face contorted in a rictus of anguish, and felt sick to the stomach. God, he really was getting too old and long in the tooth for this kind of bloody lark.

Bell had taken a hit in his arm and doubled over in pain. 'The bastard got me!' he cursed.

'Are you okay?'

Bell straightened himself up. 'I'll be fine,' he said, clutching his arm.

'You don't look it, stay here!' she commanded.

It hurt like hell; blood was seeping down over his hand.

'Do you need a tourniquet?'

He shook his head.

'Go back, find Garvan, and tell him what's happening.'

Bell didn't need asking twice. 'What about you?'

But Virginia was already heading down the iron fire exit, the trouble was by now Taylor had a march on her, she'd seen him disappear into a doorway at the foot of the stairs. He'd obviously landed badly, so she figured that it might slow him up a little, for he obviously knew the layout of the building like the back of his hand.

Taylor painfully hobbled his way down toward the shelter; it was his only realistic chance of escaping. He knew they'd have the building surrounded, but hoped that he just might still have the edge over them, He was pinning his hopes that they didn't know about the bomb shelters exit out onto St. Mary's Walk, a street away from the flats.

Taylor had done his homework well; the unprepossessing doorway leading to the shelter belonged to an adjacent office building, and to all intents and purposes was totally un-connected to the block of flats. As he made his way down toward the bowels of the building, he suddenly saw a figure swirl round, reach inside his overcoat, and in one swift movement, Spencer thumbed back the safety catch of the PKK and a shot rang out. Taylor flinched, and swung round. It had been a long time since he had looked into those deadly shrewd piercing blue eyes. The ruggedly handsome face hadn't changed that much, only the shock of salt and pepper greying hair came as a surprise, but the eyes still retained the same deadly menace, and the same detached manner. In the past he'd had a rare talent for crashing in where others dare not tread, it was a combustible combination that Taylor had found intriguing.

To Taylor's mind, it was nothing short of a miracle that he'd managed to hold onto being the Head of MI5 for as long as he had, at least not without upsetting the fragile sensitivities of his political masters. He wasn't by nature a Whitehall warrior or diplomat, but a field man, with a history for taking no prisoners.

The way Taylor saw it, he could either fight it out with him or throw down his weapon, clasp his hands behind his head and surrender. It was the easy way out of course, but he simply couldn't do it, couldn't give Spencer the satisfaction of surrendering to him. There was too much history between them, no, he'd rather die in the attempt, but more than anything he needed somehow to take Spencer down with him.

Try as he might Taylor couldn't quite manage to disguise his feelings, and looked at Spencer with smouldering hatred. His expression was taut, his eyes steady on his ex-brother in arms, but since his dismissal from British Intelligence, Spencer had been his sworn enemy, his nemesis. In a split second, it would all be over, but Taylor hesitated as Spencer unexpectedly lowered his PKK.

'Are you beginning to lose your touch, *Charlie*?'

It wasn't so much a question, as a statement. Taylor held his gaze, and said 'Well I reckon that's the chance you've got to take; let's face it, Spence, you've been out of the field driving a desk for what, five, six years now, and I reckon you're probably getting a bit rusty yourself by now.'

'Really?' he replied deadpan.

'As I remember *you* used to be pretty slick with that PKK.'

Spencer didn't respond but said. 'I am addressing Agent Pegasus, aren't I?'

Taylor didn't demur; it seemed pretty pointless to do otherwise. When he spoke, his voice was tinged with bitterness. 'Maybe we're both getting a little too old for this game.'

'I guess there's only way to find out.' Spencer's tone was cold; it had always been cold. 'But maybe you have a point; maybe I am losing my edge.' He didn't say it but he still, if possible, wanted to take the bastard alive. 'In the old days you'd have been dead by now, my motto was always to shoot first and ask questions later, it's what made me good at my game.'

Taylor felt he was playing with him, it was what he did.

'What's this really all about Charlie?

A bleak, wintry smile transcended his face. 'It's always been about *you*, Spencer, hasn't it?'

Spencer's expression gave nothing away. 'Me,' he said, blankly, 'why me?'

'I know that I've whored my way across Europe and America for the right price and to the highest bidder, but this one was different, this assignment was personal and impossible to resist,' he paused for effect, before adding, 'taking this one was a way of finally getting even with you.'

'That's as maybe, but let's face it Charlie, the KGB have played you like a fiddle.'

'Have they?'

'To them, you're nothing more than a fall guy, you were set up. How were they going to get you out of the country? Let's see, did they promise you a plane, some flight from a private airfield?'

Taylor nodded curtly.

'Did you believe them?'

'I can't remember the last time I trusted anyone let alone the KGB.'

'We both know they'd never have allowed you to live,' Spencer commented drily. 'Even if you'd managed to assassinate Haining, you were always going to be a liability to the Soviets. They wouldn't have risked that someday you'd spill the beans and tell the authorities. In your shoes, if I'd been caught, I'd have sung like a canary, and plea-bargain in the hope that I'd receive a lesser sentence.'

'I can't say it hadn't crossed my mind,' Taylor responded languidly.

'One way or another, Charlie, you've always been a sly bastard!'

'Coming from you, I'll take that as a compliment.'

'You can take it as you bloody well like.'

Spencer was right, he knew that. Taylor stared at his old adversary with a mixture of fear and defiance.

'To the KGB you were the perfect catch,' Spencer continued, 'a disaffected British agent with a chip on his shoulder the size of the Grand Canyon.' He passed him a quick, tired flicker of a smile. 'I don't deny they believed you were at the top of your game, but you broke the two cardinal rules of engagement.'

Taylor had a look of resignation on his face. 'Did I?' He asked indifferently.

'Your first mistake was in accepting a contract, not just for the money, but because it was personal to you.'

'So what was the second?'

'You so needed to get even with me that you failed to factor the KGB's end game, that you were expendable.'

Taylor chuckled. 'Am I missing something?'

'You tell me.'

'I might have got it all wrong, but from where I was standing I was under the impression that British Intelligence believed I was expendable. We're not fools; we both know that whether or not I accepted the KGB's contract, either way, I was a dead man walking.'

Spencer gave him a long hard look. 'Expendable,' he said, thoughtfully, 'yes, I suppose you were, but only because I'd always considered you to be in the second eleven, and that after the war you were never quite going to make the grade.'

In many ways, it was a blatant lie, but there was no denying that Spencer had long harboured a belief that Taylor had been psychologically scarred by the war, and had therefore become a liability. He'd voiced his concerns, but at the time had never been able to prove it, but his racketeering had been little short of a godsend and had finally given him licence to dismiss Taylor from British Intelligence.

He knew that beneath the veneer of arrogance, lurked the demeanour of an agent who was once considered to be almost irreplaceable, whereas Spencer, was still more powerful and dominant than before, it made for an uneasy mix between them. Although Taylor had carved out a successful career for himself since being fired from the Service, Spencer's own path had catapulted him to the very top of their profession. Love or loathe him, and Taylor loathed him with every fibre of his being, there was no denying his past as a tough, uncompromising agent, and his reputation on both sides of the Pond was second to none.

From Taylor's perspective, the slick suits still couldn't quite disguise what lay beneath the newly found sophistication. His ice blue eyes glistened, and when he spoke, it was in a menacingly deadly whisper. The desk job obviously hadn't softened the hard man that he remembered so well both during and after the war. As Spencer moved closer, his PKK now aimed at Taylor, he was every bit as intimidating and spoke with a politeness that was almost unnerving, as if he was holding back a cauldron of anger.

'Admit it, Charlie, you've screwed up for the last time,' he said coolly.

'Maybe,' he shrugged indifferently, 'but, at least, I have one small consolation, I've finally taken out that arsehole Stein.'

Spencer wouldn't allow him the satisfaction of provoking a reaction. He'd always believed that deep down Taylor was beset by an ingrained sense of self-doubt. Admittedly, he hid it well, but it was there all the same.

Taylor was on a roll and snarled. 'You've always been a bastard!'

As he raised his Luger a shot rang out, Virginia had managed to track them down. Taylor flinched instinctively as the shot thudded harmlessly into the door behind him; catching him off guard Spencer slammed his full weight into Taylor, propelling him into the wall, the sheer force took his breath away, and the rifle case clattered to the floor. There was a moment of chaos, Taylor's nose was broken, and blood poured down his face. Although doubled over in pain, he knew that he had to somehow fight back. Having managed to keep a grip on his pistol, Taylor suddenly thrust upward with his right hand and smashed the butt into Spencer's face.

Spencer found himself reeling under the force of the blow and crashed awkwardly to the floor, his teeth were red with blood, and his jaw hurt like hell. In the gloom Virginia hesitated, she couldn't get a clear shot as they grappled together in the corridor, so she began to edge her way forward, she could see Spencer's PPK was on the floor, and he was desperately trying to make a reach for it, but Taylor just managed to kick it away from his grasp.

Catching her out of the corner of his eye, Spencer shouted at Virginia to stay back, to stay where she was, he needed, at least, one of them to get out of this alive; he couldn't risk losing her. Taylor made a sudden bid for the door at the end of the corridor. Staggering to his feet, Spencer took an insane forward dive at him; the momentum hurled them into the heavy metal door leading down into the bowels of the building, and to the old wartime air raid shelter. If he could just get through it in one piece, then Taylor knew that he had a chance of making it outside to the side turning beyond where he'd parked his car up earlier.

It was his only hope of escape, somehow he managed to break free from Spencer's grasp, and as he stumbled forward to the door, made a half-hearted defensive shot in a desperate bid to keep both of them at a distance. Spencer ducked instinctively; he'd hurt his right hand in the fight, so steadied the PKK with both hands and fired off two rounds, but Taylor just narrowly managed to slip behind the door as the bullets thudded into it, and down a flight of stairs.

Taylor was limping badly, he gave a small groan, the pain from his jarred ankle caught his breath, but fuelled by a mixture of adrenaline and the will to live, he managed to keep going for he now had a slight edge on them again. He knew the dark, dank subterranean bunker like the back of his hand. At the top of the stairs, he flicked a switch to turn on the dim emergency lighting. For safety reasons the building's developers had requested that the electrics were to remain connected to the mains until the demolition works began in April.

After years of neglect, the once pristine shelter was now damp with dripping water seeping across the concrete floors from broken pipes. The walls were covered in patches of slimy green moss, faded wartime posters and signage. The shelter was infested with vermin, and it stunk to high heaven.

Taylor's heart was pounding, he tried to quicken his pace, but his jarred ankle brought him up sharply again. His face contorted and was grey with pain as he hobbled toward the exit. Behind, he could hear Spencer and Virginia working their way warily through the sludge and rubbish littering the floor. The emergency lighting threw strangely ethereal shadows across the myriad of interconnected tunnels that had once housed frightened Londoners from the deadly inferno raging in the streets above their heads.

Virginia eyed Spencer uneasily and whispered. 'Are you in a bad shape?'

His blood splattered face was battered and bruised. 'No!' he hissed back through gritted teeth. 'I'm fine.' It was a lie. 'There's got to be another exit, but how many?'

'God only knows, but he sure knows his way round.'

'He'd be a ruddy fool if he didn't,' Spencer grunted. As he led the way through the shelter, he briefly glanced back over his shoulder at her. 'Promise me something.'

There was an edge of anxiety in his voice, Virginia nodded.

'If we manage to get out of here in one piece, I need you to find Garvan.'

She hesitated.

'Do you *understand?*'

'Yes,' she said, in a lowered voice.

He didn't want to risk any heroics, even if Taylor took him out; their best hope of closing the net was for Virginia to touch base with Garvan. He needed her on side, didn't want her to take any unnecessary risks, she was fearless, and he knew her natural instinct would be to fight it out at his side, but there was simply too much at stake.

As Taylor finally made it to the emergency exit and forced open the heavy old door, a shaft of stark, unforgiving light suddenly enveloped the surrounding tunnels. He crouched down momentarily and let off several random volleys back into the shelter before scurrying out into the cold winter air. This was his one and only chance, even though his stomach turned with pain, he sprinted as fast as his ankle would allow toward the Jaguar XK, it had been something of an indulgence, but a necessary one, with a top speed of 135mph it was the perfect getaway car. He'd taken a chance by leaving the key in the ignition, but it was thankfully still there.

Spencer soon made daylight behind Taylor. He pulled the door open softly toward him and refilled the shells into the chamber, but found himself momentarily disoriented, where the hell was he? He'd fully expected to find himself on one of the streets surrounding the block, but had instead emerged from an inconspicuous looking door belonging to a smaller mansion block, at least, a street or so away. He glanced briefly up at the street sign; St. Mary's Walk. During the war, the myriad of tunnels had obviously been designed to provide a communal bomb shelter for the residents in the surrounding area.

'Find Garvan.' he yelled at Virginia before heading down the street after Taylor.

Injured ankle or not, he'd made some headway on them and was already opening the door of the racing green coupe. Taylor half swung round and fired off another desperate defensive volley. Spencer threw himself behind a parked car. As the shot dangerously whammed over his shoulder; it hit the road before ricocheting with a harmless thud into a nearby wall.

Taylor turned the key in the ignition, and the powerful 3.8-litre engine immediately growled into life. He then hurriedly thrust it into gear and tore the wheel around just as Spencer managed to hammer a bullet into the bodywork. But he was gone, heading off through the backstreets before finally re-emerging half a mile or so onto Cleaver Road. It ran parallel to Kenton Road, and had likewise been affected by the nearby roadworks, so the traffic was far lighter than usual; however there was still a steady stream of vehicles.

As Taylor pulled out sharply of a side turning onto Cleaver Road, someone in an open backed truck slammed on the brakes and swerved to avoid a collision. Taylor simply hadn't seen him coming, but didn't miss a beat and accelerated through a red light; with any luck, he might yet have given them the slip.

As he clenched his hands on the Jaguars steering wheel, it flashed across his mind that his old self, the war hero, the once renowned British field agent had long since receded into oblivion. Jesus Christ, where had it all gone so wrong. Somewhere along the line, he had managed to disconnect his own duplicity and that as far as British Intelligence were concerned he'd gone completely beyond the pale, and that there was no coming back. For at the time he'd not only upset his own Head of Station in Berlin but had also come to the attention of the CIA and the ultra-efficient Stasi. As a

211

consequence, Spencer's hand had been forced, albeit, it was an opportunity that he'd been waiting for.

Taylor checked his rear view mirror, he guessed, that Scotland Yard would have saturated the area by now, and unless Spencer managed to get the word out quickly, he figured that he still had a little leeway before they connected him to the Jaguar. He'd toyed with buying something a little less understated, it was a beauty of a car and might well attract a second glance, but it was the chance he needed to take.

*

Garvan was at the wheel of a Rover 105; he pulled up beside Spencer in St. Mary's Walk, and wound down the window. Virginia was in the back, alongside her was Martin Bell; his arm was now strapped up in a temporary sling, strung together with five knotted handkerchiefs.

Opening the passenger door, Spencer asked anxiously. 'How's Jack'?

Garvan said. 'He's at the hospital, the doctors reckon he should pull through, but he's going down to surgery.'

Spencer got in the car beside him, and as he slumped into his seat, let out his breath, his face still hurt to blazes, and he was nursing his right hand. He didn't think anything was broken, but it was badly swollen.

Garvan still hadn't quite managed to wipe the undisguised look of horror off his face at Spencer's battered appearance. Before he had a chance to saying anything Spencer raised his left hand to silence him.

'You really don't have to tell me.'

As they set off down the road, Garvan snorted. 'You look like you've just gone ten rounds with Floyd Patterson.'

Patterson was the current Heavyweight World Champion. Spencer checked out his reflection in the rearview mirror.

212

'Yeah, well you should see the other bloke. Where are we heading?'

'One of Mackenzie's patrols has just picked up on him, he's heading south, they'll keep us posted on the blower,' he said, inclining his head toward the receiver on the console.

Spencer rasped angrily. 'I messed up back there!'

'What do you mean, messed up?'

'Five years ago he'd never have walked out of there alive; it just wouldn't have happened. Maybe I've been at the Office too long, or maybe I'm getting past it.' There was an edge of bitterness in his voice tinged with anger at himself.

From the backseat, Virginia hissed dismissively. 'Jesus Christ, Spence, get over it, shit happens, move on!'

Bell gave her a sideways glance; he hadn't known her that long, but she sure as hell frightened the life out of him, the fact she'd somehow managed to shut Spencer up spoke volumes.

As they headed out and along Cleaver Road, Garvan asked Spencer to pick up the phone, without hesitating he reached forward to the console. It crackled into life; a voice answered; it was Scotland Yard's control room. Mackenzie's Special Branch officers were tailing the flash Jaguar XK 150.

'Is it racing Green?' Spencer queried.

'Yes, sir.'

'That's the one,' he responded, and carefully repeated the control rooms instructions to Garvan. 'Take the next left out of Cleaver Road; he's heading toward the main road toward the south coast. Still clasping the receiver Spencer glanced over his shoulder at Virginia. 'Hand me over the Sterling.'

Looking at the mangled state of his right hand, she hesitated; the submachine gun was resting on the seat beside her. 'Are you sure?'

His gaze bored into her eyes. 'What do you think?'

*

It hadn't taken Taylor long to suss out that they'd picked up on him and that he was being tailed. He'd taken evasive action, every precaution by doubling back on himself before slamming the accelerator to the floor again. He'd managed to lose one of the surveillance teams, and was almost on the point of beginning to believe that he'd shaken them off when he noticed in his wing mirror a large Rover 105 speeding up behind him. It was a big beast with a 2.6 litre engine, but not a serious match for the Jaguar, even so, he hadn't bargained on the fact that all Special Branch pool cars had supercharged engines, and try as he might the dark blue Rover was not only keeping pace, but sticking to him like glue.

Whoever was at the wheel was pretty slick. Taylor continued to keep a wary eye on them in his rear view mirror. The Rover had the occasional opportunity to overtake, or, at least, draw alongside, but for whatever reason held back. Garvan was waiting, waiting until they reached the leafy suburbs of outer London, where the roads were not overly crowded, and beyond lay the sprawling open countryside of southern England, and perhaps a realistic chance of taking him out without endangering the lives of innocent bystanders.

Taylor had originally intended driving directly to Shoreham airport down in Sussex, but the Rover's persistence had forced him to change tack, try as he might; he simply couldn't shake them off. So he headed up into the Surrey Hills, it was an area he knew well from his childhood. The steep gradients and the beautiful countryside were criss-crossed by meandering lanes and pretty villages. What he hadn't realised was that by heading into the Hills he'd inadvertently played into their hands.

The deep throbbing of the XK's engine changed to a shattering roar as he seriously opened it up, but the Rover was still coming up fast behind. Taylor cursed silently beneath his breath, and suddenly propelled the steering wheel to the right and rounded a sharp corner. He almost lost it, but the Rover had somehow gained ground and was even closer on his tail, and he could clearly make out that Spencer was on the front passenger seat.

On a quiet stretch of road bounded by trees, Spencer leaned out of the passenger window and let rip with a rapid round from the Sterling that he'd been patiently nursing on his lap. In a split second, all hell broke loose as the Jaguars rear and front windscreens shattered. The spray of bullets hadn't only ripped through the interior of the XK but had also sliced through Taylor's body. He slumped forward over the wheel, and the out of control Jaguar clipped the kerb, before somersaulting onto its roof and slewing across the road sending up a spray of sparks off the tarmac before finally hammering into a tree and coming to rest.

As Spencer let rip with the Sterling Garvan had jammed on the Rovers brakes to avoid colliding with Taylor's car. As they skidded to a halt, Spencer climbed out of the car and moved across the road to the upended Jaguar.

'Stay where you are!' Virginia snapped at Bell as she followed Spencer across the road.

Bell sat tight, he'd no intention of getting out of the car anyway, he'd had more than enough excitement for one day, in their world he was a minnow, and right now, he was happy to keep it that way. He glanced through the side window as Spencer crouched down and looked inside the battered Jag; it was obvious that Taylor was dead. He turned back toward the Rover and shook his head.

Garvan reached forward and picked up the receiver off the console.

'Benton Lane, Leaf Hill, Surrey, it's a clean-up job. Pegasus, repeat Pegasus is dead.'

*

Some three months later Jack Stein placed a call to the Office in London. An intercom light, a red one, flashed on Spencer's desk, he picked up the corresponding red scrambler phone; it was Dawn, his secretary.

'I have Mr Stein from Langley on the line for you, sir.'

'Thank you, put him through.'

'How yer doing,' Stein drawled down the phone.

'I'm doing just fine, but I thought you were still on your sickbed, are you doing okay?'

'Brennan was missing me,' he chuckled.

Spencer was aware that Stein and the Director of the CIA often didn't see eye to eye, and that they had a somewhat volatile working relationship. He said. 'I reckon it'd be a cold day in hell before Brennan started missing *you*?'

Stein threw out a laugh. 'Yeah, you might have a point,' he grunted, drawing heavily on his cigarette. 'If you really want to know I was bored to death sitting on my ass all day.'

Now that, Spencer could believe. 'So Jack, how can I help you?'

'Brennan's asked me to run a security report by you.'

Spencer eased himself back in his chair, and calmly lit a cigarette. 'What kind of security report?'

'It's something our guys picked up on the diplomatic circuit.'

It was a loaded question. 'What's it about?'

'Well that's why I'm calling you, they've heard rumours in London that your Prime Minister Haining is about to expel some Soviet diplomats.'

Spencer knew instinctively that the report hadn't derived from a top-flight politician or high ranking civil servant, his best guess was that the CIA's source was probably some fairly junior Foreign Office diplomat, who'd become a little too loose-tongued over one too many gin and tonics at some fancy London club with an American acquaintance, someone who was bragging, and needed to impress. He'd certainly need to check out who the idiot was before they managed to do any serious harm. Reading between the lines, Stein wanted to know why Washington hadn't been officially informed of the British Government's decision. Expelling the Soviets would cause a ripple effect and severely strain not only Anglo-Soviet relations but also between Moscow and Washington. It wasn't that the White House hadn't been expecting some kind of retaliatory action, it was only a matter of time, but the news of it coming via an unofficial source had surprised them.

Spencer snapped his lighter shut. 'The PM only signed off on it this afternoon.'

'Signed off what?'

'He's arranged to place a personal call to the President tomorrow morning.'

'Well that's just, swell, but is it true about the expulsions?'

Spencer drew heavily on his freshly lit cigarette and bided his time answering. The British Government's announcement was officially embargoed until after Haining had a chance to discuss the decision with the President, but he figured there wasn't much point in holding out, Stein would find out soon enough anyway.

'It's off the record,' he said.

Stein grunted down the phone. 'Spencer, we've always been off the record!'

'The Soviet Ambassador and his chargé d'affaires are going to be summoned to a meeting with the Foreign Secretary tomorrow afternoon.'

'And then what?'

'They'll be read the riot act.'

There was a slight pause down the line, Spencer knew Stein had his own agenda, it wasn't unexpected; they both had. Stein didn't want to press too heavily, their post-war relationship had been built on a quid pro quo basis, but even so, Stein was mindful that as the Director General of MI5, Spencer needed to play his cards close to his chest, sometimes it was difficult enough to get Brennan to open up, let alone a friend, even a close one, from a foreign intelligence agency.

There was a slight pause down the line before Stein said. 'Is this gonna cause problems our end?'

'Would I do that to you?' Spencer said, playfully.

'Not willingly, but we know how the game's played!'

'Don't' worry, I've run it by the book, the Foreign Secretary's brief is short and to the point, he'll let Sergei Topolski, their Ambassador know that we know that Bukin was Taylor's KGB contact in London and that one way or another we pretty well know everything there is to know about the plot to assassinate the Prime Minister.'

Stein didn't respond, but it had taken a whole weight off his mind.

'If you remember I sent you a copy of the story we planted in the National Press about Taylor's death. It was along the lines that the man police suspected of being involved in the murder of Donna Webster had died in a car crash near Leaf Hill.

He'd seen a copy.

Spencer took a long considered drag on his cigarette. 'Well, Jack, at that point the Soviet's would have to be deaf, dumb and blind not to realise something wasn't afoot.

'I guess so,' Stein pondered.

Although the expulsion of the Soviet diplomats would severely strain Anglo-Soviet relations, and cause a tit for tat expulsion of British diplomats in Moscow, Haining was justifiably incensed but knew that he needed to act swiftly, to retaliate. For if he didn't, the diplomatic fallout of not doing so could potentially damage Britain's standing on the world stage. Perhaps more importantly, he also wanted to send out a clear signal to Moscow, that the government would not tolerate diplomats dappling in covert activities incompatible with their status.

Stein smiled to himself. 'It sounds like you're reading from the script.'

'I have it in front of me, the entire script.'

'Are you going public about the plot?' Stein pressed him.

'I've persuaded them against it; they've come round that we've got too much at stake' Spencer countered. 'I told the PM that whatever happened we needed to protect our sources, especially the CIA's source in Moscow.'

'Freda, yeah, well that would have been a stumbling block.'

'I had a feeling that it might.'

'So how are you planning on playing it with the Soviet Ambassador?'

'Counter-bluff them.'

Stein's face registered surprise. 'How exactly are you gonna do that?'

'Tell them Taylor was an MI5 plant all along.'

'Will they buy it?'

'Why wouldn't they? We now know Bukin was against taking him on in the first place. Besides, even their Ambassador, Sergei Topolski wouldn't question it, why would he? It's way too late in the game for them to start kicking up rough.'

'I guess you're right. So how many Soviets are going to be packing their bags?'

'Well, it's not been easy.'

'Nah, I don't suppose it has.'

'I've had to rein Haining in a little; it's certainly not as many as he'd like.'

'Give me a ballpark figure.'

'We've managed to narrow it down to twelve.'

Even so it was more than he'd expected. Stein pursed his lips together and let out a low almost inaudible whistle. 'Anyone I know?'

Spencer let out an involuntary laugh. 'I suspect all of them. No names, no pack-drill, but as Bukin's dead and buried already, we've decided to round up the rest of the Cultural Secretary's Department, there's also a couple of businessmen on the list, you know the type, trade delegates, and just to stir things up a little I've added the air and naval attachés to the list.'

Spencer had more than stirred up things a little, it was political dynamite, but with Haining on side, he'd finally been given a free hand to clear out London's Soviet Embassy of its leading agents. It was a temporary fix but was a master stroke all the same.

'Well,' Stein laughed down the phone, 'come tomorrow, the shit's certainly going to hit the fan.'

'That's the general idea.'

'I owe you, Spence!'

'You've always owed me!'

*If you liked this book you might also wish to read the other books by the same author; they are all Free on Kindle Unlimited – **FIVE STAR RATED REVIEWS ON AMAZON AND GOODREADS***

Codename Nicolette
Review from Amazon UK

A really absorbing story which screams out to be made into a BBC produced series or British produced film (to catch the atmosphere of the like of Tinker, Tailor). The author gives the real feel of how we were "up against it" and that the strategies of the intelligence services, when needed most, played a critical part. It looks as though DCI Garvan is in the position to provide further adventures into the doings of the cloak and dagger brigade and I look forward to reading them.

Mission Lisbon the V-1 Double Cross
Review from Amazon UK

This is a very well researched wartime novel with believable characters and a twisting storyline. It is a gripping story of espionage during World War II, and I hope there will be another book in the series as it leaves the reader on a cliff-hanger.

Dead Man Walking - A Spy Amongst Us
Review from Amazon.com

Fans of British WWII espionage intrigue will love Dead Man Walking, A Spy Amongst Us by Toby Oliver. A British cabinet member is murdered, and the evidence points to infamous double agent, Toniolo, as the perpetrator. The author is a master at weaving deception and conspiracy at every turn of the page. It is a fascinating backstage look at the relationship between England, Germany, and the Soviet Union during the war. The author blends meticulously researched fact with fiction and will keep your interest until the very end.

Buy this book if you love spy novels, and you won't be disappointed.

CPSIA information can be obtained
at www.ICGtesting.com
Printed in the USA
LVOW13s1923211116
513933LV00027B/671/P

9 781517 038380